The Key of Kilenya

Books by Andrea Pearson

Kilenya Series:

The Key of Kilenya
The Ember Gods, Kilenya Series Book Two
August Fortress, Kilenya Series Book Three
Rise of Keitus, Kilenya Series Book Four
Eyes of the Sun, Kilenya Series Book Five (coming soon)
(Kilenya Series Book Six – title and book coming soon)

Kilenya Romances:
Samara: A Kilenya Romance

Katon University Series:

The Music of Anna Morse
Britnell Manor
Whistle, and I'll Come

The Key of Kilenya

by

Andrea Pearson

The Key of Kilenya

Book design and layout copyright © 2013 by Andrea Pearson
Cover design copyright © 2013 by James E. Curwen

Copyright © 2013 by Andrea Pearson

ISBN-13: 978-1463671839
ISBN-10: 1463671830

Printed in the United States of America
Year of first printing: 2011
Third Edition printing: 2013

Summary:
    Two monstrous wolves drive fourteen-year-old Jacob Clark down a path to a different world near his small-town home. The inhabitants of this new world are peculiar, and he is surprised to learn that they know everything about him. Even the evil, immortal Lorkon, who stole the Key of Kilenya. They are jealous of Jacob and wish to control powers he doesn't know he possesses.

To Josh.

This story was, is,
and always will be
for you

Pronunciation Guide

For those difficult-to-say names and words

Akeno:	ah-KAY-no
Aldo:	ALL-doe
Aloren:	ah-LOR-en
Ara Liese:	AR-uh Lees
Arien:	AR-i-en
Brojan:	BRO-zhun
Canush:	KAN-ush
Danilo:	dan-EE-lo
Duana:	do-AH-nuh
Dunsany:	DUN-suh-ni
Eachan:	EE-kun
Eetu:	EE-tu
Eklaron:	EK-la-RON
Ezra:	EZ-ruh
Gallus:	GA-ll-us

(NOT like tall, ball, etc, but like CALifornia)

Gevkan:	GEV-kun
Jaegar:	JAY-gar
Kaede:	ka-ay-day
Kaith:	KAY-th
Kaiya:	KIGH-ya
Kenji:	KEN-ji
Kilenya:	Keh-LEN-yuh
Lahs:	Law-s
Lasia:	LAY-zhyuh
Lirone:	LEE-row-n
Lorkon:	LOR-kan
Makalo:	muh-KA-low
Maivoryl:	MY-vor-ul
Molg:	molg. :-)
Rezend:	RE-zend
Shiengol:	SHEEN-gull
Troosinal:	TROO-si-nal
Wurby:	wur-bi

Table of Contents

Chapter 1.   Into the Woods   1

Chapter 2.   The Rog   12

Chapter 3.   The Key of Kilenya   23

Chapter 4.   Maple Syrup   34

Chapter 5.   Speed of Light   44

Chapter 6.   Infected   60

Chapter 7.   A Bucket Full of Nuts   79

Chapter 8.   Mud Bubbles   90

Chapter 9.   Minyas Up Close   104

Chapter 10.   Macaria   114

Chapter 11.   Grrr   132

Chapter 12.   Storm's a Comin'   153

Chapter 13.   Caves and Bones   170

Chapter 14.   The Fat Lady   190

Chapter 15.   Stone Barricade   205

Chapter 16.   Deformities and Eerie Lights   223

Chapter 17.   Breakneck Speeds   247

Chapter 18.   Bacon and Pancakes   267

About the Author   289

Acknowledgments   290

Book Club Questions   293

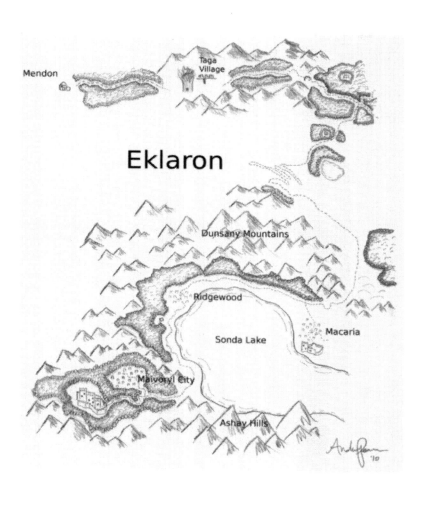

Chapter 1

Into the Woods

~ Journal Entry ~

Would a man kidnap his own daughter-in-law? The castle is in ruins, its people bloodied and broken. I suspect my father was behind it. We are counting the dead and missing, and I'm in despair because I can't find her anywhere. My beloved Princess Arien, eight months' pregnant with our first child—and such a difficult child to come by, after years of trial and loss.

Aldo and Ezra have instructed me to meet them at their mother's cottage, nearly a mile from the castle. They believe the princess was indeed kidnapped, and that her captors will demand ransom. What else would they want from the royal family?

Jacob tossed his favorite hand-held video game onto his bed, then grabbed his basketball and dashed down the stairs. As he entered the kitchen, he paused, glancing out the window to check on Amberly—still playing in the sandbox out back—then turned and bolted through the front door, eager to take advantage of the last rays of sunlight.

Matt, Jacob's sixteen-year-old brother, was working in the garage. "Hey, I wanna shoot too," he said as he popped his head out from under the truck.

"Fine, but I really need this practice. So challenge me."

"Don't I always?" Matt said with a laugh.

They played a quick game of one-on-one, with Jacob barreling past Matt and leading the game consistently by fifteen points or more. He ended it with a spectacular three-point shot and bent over panting, hands on knees.

"Yeah, well, I can still beat you at football." Matt grinned.

Jacob laughed, then tossed the ball to his brother. "Here. You need to practice more."

"You still trying out tomorrow?"

"'Course—I have to."

"Uh-huh." Matt tucked the ball under his arm and glanced at Jacob. "You know . . . letting Kevin win at something might not be a bad thing. 'Sides, you could both make it."

"No, we couldn't. You know Coach—he's not going to let two fourteen year olds on varsity."

A rustle in the trees next to the driveway made Jacob turn his head. It sounded like a large animal or a person. "You hear that?"

"Hear what?" Matt was back to shooting hoops again.

Jacob motioned for Matt to stop and took a step closer to the trees, squinting to see better. But the sun had already set, and the brush was dark. "Hey, turn on the light. I think something's in there."

Matt's footsteps faded, then light flooded across the concrete driveway, deepening the already ominous shadows in the forest. That wasn't much better.

"Hello?" Jacob called.

Matt came back and stood next to him for a moment. "Nothing's there, man." He dropped the ball at Jacob's feet. "I'm gonna go work on the truck some more."

Still unsure, Jacob slowly picked up the ball and started shooting again. After several satisfying *swishes*, he forgot the sound in the trees, picturing himself on the court at Mountain Crest High School, playing in front of Coach and the varsity team. He had to make it. He just *had* to. He'd never live down Kevin's teasing and Coach's patronizing glances of pity if he didn't.

Thirty minutes later, he dropped the ball, caught it with his foot, and pushed it up the driveway, watching it roll toward the open garage door. It bounced off the truck's tire closest to Matt. Jacob was ready for tomorrow. He could do this—he really could. He just had to make sure he got plenty of sleep that night and warmed up before tryouts began.

"Matt," he called into the garage, "we need to get Amberly inside and to bed."

A grunt came from under the truck. Jacob pushed the hair off his forehead and wondered what his mom would say if he bleached the tips while she was gone.

Leaves rustled in the forest again, a twig snapped, and he jerked to the right. A large form shifted in the moonlight, then froze. Light flashed across a pair of eyes almost level with his. He'd been right—something was there! The form moved again. It was too bulky to be human. Jacob stepped back, fumbling for his pocketknife. Nothing that big lived in this part of the mountains.

A scream raked the air—Amberly!—and he nearly fell over, stumbling away from whatever it was that had been watching him from the forest.

"What's going on?" Matt asked, scrambling out of the garage.

"Amberly—back yard!"

They raced around the garage and jerked to a stop as they spotted the sandbox, lit by the back porch light. A monstrous black wolf towered over Amberly as she sobbed, with her shoulders hunched and hand held up as if to shield herself. It sniffed her hair and clothes, then growled at Matt and Jacob. Footfalls sounded behind them and they whirled—another huge wolf lurked at the forest edge.

"What do we do?" Jacob asked under his breath.

At the sound of his whisper, both wolves bared their teeth. The one closest to Amberly lifted its nose, then took several steps toward the boys. Jacob almost stopped breathing as he waited to see what it would do. Intelligent green eyes locked with his. He tried to look away, but couldn't. Neither wolf paid attention to Matt as he edged closer to Amberly. Jacob wondered if he should follow, but something about the wolves' behavior made him decide to stay in place.

The gentle August breeze ruffled his hair. Both animals sniffed the air, then stiffened. The one closest to Amberly snarled and took a few steps in Jacob's direction. Suddenly, to his horror, both of them lunged forward, pouncing straight for him.

Matt made a run for Amberly, while Jacob had a split-second decision to make—his only escape route was through the forest that bordered their property on most sides. A low fence separated the yard from the trees.

The decision was made. In an instant, he had hopped the fence and was racing through the forest, running as fast as he could into the darkness. He glanced over his shoulder—Matt grabbed Amberly and dashed toward the house, and both wolves leaped over the fence and bounded after Jacob. Amberly's screams were cut off by the slamming of the back door.

Jacob's breath came fast, and his lungs were starting to burn. He dodged trees and darted through tight spaces and underbrush, looking back every so often in the hopes that he'd lost the wolves. There was no way he'd be able to outrun them.

He heard the wolves' paws thundering on the ground behind him, and adrenaline shot through his veins as he realized how close they were. They growled and snarled, but didn't leap. Jacob gripped his pocketknife tighter, not sure it would do any good, but wanting something—anything—to use to defend himself. The weight in his hand was comforting.

Stumbling onto a game trail, he veered a sharp right, hoping to have an easier time maintaining his distance from the wolves. The trail led him toward a small canyon. The moon offered just enough light for him to see, and he searched through the darkness for a place to take shelter. Why hadn't they caught up with him yet? He risked another glance backward—they weren't there anymore. Where'd they go? He continued running a minute longer, just in case they showed up again.

The path became springy under Jacob's feet, the bushes on either side of him thickening. The rich smell of old wood assailed him, and he looked up in surprise. The aspens and evergreens had given way to maples and magnificent oaks— trees he'd never seen in this forest. Had he gone farther now than he'd ever been before? How was that possible? He and Matt had thoroughly explored these forests on numerous occasions. For a moment, hysteria nearly overcame him. He started to look for markers, familiar trees, other *paths— anything* so he could find his way back.

Jacob's foot caught on something and he tripped, falling onto the rocks, knife flying through the air. Groaning and gasping in pain, he rolled over and squinted as lights flashed before his eyes, his head pounded, and his breaths came in short, shallow bursts.

After several moments, he propped himself up, moaning as something warm trickled down the side of his face. He touched the liquid and held up his hand. The exact color was hard to tell, but it looked like blood. A wave of nausea suddenly hit, and he put his head between his knees.

The sick feeling was soon replaced with panic, and Jacob hurriedly pulled himself to his feet. The pounding in his head nearly forced him back to the ground, but he leaned against a tree and bit his lip to keep from crying out.

Jacob's mind became clearer with each breath he took, and soon he was able to straighten again. Blackness was everywhere and the path was overgrown—he couldn't even tell which direction he'd come from.

Suddenly, the sensation that he was not alone swept over him once more. Something was watching him. Was it the wolves? His muscles tensed and he held his breath. Could they hear his heart pounding? He didn't move—maybe they'd leave him alone. Small flickers of moonlight shone through the dense scrub oak, and it wasn't difficult to imagine animals watching as the shadows danced around him in odd shapes and sizes. Something, either blood or sweat, tickled his forehead, but he didn't want to move to wipe it away.

Something rustled in the brush. Jacob spun around, ignoring the throbbing pain in his head. There was a glint of light from a pair of eyes, followed by movement and a growl. As he gingerly took a step back, a bird startled from the branches behind, and he raised his hands to shield himself from its beating wings.

A howl pierced the still air, and was answered by a closer howl. He tried to swallow, but couldn't get his throat to function.

Then a growl came from what sounded like only ten feet in front of him. Should he run? How many wolves were there? The underbrush rustled again, much louder this time, then another long growl sounded, coming closer, and fast. Something was racing at him through the bushes.

Jacob turned and ran. Thistles snagged at his clothes as he sprinted, and a branch whipped him across the face.

As he struggled forward, he could sense the animal closing in from behind. Right when he thought it was over, he burst through the trees and fell into a moonlit meadow.

A huge tree stood in the middle of the clearing. He lurched forward, head pounding, guided by the moonlight.

As Jacob got closer, he was surprised to see that the tree was as big as a house. It was old and its branches were large and twisted, without a single leaf. He ran toward it as fast as he could and circled to the left, looking for a low branch to climb.

As he approached the tree, he was surprised to see a door in the trunk swing open, revealing a hollowed-out interior. He stumbled in shock—a door in a tree?—but then let his breath out in relief. This was better than climbing. He changed course and made a dash for the door.

The two black wolves, bigger than bears, raced across the clearing, followed by several smaller, gray ones. The two wolves in the lead tried to cut off Jacob's escape from the right, but were too late. He scrambled through the doorway, swung around, and slammed the door shut just as the wolves came within leaping distance. Leaning into the door with all his weight, he pushed as hard as he could and heard the latch click just as the animals collided at full speed with a deafening thud.

He pressed his shoulder into the door a moment longer, hoping it would hold. It did, but he could still hear the wolves snarling and clawing to get in.

It was darker than coal inside the tree. Jacob put out his hands to feel around, searching for a way to bolt the door, but there was nothing but the knob. The inside of the tree smelled musty. It reminded him of woodshop class on the first day of school—the scent of projects from years long gone. Several seconds passed as he listened closely at the door—it was now quiet outside. The wolves must have left. Slowly, Jacob turned around.

Everything was completely silent. From the hollow sound of his breathing, the tree seemed spacious. He tested the air in front of him with an outstretched hand and took a step forward. He grunted when his shin bumped against something hard. As he bent down to rub the spot, blood rushed to his injured head. He was overwhelmed by the intense throbbing and, forgetting the pain in his shin, straightened and took some deep breaths.

Jacob couldn't stay in the tree—he had to get back to help Matt with Amberly. Were they okay? What would Matt do if he were in Jacob's place? He always knew the best way out of tough situations. He'd find a weapon—some way to defend himself. Jacob had to think like Matt. He put his hands down low in front of him, feeling his way in the dark until his fingers brushed against a short, small table. A table? Obviously, it was unusual to find a tree with a door in it. But furniture?

Then it occurred to him he might not be alone. "Hello?" he called out.

Several seconds passed. No response.

Moving as quickly as possible, he found a small chair next to the table and lifted it to see if it would work as a weapon. It was too awkward, so he resumed his search, wishing he hadn't dropped his pocketknife. A little ways past the chair, he found what seemed to be a bookshelf and shuffled around it in frustration. There had to be something he could use!

Finally, Jacob's hands wrapped around something that felt like a walking stick. Perfect. Despite the disorienting darkness, he returned to the door without further injury. Stick in hand, he readied himself, then pulled the door open slowly, an inch at a time.

Nothing happened.

A moment passed, then Jacob took a step through the frame. A growl alerted him right before one of the gray wolves jumped into view. He scrambled back into the tree and slammed the door shut, making sure it clicked again.

Breathing hard, he turned around, putting his back against the door. Stupid wolves!

He frowned, wiping the sweat off his brow. What were his options now?

He could go back outside and use the stick as a weapon. His heartbeat raced at the thought of that, making his head hurt even more. Could he face four or five wolves, exhausted as he was, and with nothing but a stick to defend himself? Probably not.

He could wait for a while until he was sure the wolves were gone, but how would he know they'd really left? Trapped in darkness, there was no way he could be sure.

Or he could wait until morning and get some rest in the meantime. That was the most logical solution, given the circumstances. Jacob moaned in frustration and impatience.

He was curious, though—why had the wolves chased him without attacking? Maybe they weren't hungry. And what on earth were wolves doing in this area anyway?

After a few moments, Jacob decided to try finding a more comfortable place to wait. He moved past the now-familiar table, chair, and bookshelf, and, in what felt like the middle of the room, found a larger table surrounded by four or five chairs. He slumped into one of the chairs. He felt around for the cut on his forehead, being careful not to touch the actual wound. It must have stopped bleeding, thank goodness.

Leaning forward, he rested his head in his hands, trying to ignore the pounding pain. Thoughts of his family helped distract him. His mom and dad had gone on a week-long vacation to celebrate their twentieth anniversary the day before. They were staying in some remote cabin halfway across the country and wouldn't have cell phone service almost the entire time they were gone. A neighbor was supposed to check on Jacob and his siblings in the meantime.

Jacob and Matt were in charge whenever Mom and Dad went on one of their frequent trips, and Matt would take good care of Amberly. Jacob shifted his position. He was so relieved Matt and Amberly had made it back inside the house. They had probably locked everything up and would be okay even if the wolves came back.

While thinking, Jacob absentmindedly rubbed the surface of the table. It was smooth and warm and had obviously been used a lot. After a moment, he pulled his hand away, staring at the wood. It was getting warmer. Was that possible? No, of course not. He counted to thirty in his head, then touched the table with his index finger, than his whole hand. It was cool. He'd obviously imagined the wood's change in temperature.

Too tired to sleep sitting upright, Jacob lowered himself to the floor near the chair and stretched out, breathing in the warm aroma that was almost pine, but not quite. As eventful as the evening had been, he couldn't imagine sleeping well, especially in a strange place. After a while, though, he was able to relax, and finally fell asleep.

But later, something startled him awake. A touch on his forehead—light as a whisper. He kept his eyes shut, trying to decide if he'd imagined it. He waited for a moment in the pressing silence, then felt a hand on his face.

Someone was in the tree with him.

Chapter 2

The Rog

I left the castle to meet Aldo and Ezra at the cottage. But when I arrived, I found that Ezra was dead. Someone had broken into the cabin and ransacked it. Aldo was nowhere to be found, and neither was his mother.

I spotted a piece of paper crumpled in Ezra's hand. Several notes were scribbled on it: "Lorkon behind attack?" "What motive?" "Pregnant." "Fury of the Elements."

What is a Lorkon? And how will I know where to find my Arien?

I plan to return to the cottage as soon as I can.

Jacob jumped with a start, hands swinging, but it was too late. Nothing was there. The tree door opened, and he was momentarily blinded by the late-afternoon sunlight before the door shut.

"Hello?" Jacob called out. No answer. He shook himself, trying to get rid of the creepy feeling that surrounded him.

A roar from outside made him jump. Oh, no, not the wolves again.

He forced himself to calm down. Wolves don't roar, and it didn't sound very close. Maybe he had time to get away! He couldn't stand the idea of being trapped again. Jacob raced to the door, but jerked to a stop as soon as he'd swung it open.

The biggest bear he'd ever seen charged at top speed toward the tree—and it was coming straight for him.

Terrified, Jacob slammed the door shut, then backed as far away from it as he could. Bumping into a staircase, he dashed up a couple steps, and tensely waited for the impact. Only, there wasn't one.

He could hear heavy breathing outside—it must be the bear. The knob shook ... then jiggled a bit. There was a thump and Jacob froze, expecting the bear to break through at any second. Another loud roar, and the knob jiggled again. Jacob stared at it, wondering if the bear had the intelligence to figure it out. He hoped not. The crack of light around the doorway shifted as the bear continued looking for a way in.

The knob turned, the latch released, and the door swung open. Jacob straightened in fright. The bear roared, opening its mouth wider than Jacob thought possible—the largest set of teeth he'd ever seen dripped with saliva. Jacob stumbled backward, nearly falling, as he tripped over the edge of the step behind him.

The bear roared again, then lunged toward Jacob, who spun around and dashed up the stairs.

Jacob felt the bear grab at his back. He expected pain, but felt nothing. Relief flushed through him, but it was short-lived. There seemed to be nowhere to hide in this tree. He kept running up the stairs, passing rooms as he did so. Beds, books, shelves—what was this place? He could feel the hot breath rushing over his neck, making his skin crawl.

The bear took another swipe at him, but again, the claws didn't catch. Still tripping over himself, Jacob finally reached the top of the stairs, a room with no exit—just windows. He ran at them, hoping to jump through, but his body merely slammed against the glass. Jacob whirled as the bear roared and pounced, knocking him to the ground. Spittle flew across his face.

Expecting to have his head bitten off, Jacob was surprised to feel large fingers grip his shoulder and start dragging him down the stairs. He jerked around, looking for the person who'd grabbed him, but only the bear was there. It had a human hand? How was that possible? More surprised now than afraid, Jacob twisted so he could see the other hand—it was human too! His surprise lasted merely seconds as pain shot up his back and rear with each step he hit on the way down. He flailed around, screaming for help, desperately trying to escape, but nothing worked. The fingers dug into his shoulder too tightly.

The bear—or whatever creature this was—dragged him out of the tree. It paused for a moment, but didn't loosen its grip on Jacob's arm. It seemed undecided as to where to take him—it looked to the forest on the left, where Jacob had come from the night before, then looked to where the forest continued on the right, leading up the canyon. Canyon walls towered above them to the front and right. Jacob hollered for help when he saw groups of people scrambling down a rope ladder that led to a large cave-like split in the rock. The meadow wasn't very big—he was positive they'd hear.

Suddenly, the creature pulled Jacob to the right. They rounded the tree, and Jacob was momentarily surprised to see that the canyon wall on that side also had a large fissure in it. People climbed down the side of the wall from the crevice, hands and feet gripping small holes in the rock.

As the creature dragged Jacob on the ground, gravel tore through his pants and started digging into the skin of his ankles, and he screamed. The creature charged into the forest, heading up the canyon, and the walls on either side were obscured.

A small group of people raced after Jacob and his captor. In the lead was a short blonde woman, followed by a small, black-haired boy wearing a top hat—a top hat? The boy raced to a tree and, in a deliberate yet unassuming manner, placed his left hand on the trunk. Suddenly, a sharp crack—like a rifle shot, but much louder—sounded through the air and the bear-like creature collapsed, releasing its hold. Jacob rolled, limbs sprawling across the ground, and cried out in pain.

The woman caught up and issued orders to the others. A group of men—all of whom were very, very short—threw a net over the bear creature, dragged it to a nearby tree, and tied it down.

"Jacob, are you hurt?"

"I don't—"

"He's bleeding, Ebony—his legs."

"Yes, I see," the woman replied.

Jacob looked down and nearly fainted. Sure enough, his pants were tattered, and blood was oozing from several deep gashes. The skin on his lower legs stung, and he could only imagine how much dirt and gravel was embedded in it.

Ebony motioned to the boy with the top hat. "Akeno, call Early and September."

Akeno ran to a dandelion head that had gone to seed, lifted it to his mouth, whispered into it, then blew the seeds away. Jacob frowned—what an odd thing for someone to do. A sharp pain in his leg made him look down—Ebony was ripping the right pant leg off, causing it to rub against his wounds, and exposing more deep cuts. She pointed to another person. "Find Jacob a pair of pants and shoes. He can't get the Key dressed like this."

Key? What in the heck was she talking about? And who were these people, anyway?

She glanced at Jacob. "You'll be fine. As soon as we call Kenji, he'll bring the Kaede Sap."

Kenji? Sap? Jacob wanted to ask what was going on, but Ebony ripped the other pant leg off. The pain of the cloth ripping from his flesh was almost unbearable. He dug his fingers into the grass, trying not to call out.

A bright flash of light blazed in front of Jacob, and he jerked backward in shock. A miniature person—no, *two* miniature people—hovered in the air. Without wings. How on earth was that possible? He must've gone crazy. He pointed at them, his mouth open. They were only about two inches tall!

Ebony addressed the little people. "September, go tell Kenji to come here as soon as he can, and to bring a Kaede Sap package and a Rog cage." One of them, dressed in green pants, saluted her, a large grin on its human-like face. Ebony turned to its companion, this one wearing a white dress. "Go tell Brojan that Jacob is awake and that a Rog attacked him." The girl flitted a couple feet away before Ebony stopped her. "Oh, and Early, when you're done, find Jaegar and tell him to get home at once—he's in big trouble."

The two creatures flitted to each other's sides and placed their palms together. Their hands started to glow and white rays swirled around them, spinning faster and faster. A burst of light engulfed them and then diminished as they disappeared. Little glitters of silver floated to the ground.

Had Jacob gone crazy when he hit his head? Somehow he'd entered one of Amberly's make-believe worlds! He touched his forehead, confused to find a bandage there. When had he fixed up the cut?

"You can remove that now, Jacob," Ebony said. "Your forehead is fine."

He winced when she pulled something out of his shin. "Huh?"

"I fixed it last night while you were sleeping."

He took off the bandage, gingerly touching the skin underneath. There was no evidence anything had happened. "You fixed it?"

"Yes. Now relax. As soon as Kenji comes—oh, there he is now—he and I will have to clean your wounds, and that won't feel very good."

Jacob sat up. A large—but short—man with curly, thinning brown hair rushed up the path toward the group, package in hand. He wore light-colored denim jeans.

"How is he?" Kenji asked, breathless.

"Hurting, but he'll be fine. Let's get started."

Ebony ripped open the package and pulled out a jug, bowl, small pouch, and several strips of white cloth. She handed everything but the cloth to Kenji and started separating the strips on the grass nearby. Her eyes were very dark—darker than most eyes Jacob had seen before.

Kenji opened the pouch and poured the contents of it, along with those of the jug, into the bowl, and mixed. He and Ebony finished their tasks at the same time and turned to Jacob.

"Lie down," Ebony said. "This will hurt—especially since you're awake."

"What are you going to do?"

"Clean your wounds." She pushed him down all the way.

Jacob couldn't see what she was doing, but felt it when she started. "Holy cow!" he said, and gritted his teeth as he tried to control the wave of pain that overcame him.

Akeno removed his top hat and scrambled to Jacob's side. "I'll talk to him, if you'd like—keep his mind off what's going on."

Ebony nodded. "Yes, son, that would be good."

"Jacob, what do you want to know?"

"I . . . " He took a deep breath, trying to ignore what Kenji and Ebony were doing at his feet. "I'm not sure." He felt dumb asking where he was, although he really wanted to know. He'd run here last night, after all, and he knew where his home was. Instead, he asked the next most important thing. "Who are you?"

"We're Makalos. We live here."

Since when? Jacob had lived here his whole life. "How come I've never seen you in school?"

"Because I don't go to your school. I'm from Eklaron."

Eklaron? There wasn't a city with that name around here, unless it was farther up north. Jacob had never heard of it before. He sighed to himself in frustration. His mind was tired, and he relaxed as Ebony continued to work and the pain started to fade.

Just then, he felt a sharp pain in his left leg and winced. Of course, that would happen as soon as he finally became comfortable. He blinked away the sudden tears. Not wanting the others to see, he closed his eyes, feeling warmth from self-consciousness spread across his face. Fourteen-year-olds don't cry about these sorts of things.

He tried to distract them from his embarrassment by asking another question. "What kind of bear was that?"

"It's a Wahberog. We call them Rogs. They're not usually this dangerous, but Jaegar and his friends like to tease them."

Jacob scowled. Rog. Weird name, and yet another thing he'd never heard of before. He thought he had watched all the nature shows ever made, but there was no way he would forget seeing a show about a bear with human hands. Speaking of which, how *did* it get hands? Jacob mulled this over for a moment, then sat up when an idea occurred to him. "Genetic mutation!" Akeno looked at him curiously. "The bear. It's been genetically altered. Though I'm not sure how you guys pulled it off." A wave of exhaustion rolled over him. "Whoa—I'm tired."

"That's normal with the Sap," Kenji said. "You can rest, if you like. We're nearly finished."

Jacob shook his head, fighting off the sleepiness. He forced himself to watch as Ebony laid the last strip of white cloth across a deep gash in his left shin. His legs were covered in fabric. She rocked back on her heels, a smile spreading across her face.

"There! You'll be good as new in just a few moments."

Jacob stared at her, all exhaustion gone. "Good as new? What did you do—give me a different set of legs?"

"Just about," Kenji said. "Wait a moment, then take a look."

What if they *had* given him new legs? Freaky idea. But being taller would be cool.

Finally, Jacob couldn't wait any longer and lifted the edge of one of the strips. He quickly forgot about his height. "How'd you do that?" The skin was nearly smooth—almost no sign that anything had happened. Just pink stripes where the gashes had been, which, as Jacob watched, faded before his eyes.

Kenji smiled. "We put on the Kaede Sap and allowed it to do what it does best—heal."

"Sap healed me?"

Ebony nodded. "Yes. Your forehead, too."

"Amazing!" Jacob lifted all the strips—his legs were, as Ebony had said, like new. "No way. I can't believe it. Why isn't this stuff used in hospitals? It's incredible."

19

Ebony nodded and glanced at Akeno. "Go check on the Rog."

Akeno left, and Jacob, with Kenji's help, got to his feet, astonished at how much his legs *didn't* hurt. He'd be okay for basketball tryouts today . . . then the realization hit him.

"I missed tryouts!" He stepped away from Ebony, who had reached to brush dirt off his shirt. "Oh, man! What have I done?" He turned to Kenji. "The wolves! This is their fault!"

Kenji frowned. "Technically, it wasn't their fault, though it might seem that way. I'm sorry."

Jacob stared at Kenji. He was sorry? He didn't even know how important this was! Jacob paused. "Do you have a phone? Can I use it?"

"We use Minyas," Ebony said. "Much better than—"

"Maybe Matt could go talk to Coach Birmingham. Maybe Coach'll still let me shoot a few hoops, and it's not too late. Oh, I can't believe I missed tryouts!" Jacob slumped to the ground and put his head in his hands.

"You're understandably upset," Kenji said. "Here, eat this. Food will make you feel better."

Jacob took the food and, without looking at it, shoved it in his mouth. The taste of jerky was familiar—one of his favorite snacks—but this time it made him feel like throwing up. He'd missed the most important day of his life, of his future NBA career. Months and months—even years—of practice wasted. He had to get home. He jumped to his feet, but was stopped by Kenji's arm.

"Hold on a minute, Jacob. We'll discuss everything—including your tryouts—soon. Let's take one thing at a time." He paused when Akeno approached.

Jacob scowled at Kenji. "Fine. Five minutes. That's all."

"Did you bring the cage, Father?" Akeno asked. "The Rog is about to wake up."

Kenji pulled a little wooden box—like a jail cell—from his pocket, and opened one side of it. Jacob smirked—how was that going to help? Was Kenji going to throw it at the Rog?

The creature roared, awake again. It thrashed around in the net, and the little men struggled to keep him in place. Kenji took several steps back and stretched his arm straight out in front of him. He made a scooping motion with the cage, then let go of it. It disappeared the moment it left his grasp while, simultaneously, a life-size cage appeared and scooped the Rog inside, knocking it off its feet.

Jacob jumped backward. "Holy cow!"

The men rushed over to lock the cage up. The Rog roared, furiously grabbing and rattling the bars with its human hands.

Jacob looked at Kenji, then the Rog, and back. "What on earth just happened?"

"You're not on Earth, Jacob," Akeno said. "This is Eklaron. It's a different world. Things aren't the same here."

"What do you mean, I'm not on Earth? You're kidding, right?" Jacob turned to face the forest. He was tired of these games. "Okay, Matt, you can come out now!"

Akeno grabbed Jacob's arm, pulling him back around. "No. I'm serious."

Was he telling the truth? Jacob bit his lip. Could he be on a different planet? Was it possible? After everything Jacob had seen this morning, he wasn't sure. Maybe something happened to his brain the night before when he had fallen.

A bear with human hands. Miniature people who appeared and disappeared with flashes of light. Healing sap. And Kenji just enlarged and teleported something! Jacob ran his fingers through his hair and stopped with his hand on the top of his head, staring at Kenji in disbelief. His mouth opened, then shut. "Uhhh . . ." was the only thing he could articulate.

Kenji gave him a sympathetic smile.

Jacob looked back at the Rog. He tried to swallow, but his throat was too dry. Finally, he managed to say in a croaky voice, "You guys are telling the truth, aren't you?"

Kenji nodded.

"I'm not on Earth anymore, am I?"

Kenji shook his head.

"Oh, man," Jacob said. He sank to the ground and buried his face in his hands.

Chapter 3
The Key of Kilenya

𝕴 returned to the cottage a short time later and, after further investigation, found another note attached to the underside of a chair—this one from Aldo. It was addressed to me, with instructions to go to the nearest Kaith tree, not far from the castle. When I arrived, I found a more detailed note protected by spells, allowing me—and only me, its intended recipient—to read it. It seems that the attack wasn't led by my father after all, but by a group of evil creatures known as the Lorkon. I was to choose several trusted companions of varying talents to embark on a journey to find my princess, who, he believes, is being held in the land of the Shiengols.

I have chosen Kelson, my closest friend. He was one of my followers when I was living under my father's rule in Troosinal. I've also chosen Kenji the Makalo. I don't know the Makalos very well, but formed a close bond with this one. These two have each recruited a few good men. In all, there are eleven of us—six humans and five Makalos.

Several of our group have been affected by the Lorkon attack. A few have lost loved ones, and five, including Kelson and myself, have been unable to locate their wives.

Arien's mother, Queen Ara Liese, is very closely associated with the Shiengols, and instructed me to bring one of them along for protection and guidance. However, we were unable to locate any on such short notice, and are still in need of a Minya. I've never found one I trusted, though, so I'm not sure what to do. We may have to use Arien's—a sour old Minya who hates me, possibly more than I detest her. I can't even remember her name.

Aldo's note, similar to Ezra's, also mentioned the elements—fire, wind, water, and earth. He believes they will be used as a deterrent to keep me from reaching my Arien.

Where should we take the Rog?" Akeno asked Kenji.

"Far away—to the other side of the farm. Knock it out again so it doesn't struggle while being transported."

Akeno put his left hand on the nearest tree. "Plug your ears, Jacob. We don't want you to experience too much hearing damage."

"Huh?"

Akeno waved at him to hurry. Jacob did as he was asked, noting that the others had already covered theirs. A loud crack, similar to the one he had heard earlier, pierced the air, and the Rog slumped inside the cage. Jacob shook his head. He felt like he'd just been in a blender—he couldn't keep his thoughts straight.

"Akeno, help them carry the Rog," Kenji said. "We'll get Jacob up to Brojan's place—join us there once the Rog has been deposited."

Akeno nodded and ran to join the others. On the count of three, the group heaved the cage onto their shoulders and lumbered down the trail.

Ebony reached for Jacob, motioning for him to follow her and Kenji.

Jacob stared at her. Her eyes were more circular than they should be, the irises too large, and she had no eyelashes. How did she keep stuff from falling into her eyes? "Uh . . . it's time for me to go home." He looked at Kenji. "I told you only five minutes, remember?"

"Jacob, you can't leave," Kenji said. "Not yet. Everyone is so excited that you're here."

Jacob paused. "How do you all know my name?"

Ebony and Kenji glanced at each other. "We need to take you to meet Brojan now. He'll explain everything."

Jacob nodded and followed reluctantly.

The Makalos led Jacob back down the trail and stopped at the edge of the meadow, near the first canyon wall Jacob had seen. He looked up at the split in the rock and watched as someone lowered the rope ladder.

"You first," Kenji said.

Jacob raised his eyebrow, studying the ladder, then shrugged and began climbing. He stopped just as his head made it over the ledge of the fissure. His eyes widened. The split in the rock was a massive natural cavity, hollowed out of the side of the canyon wall. It was filled with little stone buildings cut into the rock—many brightly colored.

A large group of Makalos stood in front of him, waiting. Their average height looked to be around four feet, and their heads and bodies were proportioned like a regular adult human. Most had blue eyes, though there were some whose eyes were green, but none with Ebony's dark hue. They watched him closely. Several nervously whispered to each other, while others smiled at him confidently. Everyone looked excited.

A few of the men approached Jacob, who let them help him over the ledge. Framed by small stone buildings, the area looked like a sort of gathering place and market area for the people.

As Jacob came closer, he was surprised by what appeared to be a wide age gap in the group. Most looked older, with graying hair and wrinkles, while the rest looked as though they were Akeno's age or younger. There weren't any in between.

The group of Makalos parted, allowing Kenji, Ebony, and Jacob to pass through the crowd. Kenji smiled at many, while several of the women approached Ebony and whispered to her. She smiled, nodding in reply.

Jacob did a double take when he noticed that all of them had something in common—their left ring fingers glowed blue. How had he missed that earlier, when Ebony and Kenji were working on his legs? He'd probably been too confused and in too much pain.

After passing through the crowd, they walked along a well-worn path—skipping around holes in the ground, skirting houses, and running parallel to the ledge and back wall of the cavity.

Jacob stayed behind Kenji and Ebony, letting his eyes wander as he took in the surrounding scenery. Above them were dark spots where the Makalos' fires had left smoke marks, and Jacob realized how similar this village was to Mesa Verde, the deserted Indian village in Colorado. There were only a few differences—painted buildings, rather than stone-colored, and people still lived here.

Jacob was amazed at the craftsmanship of the buildings. Drapes hung at windows made of what looked like real glass.

He spotted a few Makalos watching him, but they quickly looked away. Children ran all over the place, climbing ladders and jumping across the closely-built roofs.

They walked for about five minutes before reaching a small red-and-blue sandstone house. Kenji strode to the door and opened it, waving the others to enter ahead of him.

The front room was dark at first, the only light coming from under one of the doors at the back. Kenji touched his left ring finger to the wall, and a strip of silver lit up in the rock. The light raced upward, where it was soon one of many streaks that crisscrossed the ceiling, illuminating the entire room.

"Wow," Jacob said. "That was awesome."

Kenji grinned broadly, and Ebony smiled. "Yes, it's how we light our buildings here."

The room was clean—stone floors with a few grass-type rugs here and there—but it smelled musty and old, like the home of the elderly lady who lived next door to Jacob's family. He wrinkled his nose.

The door in the back opened, and another Makalo entered the room. Jacob figured it must be Brojan. He looked much older than the others, with a very wrinkly face and long, gray, curly hair. He was a little overweight, but stood tall—though still shorter than Jacob. He approached, hand extended.

"Jacob, my name is Patriarch Brojan, and on behalf of the Makalos, I welcome you to both Eklaron and Taga Village."

Jacob shook the older man's hand, then followed as Brojan motioned the group to join him in the other room. The patriarch sat at the head of a large, rectangular table surrounded by chairs. Everyone took a seat.

He leaned forward. "I'm going to get right to the point. Two weeks ago, an object was stolen from our village. It's a magical key that was made hundreds of years ago, along with one other, which has also been lost. This key was created to save a princess from an evil king."

"What does it do? Open a treasure box or something?" Jacob asked.

"Yes—every treasure box ever made, and more," Ebony said. "It's a powerful instrument. When placed into any lock and turned to the right, it opens the door—or box—regardless of the spells or locking bolts used. When turned to the left, one can go through any door, anywhere, regardless of one's current location."

Kenji nodded. "Because the Key is magic, an evil race called the Lorkon sought after it. They started a war about fifteen years ago that almost destroyed the entire Makalo civilization. That was not an easy feat—Makalos used to rule over the lands and people in our world. Millions died. We are all that remain." He paused and stared off into the distance. "It was horrendous. So much bloodshed and destruction."

The room was silent for a moment. Jacob couldn't imagine a war like that. He'd seen things in movies before, or heard stories in his history classes, but still, it was difficult to process. And it was obvious these Makalos had lost many loved ones—the pain was written across their faces. Fifteen years wasn't enough time to lessen their suffering.

Kenji met eyes with his wife. "Many of our loved ones were murdered. Slaughtered."

"We hid here, in Taga, to protect the Key of Kilenya from the Lorkon," Brojan said, leaning back in his chair. "But they were able to break through our safeguards and steal it. Our alarms didn't even sound."

Akeno entered the room, top hat in one hand and a book in the other. "We deposited the Rog on the far side of the corn fields." He handed the book to Brojan. "What did I miss?"

"Not much—have a seat," Brojan said.

Akeno sat next to Jacob and smiled at him.

"The fact that the Key opens any door anywhere isn't the only reason it can be dangerous, though," Kenji said. "It creates links between worlds."

Jacob frowned. "Are you telling me whoever has the Key could use it to get to Earth?"

"Yes."

"But why is that bad?"

"Because the Key is in the possession of the Lorkon," Kenji said. "And they seek power. Your world is far more advanced than ours, and they want knowledge and technology. They won't ask for it—they'll take it, and make sure your people don't get in the way."

Jacob smiled. He knew too many people obsessed with their game stations to let *that* happen. "How?"

"Violence. Murder. Destruction of everything."

"Is that possible? We have a pretty good military in my country."

Kenji leaned forward. "There aren't many Lorkon, and yet, in a matter of weeks, they were able to annihilate nearly the entire Makalo civilization. Millions died in the first week. So, yes, they could do it."

"If the Key is in their possession, shouldn't they have already come and gone from Earth?"

Kenji shook his head. "We put protective measures on it a few years ago, and they must be holding up, but we don't know how much time we have before the Lorkon figure out how to get through the spells."

"What does all this have to do with me?"

"We need you to get the Key for us."

Jacob paused. "Wait, what? You can't . . . there's no way. I . . . I can't do that."

A sympathetic expression crossed Ebony's face, and she and Kenji exchanged a glance.

"We're unable to get it, Jacob," Kenji said, rubbing his shoulder. "How many youth have you noticed here? The war killed them all off. We who remain aren't in any position to go on a trip like this. We're old—slow. We need someone fast and powerful."

Jacob shook his head. "Powerful? You must be confusing me with someone else—Matt or someone. Matt's captain of the football team and he's only sixteen. He can date any girl he wants. He's strong. And he figures things out faster than anyone I know."

Ebony leaned forward. "Jacob, you are not yet aware of your abilities. Magic resides within you, waiting to be unlocked. We want to help you find it—we want to know what skills you have."

Was what Ebony said possible? Did Jacob have Magic? He frowned, trying to remember if anything special had ever happened to him. Nothing came to mind. "But . . ." Jacob paused, then squinted his eyes when something occurred to him. "Why do I feel like I'm being used?"

"You are." Brojan shrugged, then spoke over the resulting noise of disagreement. "But only with the best of intentions. Jacob, you're a celebrity here. We've known of you since your birth, and have watched you closely."

"You have? That's really creepy. Why? And how?"

"We have ways," Brojan said. "Besides, you're the only one who *can* get the Key, since we haven't been able to leave this part of Eklaron for years—we can't get more than several feet past the entrance."

"Oh? How come?"

"As you'll see, when the Lorkon came, they tore through the barrier. But they did something to the forest on the other side of the entrance—weird things happened to us the instant we stepped through the tunnel. Our minds were rendered useless, basically. Self-doubt and fearful memories from the past started surfacing. We think it's because of our age, as it didn't happen to the younger Makalos."

Kenji leaned forward. "Our people believe in you—they feel hope when they see you. Didn't you notice how excited they were?"

Brojan didn't wait for Jacob's response. "And don't think we haven't tried other ways to get the Key—we have. We tried to contact old alliances, but to no avail. Aldo, for example. He stayed back in Gevkan to guard the entrance to Taga. But none of the Minyas we sent could make contact with him, so he's either sick, dead, or has been kidnapped. And we don't want to send more Minyas because the last time we did, one of them perished. Anything could be out there."

"And . . . if I agree? How am I not going to die?" Knowing Jacob's luck, he would. He took a deep breath. He couldn't believe they were asking him to do something so dangerous. "This sounds like a plan for failure."

"Don't underestimate your abilities," Ebony said. "You are more powerful than you know."

Jacob slumped in his chair. Their confidence in him was overwhelming. What would they do if he couldn't get the Key? "How long would it take?"

"Not long—maybe four or five days," Kenji said.

"I still can't imagine that you guys wouldn't be able to do it on your own. I've seen what you can do. Akeno knocks out Rogs, Kenji makes things bigger, and Ebony heals with sap."

"But if we can't even get past the forest?" Kenji asked. "There isn't another way to travel—not without the Key."

Jacob rubbed his eyes. What a nightmare this was becoming. "What about my family? How would I explain all this to them?"

"We had a couple of Minyas give Matt instructions to let your parents know where you are as soon as they call in to check on you. And he's pretty capable with your sister, isn't he?"

"Yes . . ."

"And school doesn't start for another two weeks—this is the best time for you to go, isn't it?"

"I guess. But this could mean the end of my NBA career—you know that, right?"

Kenji sighed. "We understand you're making sacrifices. We know this won't be easy for you."

"Yeah, it . . . it won't be." Jacob pushed his chair away from the table. "I need to . . . I need to think things over."

"We'll be here when you return."

Jacob left Brojan's house and turned left, skipping the path altogether. He went around the houses until he reached the ledge, then leaned against a stone wall and looked down at the meadow and the big tree with the door.

A gentle breeze swept his hair off his forehead, and a faint smell of spice lingered in the air, mingled with the mountain freshness. The sun was about to set and Jacob closed his eyes, enjoying the warmth on his face.

He was so confused—there were too many new things to think about, too many new ideas. What if he really did have magical abilities? Impossible. He wasn't Harry Potter.

He ran his hand through his hair, then smiled, momentarily distracted. Matt was always getting on his case about playing with his hair. *Chicks don't dig guys with hair that stands up on end. They prefer perfectly messy hair—gelled, you know—like mine.*" It seemed like forever since Jacob had last seen his brother, and he wondered how Matt and Amberly were doing back home.

There was no way he could get the Key—regardless of what the Makalos thought or said. They would quickly discover how badly they'd misplaced their trust, how he didn't have any magical abilities. The only power he had was in basketball. He'd been playing for as long as he could remember—since he'd learned to walk. And he didn't want to miss the opportunities that had come his way because of years of dedication and practice.

He left the ledge, heading toward the rope ladder and the path back home. The Makalos would have to find another way to get the Key.

Chapter 4

Maple Syrup

Our journey has finally begun, after a week of preparation. It was with much trepidation that I bade farewell to King Roylance and Queen Ara Liese. Neither of them is in good health, and with the stress of their daughter's kidnapping, is it any wonder?

I've been trying to get in contact with the Makalo Patriarch. It would be wise to have his opinion on the situation. I hope he will help us.

Jacob had nearly made it to the tree when Akeno caught up with him, hand on his top hat to keep it from falling as he ran.

"You didn't come back. They were worried—sent me to check on you."

"Yeah, I'm heading home. Let them know I'm not going, and tell them I said good luck."

Akeno stopped walking, then hurried to catch up. He met Jacob's pace, glancing sidelong at him. Jacob ignored him. He wasn't about to let the Makalo convince him to stay.

"Well . . . I'll come with you."

Jacob looked at him in surprise, but continued on. If that's what Akeno wanted, that was okay. The Makalo would have to explain to Jacob's family why he was there— some random alien in their town. That would definitely make the news.

They entered the forest, walking in silence for a while. It wasn't nearly as awkward as Jacob had expected it to be— Akeno didn't act disappointed or disapproving.

After some time, Jacob groaned in frustration. "I don't understand why *I'm* the one they chose to go. I mean, Matt's older, stronger, and he always knows what to do. So, why me?" He hesitated, but Akeno didn't say anything. "I mean, this isn't even my planet. And it's not my problem. I'm not the one who lost the Key, and I'm not the one who thinks it should be protected. And I *don't* have magical abilities!"

Jacob paused to think. "Besides, I've got my own things to deal with. I was supposed to try out for varsity today. And I know I would've made it. I'm actually really good at basketball. If it weren't for those . . . those stupid wolves . . ." He let out a long breath. "Oh, forget it. It doesn't even matter."

Another silence. Jacob guessed they were about halfway through the forest. Akeno stopped, and Jacob slowed to see why.

"Hold on a second," Akeno said. He plucked a couple leaves and sat on the ground. Rummaging through a bag strapped across his chest, he pulled out a tape dispenser and started taping the leaves to his shoes.

Jacob's eyebrows went up as high as they could. "Tape?"

"It keeps the leaves on my shoes, and the leaves keep the dust off me. I use my Rezend—which is our form of magic—and as long as the leaves are fresh, they do what I ask them to do."

"But . . . where did you get tape?"

Akeno glanced up. "From the humans. They gave me a lot of it last time they were here, along with a ton of books—I love reading books from your world."

"Humans? What humans?" For some reason, Jacob had assumed he was the first human to step foot on this world. The fact that there had been others caught him off guard. Were they like him? Did *they* have special abilities? And why did Akeno care if some dust got on him?

"Oh, they didn't tell you? Humans used to live in the tree. That's why it's human-sized."

"What? Where'd they go?"

"They moved. They used to visit, but it's been a long time—several years, in fact. We still keep in contact with them through the Minyas."

"Oh, yeah, Minyas. You guys sent them to tell Matt where I was, right?"

Akeno taped the last leaf to his shoe, put the tape dispenser back in his bag, and got to his feet. "Yeah. It took them a while to convince Matt that they were real, living things. And even longer for him to believe you were safe."

Jacob turned, but Akeno grabbed his arm.

"What?" Jacob said in irritation, facing Akeno again.

"The wolves." Akeno gestured with his other hand. "I should've made sure they weren't here before we entered the forest."

Jacob looked ahead and froze. The two black wolves were sitting on their haunches about twenty feet away, just staring at them. There was a rustling sound on either side of them, and at least ten more wolves—the smaller, gray kind—appeared, stepping forward to form a semi-circle around the boys.

"What's going on?" Jacob whispered.

"I don't know." Akeno's low voice had taken on a high pitch.

Jacob didn't blame him. He was so scared he could barely breathe. "What do we do?"

Akeno shook his head. His whole body was shaking.

Jacob stared back at the wolves, unflinching, waiting to see what they would do. Nothing happened. Why weren't they attacking?

"Should I knock them out?" Akeno asked.

"No—don't. They're not doing anything."

"Maybe we could go around?"

Jacob shook his head. The last thing he wanted was to step any closer. "You think we should?"

"No . . . but what else is there?"

Jacob's emotions were conflicted. Fear—that was the strongest. The night before had been horrendous. He hadn't been that afraid in a long time—if ever. But he also wanted to go home—desperately *needed* to go home. He wanted to play basketball, yes, but more than that, he just wanted the comfort of his house and family. He wanted the last twenty-four hours to be erased—rewound, if possible. He wanted to be normal. He wanted to forget all about this other world.

Jacob took a deep breath. Go around. That's what they should do. He took a step to the right. Nothing happened.

His heart was racing, and he willed it to calm down. What were the animals doing? It seemed unnatural for them to sit so quietly. Then he remembered Kenji saying that the Lorkon had sent the wolves to get Jacob. Was it possible that's what they were trying to do? And they wouldn't let him pass? That didn't work for him—he had to get home, and no "otherworldly" creature was going to stop him.

He cautiously took another step, trying to make a wide arc around the wolf formation. Akeno stayed close, only moving when Jacob did. A low grumble came from one of the wolves, but still, none of them moved.

"Maybe they'll let us pass." Jacob doubted it, but hoped that saying so would make the Makalo feel better.

He took another step. This time, one of the black wolves growled and jumped to its feet. Jacob nearly fell as his knees went weak in fear, and Akeno jumped. It took a moment for Jacob to realize what was going on. The wolf stood, pointing its muzzle toward Taga. The message was clear: *go back*. Jacob's heart pounded so hard he felt he would have a heart attack.

"What are they doing?" Akeno asked.

"Stopping me from going home."

Akeno took a deep breath. "They can't stop you. They can't force you to do anything."

"So . . . what do they want you to do?" came a voice from behind. Jacob whirled, half expecting a ghost or Lorkon or something to be standing there. It was only two Makalos—a shorter one, and one with lots of facial hair.

"Don't *do* that!" Jacob hissed. "You scared the heck out of me!"

The hairier Makalo grimaced. "Sorry. We . . . uh . . . heard your voices and came to investigate."

"Jaegar, aren't you supposed to be home with Mother?" Akeno asked.

The shorter Makalo looked away. "Yeah, well, I . . ." He cleared his throat. "What're the wolves doing?"

Jacob looked at the animals. "Trying to keep me from going home, I'm guessing. They want me to turn back."

As if in response, the other black wolf jumped to its feet and stepped forward to join the first.

"You don't want to go back to Taga?" asked the hairy Makalo—or Butch, as Jacob decided to call him. "Then don't. How are they going to stop you?"

"Oh, I don't know. Kill me, maybe?"

A concerned expression crossed Jaegar's face. "They can't kill you. You're too important to everyone here. We wouldn't let them."

"Okay, well, it's probably better if I go on alone." Jacob nodded to Akeno. "Thanks for trying to come with me. Maybe I'll see you around."

He took one full step away from the Makalos and toward the wolves. The wolves responded by growling and shuffling closer together as if to form a wall. It felt like they were pushing him back. Well, he wasn't about to let that happen. He took a few strides forward, almost a jog, but came to an abrupt stop as the two black wolves leaped in front of him, blocking his path. Then the gray wolves rushed at the Makalos. Jacob whirled in time to see some of the wolves chase Butch up a tree. Others charged at Jaegar, who spun around, trying to shield himself with his hands. Jacob sprinted toward them, but it was too late—Jaegar was already pinned to the ground, with two wolves on top of him, barking and slashing with their teeth and paws.

"No!" Akeno screamed. A loud crack filled the air, and all the wolves fell to the ground.

"Help me get them off!" he shouted. "We've only got a few seconds. The effect doesn't last as long on them."

Jacob caught up with him—two wolves had collapsed on top of Jaegar, who was unconscious. Together, Jacob and Akeno rolled the wolves off.

Already the beasts were beginning to stir. Jacob lifted Jaegar's small frame in his arms and ran with him toward Taga, following Akeno.

Butch climbed down from his tree as Jacob ran past, then trailed behind. He wasn't as fast as Akeno or Jacob, and it wasn't long before Jacob heard scuffling. He stopped, knowing the Makalo was in trouble, and turned around. The wolves had attacked.

"Knock them out!" Jacob shouted to Akeno.

"I can't—it's been too soon. It loses effectiveness."

"Then take him and run!" Jacob shouted as he shoved Jaegar into Akeno's arms. He ran back to Butch and the wolves, trying to distract them by flailing his hands wildly. Seeing him, the gray wolves snarled and leaped, but were stopped by the black wolves.

With the black wolves in front, the pack backed away as Jacob neared. He held his hands out in front, ready to defend himself if the wolves decided to charge. Keeping a distance of about twenty feet, they snarled and showed their teeth—seemingly dissatisfied, but unwilling to move any closer. Jacob scooped up Butch, glad Makalos were smaller than humans. Butch was bloodied, but awake.

"Sorry, man . . . I tried to . . ."

"It's okay."

With Butch in his arms, Jacob backed up, then turned and ran as quickly as he could through the trees. It wasn't long before he could hear the yelps of the wolves behind him, once again in hot pursuit. His breath heaving, he nearly dropped Butch a couple of times. This Makalo was much heavier than Jaegar.

As Jacob entered the meadow, he spotted Akeno halfway across, running toward the edge of the village opposite from Brojan's place. He made a beeline in that direction. He was almost at the tree when he made the mistake of looking back. As he did, his stomach tightened in fear and he nearly tripped.

The wolves were gaining on him quickly, having already gotten to the edge of the meadow.

Akeno had reached the stone wall. No ladder there, handholds had been carved into the wall. He shifted Jaegar to one shoulder, attempting to climb, but failing when the boy's body got in the way. Jacob put Butch down, took Jaegar from Akeno, and motioned for Akeno to climb the wall. Akeno scrambled halfway to the top. With one hand securely anchored in a handhold, he bent and took hold of Jaegar by the arm. He lifted the injured boy as high as he could, and a Makalo from above reached down and hoisted Jaegar to safety.

Jacob picked up Butch and shoved him up the wall to Akeno, who tried pulling him up as he'd done with Jaegar.

"You gotta help," Akeno said to Butch, grunting. "You're too heavy."

With Akeno's help, Butch hauled himself up, crying out in pain.

"Hurry!" Jacob said. The wolves were only yards away. The same Makalo from above grabbed hold of Butch and, with some effort, pulled him the rest of the way.

Akeno climbed up, then leaned and offered his hand to Jacob. Jacob took it and hoisted himself over the edge, with the wolves snapping at his heels.

Kenji stood with Jaegar in his arms. Jacob looked around for Butch and saw him with an elderly man who was supporting most of Butch's weight. They hobbled to the right, disappearing between the buildings.

Kenji addressed two of the Makalos who were anxiously peering over the ledge. "Watch the wolves. Tell me when they leave." He turned and headed swiftly down the path to his left, Jaegar limp in his arms. Jacob and Akeno had to jog to keep up with him.

"My son, my poor son—" Kenji said to no one in particular, the pain in his voice evident.

"I'm so sorry," Jacob said.

"If he dies, I . . ." He cleared his throat. "Jacob, before you came, the wolves never dared enter Taga Village."

Jacob bit the inside of his cheek, avoiding looking at Kenji. If only he'd listened to the Makalos, none of this would've happened.

They entered a stone house, painted bright blue, with streaks and spatters of white. Kenji gently placed Jaegar on a large table situated along the left wall of the room. Ebony burst into tears at the sight of her tattered young son.

"What happened?" she asked.

"The wolves attacked while . . ." Akeno started.

"While I was trying to go home," Jacob finished. Guilt poured over him again.

Disappointment flushed across Ebony and Kenji's faces before they turned their attention back to Jaegar.

"Oh, Jaegar, Jaegar . . ." Ebony said. "What if those wolves were poisonous? Will sap help?"

"We'll need to work quickly," Kenji said. "This is hard, but I need your help. Gather yourself. You know what to do."

Ebony nodded, sniffling as she tried to hold back the tears, and ran from the room. She returned moments later with some familiar items—a small package, an armful of cloth, and a bowl.

Kenji mixed the sap while Ebony separated the cloth. Most of it had been cut into strips, but there was one piece that formed a sheet.

Jacob leaned forward, curious to watch everything they did, since last time he had been the injured one.

Kenji poured the contents of the jug and the small package into the bowl, creating a thick, brown liquid. Jacob recognized the smell immediately. Maple syrup. Why on earth would they use maple syrup?

Akeno and Ebony hurriedly cut off Jaegar's shirt, revealing severe bites all over his chest and arms. Jacob shook his head, shoving his shaking hands into his pockets. He should have listened.

The Makalos saturated strips of cloth with the mixture and laid them on Jaegar's wounds. Very soon, Jaegar was almost completely covered in cloth pieces. Ebony let out a worried breath as she and Akeno stepped back. Kenji covered Jaegar with the larger sheet, and the three of them looked on as they stood near Jacob.

"Was it too late? Will he die?" Jacob asked, but Ebony held up her hand.

"Give it time."

Every few moments, she lifted the edge of one of the strips and looked under, a deep frown on her face. Kenji paced near the front door, hands behind his back.

At first, nothing appeared to be changing. But a few moments later, Jacob was relieved to see that the wounds were healing and disappearing.

After what felt like forever, Ebony let out a breath, this time of relief, and pulled off all the strips. Every single wound was gone, leaving only pink skin underneath. Jaegar's breathing was now steady.

"All right," Kenji said. "Now he needs to rest." He picked Jaegar up and carried him out of the room.

Chapter 5

Speed of Light

*T*oday we encountered the first element. It was lucky we were not killed. Or drowned, I should say. The Lorkon had placed a magical waterfall to completely bar passage from the castle and neighboring city to anything beyond. The water was totally invisible and difficult to feel. Perhaps it would be more correct to say that it was mostly invisible. When riding up to it, it appeared as a great wall of air, shimmering in the hot sun.

One of our men entered first, and he and his horse started to drown before our eyes. It took several seconds for us to realize what was happening. They were standing as if in plain air, and yet could not breathe. We acted as quickly as we could and pulled them out, barely in time.

It took us at least an hour to discover the true size of the waterfall. It rose miles upon miles into the air— Arien's Minya was unable to reach the top—and it was at least four hundred feet thick, most likely more. We couldn't measure. We knew the Lorkon must have created a means of escape, as they'd returned to attack Aldo and Ezra, so we searched for a way through. By trailing my *hand in the water as I walked alongside it, I found a tunnel of air that led us and our animals to safety.*

Once we reached the other side, we were surprised to find that Arien's Minya was unable to go back through the tunnel, even though she now knew where the entrance was. Her magic will no longer allow her to find it. What is this the Lorkon have done, and how will we communicate with the king and queen?

Jacob, Akeno, and Ebony were left standing in the front room, waiting for Kenji to return.

Jacob fidgeted with his hands, afraid to look at the other two. "Jaegar's friend got hurt, too."

"Oh, dear," Ebony said, sounding worried. "Is he being taken care of?"

Akeno nodded. "They took him to his home—I'm sure Mara is doing everything she can."

"Good. He is lucky to have her for a mother." She paused and took a shaky breath. "Jaegar has lost a lot of blood. It will take several hours for him to completely recover. If there was any poison in those wolf bites and scratches, hopefully it has all been removed." She grabbed a rag and wiped the table down several times, scrubbing at food stains that wouldn't go away.

"Are wolves here usually poisonous?" Jacob asked. He'd never heard of poisonous wolves. Though, this world wasn't the same as Earth, and anything could be possible.

Ebony paused. "No, not usually. And I really hope these weren't. There wasn't any pus, no redness around the wounds." She scrubbed for a moment longer, then spoke to Akeno. "I can't stand this. Jaegar will be fine with your father here. Let's take some sap to Mara."

Akeno nodded, scurried out of the room, then returned, holding a Kaede Sap package.

"We'll be back in five minutes," Ebony said before shutting the door behind her and Akeno.

Jacob took a deep breath and studied the room. Everything in the small house was beautiful, including the windows. The glass had a silver sheen that made it sparkle. The stone walls were painted scintillating shades of yellow, red, orange, and blue, with silver streaks. The doors were large and wooden. The stone floor was painted red, with a bright blue mat on it, and the wood furniture, which was lower than what Jacob was used to, was simple, yet elegant. The ceiling was plenty high, even for him, and Jacob looked at it in awe, studying the intricate design created by the streaks of metal. The room glowed from the silver in the stone, and Jacob found himself wishing his room back home could be given light from the same source. It was really cool.

He walked to the closest wall to trace one of the streaks of silver with his finger. He felt warmth in places and stopped tracing, putting his whole hand over one of the spots. The heat increased considerably where his palm touched it and he recoiled, looking at his skin. This was the second time he'd felt warmth like this. Was there a reaction between his skin and the materials in this world?

It hadn't hurt, so he ran his hand along the wall again. After a moment, he noticed that the longer he held his hand in one spot, the warmer that place became. Holding still for several seconds, he closed his eyes, enjoying the heat.

A door behind him opened, and Jacob jumped when someone chuckled.

"It looks like you've decided to leave your mark here," Kenji said with a slight smile, stepping through the door to the back of the house.

Jacob looked down and felt himself blush when he saw there was now a deep handprint in the wall. He lowered his arm. "Oh, I'm so sorry! I . . . I didn't mean to—I was just feeling the warmth."

Kenji frowned, crossing the room to Jacob. "What warmth?"

"Right here."

The Makalo felt the spot where Jacob's hand had been. "I can't feel anything. Has this happened before?"

"In the tree last night, but I don't think I left a mark." Jacob frowned, trying to think of something he could do to remove the print.

"And before then?" A smile played at the corners of Kenji's mouth.

"No, that was the first time." Jacob shook his head. "I'm really sorry."

There was a twinkle in Kenji's eyes. "That's fine—it's a nice addition to the décor of the room." Interest flitted across his eyes. "See if you can figure out why you felt heat. That is definitely fascinating."

The front door opened, and Ebony and Akeno entered the room.

Kenji put his arms around his wife. "Jaegar will be fine, but we need to talk." He led her to the table, and Jacob and Akeno followed.

Kenji addressed Jacob after sitting. "What happened out there?"

Jacob couldn't meet his eyes. "I . . . I left. I wanted to go home. Akeno came with me. The wolves stopped us and attacked."

Kenji nodded. He didn't question Jacob's decision to go home, which made Jacob feel even more uncomfortable. The need to defend himself rose—even though it was apparent

47

he didn't need to—but he didn't dare say anything. He'd almost been responsible for the loss of two lives.

Kenji finally broke the silence. "Jacob, I do not believe the wolves will leave the villagers alone until . . ." He sighed, then looked at Jacob, a worried but tender expression on his face. "Until you leave to get the Key. If they won't even let you go home, there really isn't another choice. It's too dangerous for all of us—you included—to have you here."

Jacob's face tightened. He stood and paced near the front door. Kenji was right. These people were in too much danger if he didn't leave. The wolves wouldn't let him go home, and they had no hesitation in attacking others to force him into following the Lorkon plan. He wanted to curse. He wanted to throw things, to rip something up. He clenched his fists, frustrated at how things had turned out. Why now? It wasn't fair. He looked at the expectant Makalos.

"Okay, I'll go. It's just so annoying . . ." He scowled. He sounded so selfish. He sat in resignation, trying to think how the Makalos must feel. They were practically helpless. "But I can't do it alone."

Relief spread across Kenji's face, but he quickly replaced it with a serious expression—the expression adults got when they were planning something important. "Akeno will accompany you, along with the Minyas, September and Early."

Jacob nodded and glanced at Akeno, who smiled back. "But you're sending more than just us, right?"

"There's no need. The four of you are enough."

"What?" Jacob frowned. "I don't want to offend Akeno, but I figured you'd also send an adult with us. At least, someone a little older than me, and more experienced."

Kenji smiled. "Actually, Akeno is older than you. He's the oldest of the Makalo youth here." Kenji said it with pride in his voice.

Jacob raised an eyebrow. "He looks like he's ten. Maybe eleven."

"He's thirteen, but Makalos age differently than humans."

Akeno leaned forward. "If I were human, I'd be seventeen or eighteen. Our bodies mature physically, mentally, and emotionally much more quickly than do the bodies of humans."

"Kind of like my dog," Jacob said. He flushed, realizing how that would sound to the Makalos. "I'm not saying that you're dogs or anything like that, or animals, or . . ." He stopped talking, wanting to kick himself for not being more tactful, but relaxed when the others laughed.

Kenji stood and walked over to the window. "The sun is about to set. You need to leave now—even though night is coming. It isn't safe for you to stay any longer."

Jacob knew he was right, and nodded. "Which way do we go?"

Kenji motioned to Akeno. "Get the map, please," he said.

Akeno nodded and left the room.

While waiting, Jacob turned to the others. "I still don't understand why an adult doesn't come with us. I'm really glad Akeno will be there, but if he's never left the village . . ."

Kenji sat at the table again. "The adults can't leave. Only the youth were unaffected by those trees outside the entrance. Plus, Akeno's Rezend is fairly strong. Stronger than most other Makalos, and he can control it really well. He'll be the best company for you."

"What's Rezend again?"

"The magic of the Makalos."

Akeno entered the room with a slab of stone nearly half his own size. He carefully placed it on the table in front of Jacob.

Jacob leaned forward, eager to see. A fragile, two-foot square piece of leather was mounted to the stone, and on it was a map drawn in ink. It was a standard-looking map, with markings to show mountain ranges, villages, and roads. He looked to Ebony and Kenji for an explanation.

"We're right here," Ebony said, pointing to a spot near the top left corner of the map. "And this is where the Lorkon live." She pointed to a spot several inches south.

"Don't let the small distance between here and there fool you," Kenji said. "Even though it's just a portion of the map, it will still take a long time to get there. Three or four days, as we said."

Kenji then showed Jacob the way to the Lorkon castle. It was fairly simple. The only thing Jacob had to remember was to head through the forest, then stick to the path that led them closest to the mountains. It was the only one that would lead to the Lorkon castle.

Kenji pointed out two cabins on the map. One of them was just outside the forest, not too far from the entrance to Taga. The other was quite close to where the Lorkon lived. Each cabin belonged to a friend of the Makalos, and Jacob and Akeno could go there for help and information.

"Remember," Kenji said, "don't spend time in the forest outside our village. Stick to the path. It'll lead you out of the woods and to Aldo's cabin. Stop and talk to Aldo—he'll give you additional information."

"I thought you said you couldn't get hold of him last time you tried."

"We hope he's still there. He's the only person we trust who is within a day's travel. We don't know anything about the Land of Gevkan anymore. It might have changed drastically since we last lived there. If he's not around, let us know."

Jacob took a deep breath, feeling overwhelmed at what he had to accomplish in only a few days. "How do you know the Key is at the castle?"

"We don't know for sure," Kenji said. "But it's a starting point."

"And what happens if it's not there?"

"We'll look into other locations—and send you back home."

Jacob nodded in relief. He felt like a wimp, but was really scared of what he might have to go through to get the Key.

A frantic knock sounded on the door. Akeno jumped to answer it and a Makalo rushed in, addressing Kenji.

"The wolves have left. They guarded the path to Jacob's town for a while, then disappeared. We waited five minutes, but they haven't returned. Now might be the best time . . ." He shot a glance at Jacob.

Kenji quickly stood. "Thank you. Continue to keep watch and let us know if anything changes." He held the door as the Makalo left. "We'll need two bags prepared—Ebony, you and Akeno do that. Gather whatever they'll need for the trip. I'll summon Early and September." He stepped out of the house.

"I'll get a Minya box," Akeno said, going into a back room.

"Grab that jerky while you're at it," Ebony called after him, then yanked open cupboards and drawers, stuffing things into one of the bags.

Jacob, not knowing what to do, stood awkwardly by the table. Kenji came back, and seconds later, Akeno raced back into the room, still shoving things into a knapsack.

"Jacob, you and Akeno will leave immediately," Kenji said. "September and Early will meet you in the morning. Send them back with updates as often as you feel is necessary. You should always have one of them with you for emergencies. Don't worry about sending messages to your family, Jacob—we'll take care of it for you. I wish we had more time to tell you everything you need to know, but we'll fill you in as you need more information."

"How're we going to keep the wolves from attacking us?" Jacob asked.

"Akeno is able to make Rezend-strengthened shelters that will keep predators out. You'll be safe while you're sleeping. And as long as you stay on the move during the day, the wolves won't harm you. But don't provoke them or stay in one place for too long."

Jacob nodded, feeling panic start to well up within him. This was seriously the craziest thing he'd ever done. Why'd he agree to it? He found himself wishing again that Matt were there. Jacob took another deep breath, put away his thoughts, and tuned in again to what Kenji was saying.

"The entrance to Taga is up the canyon from here. Akeno will lead the way, using Rezend to distract the wolves. You will need to stay close to him and do exactly as he says. Find a safe place to spend the night between here and the barrier, and once you get there, send a message back to us." Kenji rubbed his left shoulder. "I'll walk you to the ledge."

Akeno put on his top hat and picked up a leather knapsack. Jacob grabbed the other, darker in color, with two straps. He put it on the way he would his own backpack.

Ebony choked down a sob and grabbed Akeno, giving him a big hug and making him promise to be careful. She then wrapped her arms around Jacob. He patted her shoulder, not sure what to say. Kenji opened the door, and Jacob and Akeno followed him through.

"The wolves couldn't have gone far," Kenji said as they hurried to the ledge. "So go as fast as you can." He gave them quick hugs. "Godspeed. Akeno, be careful when shrinking or enlarging things. Stay together. As long as you follow my instructions, you should be safe. Now go!"

Jacob had to scramble down the canyon wall to keep up with Akeno. They stood still for a moment, watching the shadows for any sign of danger.

Seeing nothing, they waved goodbye to Kenji, who watched from above. Once they reached the sparsely vegetated forest, Akeno took off down the path, and Jacob almost tripped as he hurried to keep up. He expected a wolf or a Rog to jump out at any moment.

After running for about half an hour, Akeno stopped and put his hand up against a tree—just listening, it seemed. "Nothing," he said, steadying himself to catch his breath. "We'll stop here to rest. I don't want to be too close to the barrier while it's dark."

Jacob readjusted his bag. "I hope the whole trip doesn't consist of us running from wolves."

He followed Akeno into the forest, and they looked around for a place to set up camp. After searching for a few minutes, they found a large, overturned tree surrounded by thick bushes. Akeno put his finger to the tree's trunk and muttered.

"What are you doing?"

"Telling the tree and the bushes to form a tent."

The branches of the tree and bushes started to move, encircling Akeno and Jacob. Jacob stared, hardly believing his eyes, then jumped out of the way as a squirrel darted across the ground, followed closely by intertwining branches.

Akeno wasn't kidding when he'd said he could tell living things what to do.

Moments later, a somewhat round little fort had been created. There was a small opening in the roof, and the walls were made of tightly woven branches. The floor of the hut was matted and springy—perfect for sleeping on.

"Will this be strong enough against the wolves?" Jacob said.

"They won't be able to get in." Akeno sat close to the wall on a bouncy section of branches. He pointed to a spot on the other side of the hut. "You'll need all the rest you can get."

Jacob agreed, and they both lay down and fell asleep.

Jacob awoke an hour or so after sunrise, feeling refreshed and energetic. He rolled over to face the other side of the hut and saw that Akeno had already left. Alarmed, Jacob jumped to his feet and started pushing against the walls of the hut, but nothing gave.

"Akeno! Hey! How do I get out of this thing?"

"Oh, I'm sorry, I didn't tell you," Akeno's voice sounded muffled through the wall. "I'll always leave a place for us to exit. Once you're out, though, you won't be able to get back in, so make sure you don't leave anything behind."

The branches quivered and shook around Jacob, and before he knew it, he stood in the open, next to the bushes and fallen tree that looked as they had the night before. It was a clear morning, and a brisk breeze ruffled Jacob's hair. A feeling hit him—excitement? Was it possible he was *excited* for this trip? He frowned, not yet ready to let go of his grudge over having to go at all.

Akeno sat on a log and put on his shoes, which had fresh leaves attached to them. "That ought to do it," he said.

"That's so weird."

"Hey—at least it keeps the dirt away." He stood, adjusting his top hat. For the first time, Jacob took notice of Akeno's other clothing. His black T-shirt had the word *"dare"* spelled out across it in bright red, and he wore brown pants. *Dare?*

"The Minyas came while you were sleeping," the Makalo said, "but I let them go play. We'll need to call them again." He walked to a dandelion plant and picked one of the bigger, fluffier heads. He whispered into the seeds and blew them into the air, turning the head so he wouldn't miss any.

Jacob watched the seeds float off. "Why dandelions? And what do the seeds do?"

"They're available during a large part of the year. The seeds carry the message to the Minyas. I don't know how, so don't ask." He smiled to show he wasn't trying to be rude. "Okay, they're coming."

"How do the Minyas fly without wings?" Jacob asked.

"They use their magic as a way to maneuver, and choose what does and doesn't affect them: gravity, resistance, laws of physics—things like that." As the Minyas arrived, Akeno motioned toward Jacob. "September, Early, this is Jacob. He's here to help us get the Key back."

"Don't they remember me from earlier? When they were helping with the Rog?"

Akeno laughed. "I doubt they do. They probably didn't pay any attention to the cause of the commotion."

"Hi, Jacob," Early said. She spoke to September. "My, isn't he a big Makalo."

September laughed, slapping his knee. "He's not a Makalo," he said. "He's a human!"

Jacob shook his head. Akeno was right.

"Oh, another one?" Early looked at Jacob, tapping the side of her face with a finger. "Why's he here?"

"Don't care. Come on!" September grabbed Early's hand, and they flitted away.

Akeno called to the Minyas to stop, then told Early to deliver a message to his parents, telling them the group was heading off.

Jacob was a little surprised when she acted thrilled to do it. After a bright flash of light, she was gone.

"How fast do they go?" Jacob asked.

"They travel at the speed of light when they combine their powers."

"Are you sure?" Jacob asked. Akeno had to be exaggerating. "That's really fast. I don't think it's even possible."

"In normal cases, obviously it wouldn't be possible. But remember that the laws of physics don't apply to them. Their magic makes them invincible to anything that might cause a resistance. There are drawbacks to using their magic, though. In order to travel that way, a Minya must have been to, or seen, the place where he or she is headed. The magic draws on their memories and propels them forward, taking them to their destination. If they don't know where the place is located, it can be very dangerous, since the magic will then take the shortest route, which is sometimes through solid objects." Akeno paused. "Oh, and don't say please to them—they don't like it."

"What? Why not?"

"Hundreds of years ago, they were slaves. You don't say please to slaves. Now it's just a weird thing about them. Honestly, no one really knows how the mind of a Minya works." Akeno looked up and frowned, searching the air. "Early should be back by now."

They continued waiting in silence. After a moment, Jacob spotted Early zooming toward them.

"What took you so long?" September said as soon as Early was close enough.

"Kenji gave me some honey. And they say hi and are happy that nothing bad has happened yet."

Akeno laughed out loud. "'Yet?' Are they expecting us to have that much trouble?"

Jacob picked up his bag. "Let's get going."

"Yes, good idea. We can eat while we walk." Akeno pulled bread and jerky from his knapsack, handing some of it to Jacob.

Jacob fell into step behind Akeno, munching on a piece of bread, appreciating the beauty of the morning and tranquility of the thin forest. The sun was bright, but not too warm, and the sky was almost cloudless. The leaves and grass glowed light green in the sunny morning light, and there were flowers everywhere.

After several minutes of walking, the trail turned sharply upward and looked like it would be difficult for about a hundred feet or so. Large weeds and underbrush grew over the path, and they had to push their way through.

"Not . . . much . . . farther," Akeno said, panting.

As predicted, the path stopped. The sheer canyon wall rose up before them, with a gaping hole in it and broken boards on either side of the hole. The boards appeared to have been ripped off, and several were strewn across the ground. The canyon wall was solid rock, and the hole looked man-made.

Jacob picked up one of the smaller pieces of board. The wood was attractive, somehow, in its coloring. It was very light brown, with silver streaks flowing through the grain and was thick and sturdy. "I'm guessing this is where the Lorkon came in."

"Yes, this is the entrance." Akeno said. He motioned to the wood in Jacob's hand. "That comes from the Kaede tree—the same tree which produces the healing sap."

"Oh, yeah. The sap smells like maple syrup. Why's that?"

"It's a type of maple tree—but don't eat it. It tastes disgusting." He laughed—probably at a memory. "The trees are awesome. They're grown naturally, but with some . . . *help* from Makalos." He smiled. "Rezend makes them grow stronger than other trees, and steel develops in the grain, making it nearly unbreakable."

"It looks really cool," Jacob said.

He dropped the board and studied the area. The ground had leveled, forming a small meadow in front of the entrance. There were only a few trees up here, and they looked as though they had some type of horrible disease. Their leaves were shriveled, the bark had a slight red shade, and the grass around them was yellowed.

"It's sad to see the trees like this," Akeno said. "Normally, Kaede trees live through everything."

"The Lorkon did it?"

Akeno nodded. "Let's get going." He walked to the tree closest to the entrance, putting his hand on it for a moment. A frustrated expression crossed his face. "I can't sense anything. I hate running blind like this." He frowned at the tree, then turned to Jacob. "Are you ready?"

"I guess so," Jacob said. "I can't tell which emotion is stronger right now—nervousness or excitement."

"Me neither." Akeno motioned to the hole. "After you."

"I've got a better idea. You go first, and I'll make sure no one kills us from behind."

"Right," Akeno said, laughing. He entered the tunnel.

The hole was the perfect height for Akeno, but Jacob had to duck to get through. It was cool and dark inside, and

Jacob's eyes had just enough time to adjust when suddenly the tunnel ended.

Akeno stopped abruptly and Jacob ran into him, squinting in the brightness of the sun. Looking ahead, his jaw dropped.

"Whoa," he said, eyes wide.

Chapter 6

Infected

We finally managed to contact the Makalo patriarch and beg his assistance. Luckily, he is just as determined as we are to remove the Lorkon from our land. The Lorkon have amassed a huge force, and the patriarch is sending an army of Makalos to assist in the war that is surely coming.

The trees on the other side of the tunnel were dead, misshapen, and shriveled. They were almost painful to look at. The land around the trees also appeared to be dead, and there were animal carcasses strewn across the ground. The stench was so strong that Jacob's stomach lurched, and a sharp feeling of nausea hit him.

All of this, however, was not what had caught Jacob off guard.

Everything—including the sky—was completely devoid of color.

Coming up beside Akeno, Jacob was disturbed to see that the Makalo, too, was colorless. Akeno's mouth was set in a grim line. He'd obviously seen this before—most likely when they tried to get the Key themselves. The Minyas were oblivious to the situation and continued flitting around in the air.

"Why is everything black and white?" Jacob asked. Even his own body was in shades of gray.

"We don't know," Akeno said.

While he was taking in the surroundings, Jacob had the slight sensation of being on a boat, rocking side to side. He couldn't put his finger on why he felt this way. He studied the forest around them, trying to figure it out. After a moment, he noticed something odd about the trees. "Akeno, are the trees moving?"

"I'm not sure." Akeno walked up to the trunk of the tree nearest them.

"Oh, wow!" Jacob said. "Did you see that? The tree leaned away from you!"

"Yeah, I saw." Akeno started wringing his hands. "But why'd it do it?"

"I don't know." Jacob joined Akeno and noticed that most of the trees shifted as they got closer. "It's as though they're trying to get away, like they're repulsed by us or something."

"I don't like this." Akeno reached out with his left ring finger to touch the tree. As soon as he made contact with the bark, a branch whipped through the air and smacked his hand, causing both of them to jump.

"Ouch!" Akeno looked down at the skin on his hand, where a large welt was already forming. "Why did it do that?" He glared at the branch that hit him. "Stupid tree!"

"Maybe it doesn't want you to touch it. Or maybe it's possessed or something." Jacob backed away quickly, careful not to get too close to the trees on the other side of the path.

Akeno shook his head, motioning in jerky movements with his hands. "I've never heard of this happening before."

"Should we send one of the Minyas to ask Kenji about it?"

"I don't know, I don't know!" Akeno said frantically. "What could he possibly do to help?"

"He might have an idea about what's going on," Jacob said, looking around at the trees.

"I doubt he would." Akeno's voice took on a shrill note. "Why didn't he come with us? Why didn't Brojan come with us? This is such a waste of time!"

Jacob looked at the Makalo. What was wrong with him? "Akeno? Are you . . . feeling okay?"

Akeno turned on Jacob. "Of course I'm not! What makes you think I would be? I just got attacked by a tree!" An anguished expression crossed his face. "If it won't let me touch it, how will I know what's going on around us? These things don't just happen for no reason! I've always been able to use my Rezend!"

Jacob was astonished to see that Akeno was almost in tears.

"Can I see your hand? The one the tree just whipped?" Jacob reached out, but Akeno jumped away from him.

"Don't touch me! What are you doing? Keep away!"

Jacob put his hands in the air. "Okay! Sorry. I won't do it again."

Akeno pulled off his top hat and crumpled to the ground, sobbing.

"I'm sorry!" Jacob said, exasperated. "I really didn't mean to upset you."

"I don't need your pity!" Akeno said, flinging his hat at Jacob.

Jacob caught the hat and turned away, muttering to himself. Someone had to act logically here.

Brojan and Kenji would know what to do—they must have some advice. He started running to the tunnel to go back to Taga, but thought better of it and turned around.

"September, go now—" He paused when he saw that September was pretending not to hear him. "Come on—it's for Akeno, not me."

September turned to him. "Fine."

"Is it possible for the two of you to throw yourselves, or whatever you do, at the same time?"

"Yes, it is," September said.

"Then you go to Kenji, and you, Early, go to Brojan. We need to figure out what's going on."

"On it!" Early said, and with a bright flash of light, they were gone. Jacob faced Akeno, who was no longer sobbing, but glaring up at him.

"Okay . . . uh . . . well, hopefully we'll figure things out soon," Jacob said, giving the hat back to Akeno.

Akeno jammed the hat on his head. "There's absolutely nothing going on that wasn't supposed to happen, Jacob." The amount of venom in his voice was shocking. "Are you so stupid you can't see that?"

Jacob tried not to look at him, but couldn't help it. "Well, uh, I'm sure this wasn't planned by anyone . . . except maybe the Lorkon."

Akeno's fist hit the ground. "You're wrong. My father and Brojan knew this would happen. They sent us here to fail."

Jacob shook his head slowly. He couldn't figure out why Akeno was acting this way. "I really don't think they did."

Thankfully, September and Early returned, putting a stop to the conversation. Early flew to Akeno and stuck her tongue out at him. Akeno snarled, his face contorted, and he jumped up, lunging at her. His hands swiped the air,

but she was already several feet away from him, grinning. He ran after her, yelling at her to come back.

Jacob turned to September, who, like Early, thought this was hilarious. "What did they say?"

September stopped laughing and turned to Jacob. "Kenji and Brojan were at Akeno's house. They said you should always keep one messenger with you and to send only one of us at a time from now on, just in case something happens and you need the other Minya's help." He looked at Akeno, who was still trying to get Early. "You need to get Akeno out of the forest right now—the trees are poisonous to him."

Jacob raised an eyebrow. "Poisonous trees? What else are we going to come across here? Animal-eating flowers?" The Minya ignored him. "At least the tree didn't hit me, too. One of us had to stay sane."

September shook his head, watching Early and Akeno. "Brojan said Akeno isn't acting that way because he got hit. The trees—their influence—are poisonous to him, like they were to the adult Makalos. He must be getting older."

Jacob rolled his eyes. Of *course* the Makalo was getting older. "Was there anything else?" he asked.

No response. Jacob waved his hand in front of September. "Hello? Was there anything else?"

"Oh, yes, there was."

"Well?"

September finally turned back to Jacob. "Brojan said, 'Absolutely do not go into the forest.' And Kenji said, 'Don't tell Akeno you're moving him. Just grab him and go.'"

"Okay. And that's all?"

"Yes, that's all."

Jacob motioned toward Akeno. "Have Early bring him back."

Akeno's ranting became louder as he and the Minyas drew closer. Jacob waved his arms. "Hey, Akeno!"

"You stay out of this, you good-for-nothing human!" Akeno screamed, spittle flying from his mouth. "Who cares who you are? Who cares where you come from? I could've done this just as well as you, only I could've done it alone!"

Jacob frowned, trying to decide the best way to move the Makalo. Bribery? He dismissed that idea as soon as it came to him. Akeno wasn't acting logically right now, and wouldn't respond well to a verbal approach. That meant there was only one thing Jacob could do. Grab Akeno and run—just as Kenji had suggested. "I'm really sorry for doing this," Jacob said, and then he rushed forward, picked up Akeno, and swung him over his shoulder.

"Put me down! Put me down right now!"

With a sudden squirm, Akeno turned and clawed at Jacob's face. Surprised, Jacob dropped him, and Akeno took off, running full speed into the forest.

"Oh, no!"

Jacob dropped his bag and sped after Akeno. He wasn't surprised when the trees started thrashing around him.

Dodging branches, dead animals, and stumps, he stumbled through the forest, doing his best to ignore the angry, moving trees. He kept his eyes on Akeno, but the Makalo was much faster than Jacob had given him credit for, and it was difficult to keep up.

The forest was much thicker now, with almost no visibility. Panic hit Jacob when he noticed that the distance between himself and Akeno was growing. He couldn't tell for sure, but it seemed that while the trees were still trying to stop him, they were now letting Akeno through. The air tasted stale and dirty, and each breath he took was agonizing. Jacob tried to limit the amount of air that entered his lungs, but the stench of death was unavoidable.

The forest grew thicker, making it nearly impossible to see, and what little light there was danced around as the branches thrashed. After only a few minutes, Jacob could no longer see Akeno, and very soon couldn't hear him, either. The trees thinned and he stopped running, not sure where to go since Akeno hadn't exactly been running in a straight line.

Something cold and smooth brushed against Jacob's cheek. He frantically wiped it off his face, spinning to see what had touched him. Nothing was there but the moving branches.

He started forward again, cautiously peering ahead. He gasped as another cold, smooth thing ran through his hair. He bent over and shook his head as hard as he could, trying to rid himself of the animal—or whatever it was.

Seconds later, an extra weight slid across his shoulders and over them, circling his neck. Reaching up to grab it, he recognized the feel of the creature. It was a snake about two feet long, and in the dim light, he could see that it was pale in color. He yanked, flinging it off. As it flew through the air, Jacob stumbled from shock as he watched it flatten and float swiftly to a nearby tree.

The trees stopped moving. With the stillness, the light no longer danced, and Jacob could see better. Nearly every surface was covered with snakes—the ground seemed to have come alive. Several of them floated through the air.

Worried that the trees had stopped moving because something even larger and scarier than flying serpents had entered the forest, Jacob peered through the darkness, gingerly treading forward. He tried not to step on any of the snakes and grimaced when he did, but they weren't reacting to him now that the trees were still.

As he walked cautiously, watching the trees in case they started to fling their branches around again, something large brushed against his leg. He looked down and made out the shape of a snake, two feet in diameter, as it slithered slowly past him, then stopped.

Jacob's body stiffened with fear as his mind raced. He flipped through all his Scouting memories—what kind of snake was this? Was it poisonous? He couldn't remember ever having seen one as big as it, with its coloring, before, even on TV. He gasped when the snake coiled around his feet. He tried to step away, but couldn't. Not only was the fear overwhelming, but his feet were being held too tightly.

The snake hissed, and suddenly it was eye-to-eye with Jacob, its intelligent green eyes piercing into him. Pressure around his knees told him the snake was increasing its grip there. He tried to move again, but couldn't—the massive serpent had coiled around his chest and tightened its hold.

The snake's tongue flicked out, barely touching Jacob's skin and hair, testing the air around him. Then its body tightened so much that it squeezed the breath out of him. Lifting him completely off the ground, the snake leaned in about a foot from Jacob's face and gave a loud, menacing hiss, revealing six-inch fangs that glistened in the dim light. It whipped its head away and started dragging him through the forest. Jacob gasped desperately for air and was finally able to pull in a short breath.

After a few moments, they were joined by a second snake just as big as the first. This snake slithered alongside them for a moment, then headed off to the right.

The forest ended as the snake reached the edge of a clearing. Toward the center was a hill with a very large manor sitting atop its crest. There was no sign of Akeno.

The manor must have been impressive in its day. The large columns looked to be made of granite, and the windows, most of which had either been boarded over or smashed open, were massive and elegant. The wide, concrete porch that circled the house was now cracked and disheveled, with vines growing unchecked through the cracks and up many of the columns. The front right corner of the foundation had begun to sink, and rotted wood lay strewn about.

In front of the house, to the right, was a large pit. Jacob thought he could hear Akeno's voice coming from it, and he struggled to break free of the snake's tight grip. But the snake ignored his attempts and continued slithering across the ground, up the stairs, and through the open front door of the house.

It was musty and dirty inside. Dim light shone through several of the smashed windows. The front entryway was spacious—at least two stories high, maybe three. The floor was marble, and there were grand marble pillars lining the edges of the room. Stained-glass windows, most of them boarded over, were placed between the pillars.

Just before they went up a large, curved stairway, Jacob caught a glimpse of a side room with sheet-covered furniture. There was a hallway at the top of the stairs, the first half overlooking the front entry and the second half lined with doors on both sides. All the doors were shut, and many of them had a slight greenish glow coming through the cracks. The snake stopped abruptly at the end of the hall. In place of the door was a silvery, translucent sheen that filled the entire doorway.

The snake paused before entering. The moment its head passed the frame, there was a loud clap, and the sheen disappeared. The snake wriggled forward a few feet, then released its hold on Jacob. He stumbled to his feet and whirled, ready to defend himself, but the snake had already slithered back into the hallway and was biting the top, bottom, and sides of the door frame. The translucent veil materialized again, sealing the doorway, and the snake slithered down the hall and stairs.

Jacob rushed to the nearest window, barely noticing the junk and oddly placed rolls of thick cloth on the floor, and watched as the snake disappeared into the forest. He waited a few moments longer, but the snake didn't return.

The pit was beneath the window. It wasn't very deep—maybe two or three feet—and Akeno was there, thrashing around with the remains of charred furniture and other debris. Jacob pounded on the window, trying to get Akeno's attention, but the Makalo didn't seem to notice.

A cold wind blew on the back of Jacob's neck, making his hair rise. He turned and nearly yelled—about a foot or so away was a partially decomposed body sitting in a chair, on the verge of tumbling over.

Afraid it would fall at any moment, Jacob kept his hands up as he stepped to the side, barely missing another body that lay across the floor with arms stretched toward the door. He jumped away from it, realizing that what he'd assumed to be rolls of cloth were really bodies sprawled on the ground, reaching for the exit.

He made his way to a clear spot and looked around.

The room was very large. There was a massive bed against one wall, a fireplace on another, and several chairs placed in random positions around bookcases, tables, and the fireplace. Nearly every chair held human remains, ranging from full skeletons to decomposing corpses that had been dead for only a few weeks at most. In one corner of the room was a table. On top were two stone jugs and bits of both fresh and moldy food.

The smell of death and decay became so overpowering, Jacob felt as though his lungs would burst. Desperate for fresh air, he steeled himself, then rushed past the dead bodies back to the window.

He grunted, pushing on the lever, trying to open the window. But it wouldn't budge.

Jacob's gaze landed on the jugs, and he grabbed one—it was heavy with water. He smashed it against the window as hard as he could. The result was water splashing all over him and the nearest body, the jug shattering, and the window remaining undamaged. He grimaced.

Then he looked down and noticed several other broken objects on the floor below the windows—byproducts of others' attempts to break the glass.

Jacob groaned. "Oh, man, I've really got to get out of here."

The sound of his own voice startled him, and he looked over his shoulder at the bodies. He felt stupid when he realized he was checking to see if they'd moved. He forced himself to take a deep breath to calm himself, and studied them. What if, like them, his only way out was through the doorway? But why hadn't the others gone through? They weren't tied up or anything. They weren't even near the door. None of them was closer than five or six feet.

Resolving to get out, Jacob crossed the room toward the shimmering doorway. He stopped about three feet away, peering at it. There was a slight movement, a few swirls in the silver. Light pink and blue mists emanated from it, and Jacob was distracted by the color for a moment—it was the first he'd seen since he got here. Reaching toward the portal, something passed over his skin as his hand went through the mist. It was cold—very cold—and a sharp pinpricking sensation started at his fingertips, moving up his wrist to where the mist stopped. Alarmed, Jacob pulled back his arm and examined his hand. No blood, no mark, nothing.

He looked up, took a step closer, and put his hand out again, this time determined to touch the shimmering barrier. The same cold, prickly feeling started at his fingertips and reached his elbow. He held his breath and plunged his arm forward. Nothing happened. But then he saw the sheen separate where he touched it.

Jacob stepped forward, pushing himself into the veil. The cold mist encompassed him, and the pinpricks covered him from head to foot. An enormous pressure enveloped his entire body, making movement difficult, and the air started to swirl around him. As the wind gained speed, his shirt got pulled up and his hair ruffled.

An intense pain suddenly hit him, starting in his chest and moving to his extremities. He felt electrocuted—he couldn't move, and his body shook. He couldn't even breathe. His fingers felt pulled from their joints, and there was no sensation in his feet. He tried to back out of the doorway, but it was as if some invisible force was holding him in one spot.

After what seemed like an eternity, but was probably only a few seconds, the feeling left him and he doubled over, gasping for breath. The pain in his muscles was replaced with numbness and he lost his balance, falling back into the room.

Jacob lay awkwardly on his side, no feeling in his body whatsoever. Had he been hit by lighting? Zapped with a Taser? Even his brain seemed paralyzed.

Sensation slowly returned to his limbs and he rolled onto his back, staring up at the ceiling. What on earth had happened? Or, more precisely, what on Eklaron had happened? *Had* he been electrocuted? And why hadn't it killed him? Did the people in the room try the same thing with similar results? He flipped onto his stomach and gradually got to his knees, ignoring the dead body only a foot or so in front of him.

He stood and turned around to face the barrier. It was the only way out of the room—he was sure of it. Did he dare try to walk through again? He grimaced, imagining going through the pain once more. Or three or four times. Who, after experiencing something like that, would volunteer for a repeat? He looked around the room at the dead bodies. There was no way he was going to stay here and die like they did. He had to get that Key. He had to get Akeno out of the forest. He had to see Ebony and Kenji and Matt and his family again. And he definitely had to try out for the basketball team before he died. A fierce determination hit him. He *would* get the Key. *Nothing* was going to stop him.

With new resolve, Jacob held up his hand and took a step, frowning as the tingly sensation moved from his fingers and up his arm. This time, however, he steeled himself against the pressure of the swirling air and pushed as hard as he could. The same intense pain began, stopping his breathing once again, but he was already moving forward and continued pushing.

A loud pop made him jump, and the pressure, the mist, the pain, and the wind were suddenly gone. There was only the simple door frame.

Relief coursed through his body and he paused, breathing deeply. Why did it work this time and not the first? Deciding to think on it later, he took one last look into the room, then sprinted down the hallway and the stairs. He crossed the front entryway and exited the house, expecting something to jump out at him any moment, and feeling relieved when nothing did.

Once outside, Jacob looked around for any sign of the snakes, but something odd caught his attention. The trees appeared to be pulsing toward the same point in the forest some distance away. And that spot appeared to be moving.

A sick feeling came over him as he realized that whatever was moving through the forest was coming his way, and that the trees wanted to be close to it—trees that had been trying to kill him earlier. His imagination spun wildly out of control, and he tried to push thoughts of thousands of snakes or huge spiders like the one in Lord of the Rings coming at him.

Jacob ran to the edge of the pit and saw Akeno randomly digging around in the pile of junk. The furniture had been burned a while ago—how long, he couldn't tell.

He quickly headed down the three-foot slope into the pit toward Akeno. Not even waiting to see what mood he was in, Jacob took Akeno's hands, pinned them tightly together, and swung the small Makalo over his shoulder.

Then he practically flew out of the pit. Ignoring Akeno's yelling, Jacob sprinted through the forest, praying he wouldn't run into either of the snakes. It was difficult to keep Akeno on his shoulder—he was kicking and flailing his arms with all his might and almost got away several times.

The trees weren't thrashing at them. Jacob figured they were distracted by whatever lay just ahead of them, and felt uncomfortable with the idea that he was running almost straight toward their focus point. But there wasn't anything else he could do. He only knew one way to get back to the path, and that was to go the way he had come.

Jacob kept Akeno's wrists pinned together with one hand. He used the other to push branches out of the way. Jumping across a flattened tree, he almost lost his grip on Akeno.

Veering right, Jacob tried to widen the space between the oncoming danger and themselves. He started to feel hopeful that they could get away after all.

As he tore through the forest, a snake flew out of the air in front of him, and he almost lost Akeno again. A memory of flying snakes he'd once seen on a science show flashed across his mind, and he had an "ahah!" moment. The snakes around him were a lot like the ones he'd seen on TV. They must've been related somehow!

Something caught Jacob's attention and he stole a sidelong glance. Completely unprepared for what he saw, Jacob lost his balance and tumbled headlong into the brush. The dark, piercing eyes of a beautiful woman had locked with his. She was at least a hundred feet away, but the trees were leaning over, almost touching the ground as they bowed to her, and he could see her clearly.

She was clad in flowing white robes that billowed in the breeze. Her long, dark hair mingled with the robes, drifting around her. She smiled mockingly at him, and it appeared as if she found his situation humorous. Her walk was graceful, and though she moved toward the house, when their eyes met, she stopped to face him.

"Danilo," she said in a whisper. Her voice was haunting, carrying across the distance with ease.

Akeno whimpered, and Jacob, distracted by the woman's beauty, realized he was probably squishing his little prisoner. Tearing his eyes away from her gaze, Jacob saw fear written all over the poor Makalo's face. He looked at the woman again and saw that she was still watching him, though now she reached toward him, beckoning him to come.

Feeling an odd yearning to do so, Jacob got to his feet, hefting Akeno and brushing himself off with the hand that wasn't holding the Makalo. What was a beautiful woman like that doing alone in the forest? There were dangerous things here, and . . . and she obviously needed him. He could take care of her. He'd even clean and fix up the manor. Akeno didn't need his help. The Makalos were probably just being pessimistic about the Lorkon and their old war. He took a step in her direction, but Akeno struggled on his shoulder, seemingly aware of what Jacob was doing.

Jacob scowled. Akeno was always getting in the way, trying to make Jacob do things he didn't want to do. Jacob glanced at the lady, and she again beckoned.

He smiled at her. The picture she created was one of serenity and elegance. He wanted to look into her eyes and say something intelligent to make her like him. He took a determined step forward, but jumped when Akeno bit him and tried to escape.

"Stupid Makalo!" Jacob said, scrambling to cover Akeno's mouth and hold him in place.

The pain made him hesitate, however, and he frowned, struggling with himself internally. Something made him long to be near the woman. But then again . . . a gross feeling started in the pit of his stomach and spread to his heart. He blinked, his mind clearing, somewhat confused by the feeling. Something so beautiful and perfect couldn't be bad, could it? But there was that feeling again. *Take a step back*, it warned him. He grunted, frustrated with the persistence of the ridiculous thought that was ruining his peaceful moment.

Finally recognizing that he couldn't ignore the warning, he closed his eyes, willing his intuition to tell him why he shouldn't go to her.

Logic entered his mind. The trees wanted to be near her, and they had been trying to kill him earier. They'd been incredibly vicious and angry toward the intruders. He scowled and opened his eyes. She was still there, patiently waiting. He glanced down at his arms, the skin still scratched and scraped from being attacked by limbs.

Jacob sighed and looked at the woman, feeling wistful. Then he saw the hundreds of snakes swirling around her ankles. That wasn't good. Snakes had taken him to a room full of dead people.

No, he couldn't go to her.

With that thought, a feeling of warmth spread through his chest, as if to confirm his reasoning, and the disturbing feeling started to leave.

He took a step back, stumbled, and almost fell. A look of anger crossed the woman's face. Again she beckoned, imploring him to come.

Shaking his head, unable to speak, he took another step back.

This time, an unmistakable expression of anger marred her exotic features. With a quick movement, she spread her arms, raised her face to the sky, and emitted a shrill, piercing scream.

Out of her mouth poured a thick, black cloud of air, made up of thousands of flying bugs and beetles which congregated around her. Dropping her head, she directed her scream toward Jacob, and the cloud came shooting across the distance between them.

No longer hesitant, Jacob took off in the opposite direction, running as fast as his legs would go.

"Faster!" Akeno yelled, still slung over Jacob's shoulder. After what felt like an eternity of fighting branches, a bright patch of light came upon them, and Jacob fell to his knees onto the trail.

Jumping to his feet, he readjusted his hold on Akeno and grabbed both their bags from where they had dropped them earlier. He saw the Minyas and pointed at them. "You, come now!"

They immediately flitted into the air, following him as ran down the trail.

The trees were now bending toward something almost directly behind them. Jacob didn't want to know if the lady was there.

After running for only a few hundred feet, he came to a crossroads. All three paths led into the forest, but one led to the south and looked less worn. Without stopping, Jacob made a split-second decision and chose that one.

Akeno yelled in fright at something behind them, and Jacob, who thought he was already running as fast as he could, put on even more speed, nearly losing his balance in the process.

The Minyas flitted alongside him. Both looked terrified and urged him to go faster. The smell of dead animals was overwhelming, and Jacob's head spun from the stench.

Jacob looked up from the trail, and before long, he could see the end of the forest fast approaching. Relief coursed through him. Only that much farther to go. He could make it—he *had* to make it.

With one final push, he sailed through the last bit of forest at what felt like breakneck speed. A few strides from the forest edge, the buzzing sound dissipated, and he chanced a look backward. The cloud of black had stopped exactly where the forest ended. There was no sign of the woman.

Jacob ran a good minute or so before he couldn't go any more. He released his hold on Akeno, who tumbled out of sight, and Jacob collapsed on his back in the tall grass alongside the trail.

After catching his breath, Jacob realized the scent of decay was fading. And he could see color again! He breathed deeply the warm fragrance of sun-baked grass and wildflowers. Rolling to his side, he reached over and grabbed a handful of the nearest flowers, pulling them out at the roots. He shoved them up against his nose, hoping the sweet aroma would remove the smell of rot that seemed to be forever imprinted on his brain.

A few minutes later, when his breathing had returned to normal, when his heart had slowed, and when he could no longer taste or smell death, he set the flowers aside and sprawled out on his back again, stretching out his sore muscles. Locking his hands behind his head, he gazed at the deep blue sky, unable to remember a time when he was more grateful to see it.

Chapter 7

A Bucket Full of Nuts

Today we experienced the second element: wind. As with the water, it was nothing like what we'd been expecting, and the form in which it came was a complete surprise to us. There was no warning at all, not even a wave of heat as before.

We were following the trail, conversing, when we noticed a pleasant scent. Kelson claimed it was his mother's bread and soup. Kenji believed it was maple trees, pine needles, and mountains. To me, it was Arien's perfume. The other Makalos and humans also listed their favorite things. Regardless of what we smelled, the effect was the same—we were made to feel completely happy and at peace.

We continued our trek, satisfied and content, and weren't surprised to find the trail free from problems as we traveled.

However, an hour or two later, I felt someone pull me from my horse and drag me along the ground. I couldn't focus on whoever it was, nor could I clear my thoughts long enough to remember what I was doing. The smell was so pervasive that my thoughts were completely centered on Arien. I'd even forgotten that she'd been kidnapped.

I felt water being poured over my head, and suddenly my thoughts were sharp again. When I looked around, I saw that I was near a small cabin, with its owner standing over me. Instead of fear, I felt joy as I realized who this woman was—a long-time friend of Ara Liese and Arien's.

The Fat Lady—as she insists on being called—drew my attention to the trail and my fellow travelers. I was disturbed to see every member of the group standing still, a complacent smile upon their faces. But what shocked me most was that during the last two hours, we hadn't moved an inch, and the horses had wandered away from us to graze. How had they done so, when we had been riding them?

Once my companions had been rescued and the horses rounded up, the Fat Lady explained everything.

The Lorkon created a type of everlasting potion and placed it in thick concentrations throughout the area. Whenever a person inhales the fumes of this potion, his mind is confounded, and he—or she—is rendered completely helpless. What was most frightening to us was this—the individual has no idea he is not continuing with his life because in his mind, he is. It is an invisible prison.

A timid voice interrupted Jacob's reverie. "Jacob?"

He sat up and focused on Akeno, who sat not too far away. "Yeah?"

"Would you accept an apology? The way I behaved was completely childish and . . ."

Jacob smiled, holding his hand toward Akeno. "It's okay, really it is."

Jacob watched Akeno closely to see if he was going to cry or start throwing punches. Satisfied by what he saw in the Makalo's eyes, he relaxed.

His mind drifted back to the forest. "Do you think that lady had an influence on what the trees were doing to us?"

Akeno shredded the leaves on his shoes. "I imagine so," he said, then scratched his head. "Good thing I have another hat at home, 'cause I think I lost mine somewhere in the forest." He looked at Jacob. "Am I really so weak I couldn't even handle a few negative emotions?"

Jacob shook his head. "No, I don't think you are. It affected the Makalo adults, too."

Akeno picked some grass near him, and Jacob pulled the petals off a flower. He could tell Akeno wanted to say something, so he waited. He hated awkward silences.

Akeno kept picking at the grass. Finally, he looked up. "Why didn't the forest bother you?"

Jacob thought back to what he had felt while in the forest. He recognized he had remained rational the entire time . . . well, except when the woman was trying to lure him. But even Matt would have given in under those circumstances.

He sprawled on his back again. Why *had* Akeno been the only one affected by the trees? Why hadn't they bothered Jacob? "Maybe the magic of your world doesn't apply to humans," he said.

"I don't think that's it," Akeno said. "But you might be immune to bad magic."

"How 'bout we not do anything to test *that* theory." Jacob wanted to avoid anything that would cause Akeno to go back to how he had acted earlier. He propped himself up on his elbow. "Why weren't the Minyas overcome by it?"

"The same reason the laws of physics don't affect them," Akeno said. "Their magic doesn't allow it. Very rarely do they come across something that does bother them."

"We couldn't enter the forest," September said, floating above them. "We tried to follow, but something stopped us—perhaps a magic."

Jacob sat up, shading his eyes from the sun. "But what if we hadn't come back?"

"Then we would have informed Brojan and Kenji," September said.

Jacob faced Akeno. "We can ask your dad about the forest and the room in the house and everything. They'd probably know why it all happened." He turned to find the Minyas. "Early, take a message to Akeno's parents and Brojan, telling them about how we saw an insane woman and found a manor full of dead people. Then let us know what they say."

Early disappeared and Jacob sat and pulled food out of his bag. He was starving, and practically stuffed his mouth full of jerky and cheese. Once they'd finished, he put the food away. "Tell me more about Rezend. How do you target the wolves' hearing?"

"I use Rezend to make a loud noise."

"Gee, I would never have guessed." He snorted. "Seriously. How does it knock them out?"

"Well, I concentrate on them while I create a sort of shockwave that targets ears. The shockwave is really powerful, and it knocks them out. It'll target almost any living thing, but if used too frequently, it isn't as effective."

Jacob took a drink of water out of the canteen, then stared at it. It looked like it came from Walmart. He smiled to himself. They sat in silence for a while, waiting for Early to return.

"What other things can you do with your Rezend?" Jacob asked.

Akeno's face turned thoughtful, and he took a moment to answer. "I can use it as a light. My left ring finger—where the Rezend is centered—will glow brightly when I want. Rezend can control electricity, and particles to an extent." He rummaged through his bag, then popped a grape into his mouth and lay in the grass. "And water, too. Plumbing, lighting, etc."

Akeno got to his knees, about to say something more, then stopped short.

The two black wolves sat on the forest edge, watching them.

"Not this again," Jacob said.

"It's definitely annoying."

"Let's just ignore them. I'm positive they're making sure we're not returning to Taga Village."

Jacob looked at the trail in the opposite direction. Not far away was a grove of trees with a small cabin in the middle. Taller trees grew beyond that. The mountains to the south were big, though not as tall as the mountains even farther than them. There were acres and acres of gently rolling hills between the forest behind them and the mountains ahead.

When he turned back, he saw that the wolves had left. He breathed a sigh of relief.

Just then, Early returned. "Kenji and Brojan didn't say a lot. They gave me honey, though! They didn't see the lady in the forest when they tried to leave Taga. But they said to go see Aldo. Ask him what he knows about the forest and the Key." She pointed at the cabin. "That's where he lives."

The group gathered their things and followed the trail to the grove, soon reaching the path that led to Aldo's place.

"Someone's home," Jacob said, motioning to the smoke that rose from the chimney.

Akeno nodded, stopping near one of the trees. "I wonder how these will treat me—I'm not feeling any negative emotions. Maybe I should check what's going on around us?"

"Yeah, do. I'll be right here to pull you away in case it tries to hit you."

"Okay, here we go."

Akeno reached his left hand to the tree, carefully touching the bark. When nothing happened, he visibly relaxed. "No danger here—the wolves must've stayed in the forest." He plucked a bunch of leaves, then sat on the ground and taped them to his shoes.

When Akeno was finished, Jacob led the way to the cabin. He knocked on the door, and after a moment, it opened. An old man with a large nose, a sparse, scraggly beard, and frizzy gray hair poked his head out.

"Squirrels said the clock was today?"

Jacob cleared his throat. "We're looking for Aldo. Is that you?"

The man straightened and put his hand on his chest. "Aldo is me? Of course it is! The smile was pretty today. Why didn't you take it?"

"Take what?" Jacob exchanged a glance with Akeno. "I don't get it."

"Sometimes, when purple raspberries come, they win plates. And you're happy to be yesterday!" The old man's lips lifted in a huge grin, revealing crooked, dirty teeth. "Children, children, children. Why even try? Squirrels are so much more effective."

Akeno and Jacob looked at each other again, and Jacob raised his eyebrow. This was weird.

Aldo beckoned them into the cabin, ushering them to a couple of chairs next to a table. The front room, which doubled as a dining room, was small and dingy.

Sitting down, the old man picked up a teapot and motioned toward some cups on the table. "Stop here with bottles? I wouldn't have gone to the store for a pixie if I were you."

"Uh, no thanks," Jacob said, wondering how long ago the man had lost his senses. No wonder the Makalos weren't able to find out what was going on with him—he probably wouldn't even let the Minyas near him.

"Oh, I forgot! Ladies! It means that they themselves once walked. Or maybe it was magic. Or perhaps it was that they couldn't leave home if they wanted it."

"Sure," Jacob said. He looked around the room, noticing that the walls were covered with knickknacks, pots, and a few old photographs. Photographs? Jacob wished he were sitting closer so he could inspect them. Trying to remain focused on the here and now, he turned his attention back to their host, but caught himself staring at the man's extremely large nose. He quickly looked away, realizing too late he should have been more discreet.

Aldo nodded. "The same place I'd be without my dazzling smile."

Jacob noticed that Aldo was staring at him as well, but with an almost knowing expression. He avoided the old man's gaze and instead glanced at Akeno, who had a big grin on his face. Jacob kicked Akeno's leg under the table, frowning at him and shaking his head.

Akeno's smile disappeared. He cleared his throat and looked at Aldo. "We were wondering what you can tell us about the Key of Kilenya."

"The sunset is really cool. But if the dispenser's broken—now, that's irreplaceable."

Jacob sighed inwardly. They were wasting their time.

Suddenly, the old man stood, knocking his chair over in the process, and left the room through a door in the back wall. Jacob heard him moving things around. Both boys jumped at the sound of a loud crash, followed by a yell and a stream of angry words.

Jacob snickered. "I understood that," he whispered.

When Aldo returned, he was carrying a bucket of nuts. He grabbed one of them, showed it to Jacob, and laughed, saying, "Squirrels don't come here. I'll show you why." Then he threw the nut at Jacob.

Jacob jumped out of his chair. "Hey! That hurt!"

"You too?" Aldo turned to Akeno, but Akeno was too fast for him and jumped out of the way.

Jacob couldn't help but laugh at the devastated look on the old man's face when he realized he hadn't hit his target.

Aldo's expression turned to one of anger. He put the bucket down, grabbed a handful of nuts, and chucked them at top speed, hitting both boys. Then he laughed gleefully and jumped up and down, clapping his hands.

"Come on, let's get out of here," Jacob said. "He's crazy!"

They ran outside, doing their best to dodge the nuts that were being flung at them. It only took a couple of seconds to reach the main trail, where they were joined by the Minyas. Looking over his shoulder, Jacob saw that the old man continued throwing nuts, even though the boys had already gone a fair distance.

"That was kind of funny, actually," Jacob said. "Did you understand anything he said?"

"No, nothing. Did you?"

"The words, yes. The context, not at all. I would've dropped to the ground laughing if he hadn't been trying to kill us."

"I really don't think we can expect any help from him."

Jacob chuckled as they slowed to a walk and exited the small grove of trees. "No, obviously not. We should tell Kenji and Brojan that he's gone crazy, though." He turned to Early and asked her to take a message to the village. She left quickly, returning a moment later.

"They were very surprised. Aldo played an important role in the war, was a great friend, and they're upset to hear what has become of him. They'd hoped he'd be able to explain more to you about this world and what to expect."

Jacob watched Early for a minute. He could only imagine the pain Kenji, Brojan, and Ebony were feeling right now. They'd have no closure, and since they hadn't left Taga in several years, they would have no way of finding out what had happened to Aldo. Jacob couldn't remember his grandparents—they died before he was born—but he knew it had been difficult for his parents. Maybe Aldo had been like a grandparent to the Makalos—Early did say he was practically a member of the family.

Jacob frowned—if Aldo couldn't help them figure things out, who could? They hadn't run into anyone besides Aldo and the woman in the forest. And from the looks of this desolate valley, it would be a while before they would. What if they never found help? Would they be killed before even reaching the Lorkon castle? It seemed likely—neither he nor Akeno had experience in this part of the world, and they wouldn't know who to trust.

Akeno seemed to be waiting for Jacob to make a decision.

"All right," Jacob said. "I guess we should just keep following this path." He dragged his hands down his face, then attempted a smile. "Hopefully we'll find someone who can tell us what to do." For some reason, he felt the need to put on a positive front for Akeno.

The trail led them south through a pretty little valley next to the tall trees Jacob had seen earlier. It was early afternoon—the sun was hot, and the scent of the wildflowers all around was refreshing. Jacob settled into a comfortable walking pace.

About forty-five minutes later, Jacob was no longer enjoying the scenery. The sun was bearing down, and the air felt humid. The wind rustled the leaves on the upper branches of the trees, but it wasn't reaching them on the ground.

Jacob tried not to focus on the sweat trickling down his back, but was unsuccessful. He felt grimy—especially after the forest and the manor.

The Minyas were playing a game of tag, flitting around Akeno and Jacob's heads, when all of a sudden they paused, floating still in the air. Early let out a squeal, and the two of them took off through the trees to the left of the trail. Jacob raised an eyebrow and looked at Akeno, who shrugged and followed the Minyas.

In the middle of the forest was a little lake with water so clear the bottom was visible. Jacob jumped forward, hoping to cool off, but Akeno stopped him. He pointed farther up the lake. A bear was partway in the water, staring into the depths. Jacob realized it was a Rog when he saw the human hands.

The Minyas flitted past, both giggling, zooming toward the Rog. There was a flash of light and the Rog soared over the water, landing with a splash. It surfaced, sputtering.

"Oh, no," Akeno said. "Uh . . . Jacob, we might want to run. Fast."

"Why?"

Akeno pointed. A huge Rog—much larger than the one who'd attacked Jacob in Taga—exited the forest only fifteen feet away. It shuffled to the water's edge and took a drink.

Just then, the Minyas flitted up to it and with another flash, thrust it into the water. Except this time, they didn't push it far enough. It bounded out of the lake, spotted Jacob and Akeno, and roared, standing on its hind legs.

Jacob spun around and ran as fast as he could. The Minyas zoomed alongside him, giggling so hard they were almost bent in half. A sudden urge to whack them out of the air nearly overwhelmed Jacob, but he concentrated on getting away from the Rog instead.

He and Akeno were nearly separated several times. That Makalo was fast! After a moment, though, Akeno grabbed Jacob and pulled him. They stumbled through underbrush, barely staying ahead.

Soon, they were able to put some distance between themselves and the Rog. Before long, Jacob couldn't see or hear it. He and Akeno ran up the slope, exited the trees, and raced down the trail, putting more space between them and the lake.

Akeno reached out, stopping Jacob. He bent, hands on knees, and panted before saying, "We probably don't have to run anymore, but we'd better keep going before the Rog figures out where we went. They're not very smart, but they are dangerous."

Jacob agreed and settled into the swift pace set by Akeno, holding his arm over the stitch in his side.

Chapter 8

Mud Bubbles

The Fat Lady sent us on our way, but not before showing us a tunnel that leads from the foothills behind her house directly to a passageway in the castle, bypassing the waterfall. Arien showed the tunnel to me once and I used it a few times, but hadn't needed it for several years. Luckily, our Minya is able to use it as a way to travel to and from the castle.

The Fat Lady also gave me information concerning the next element. It's in the form of a person—a Fire Pulser named Lasia. I've heard horrible stories about Fire Pulsers and have no confidence in my ability to defeat one. However, the Fat Lady did give me instructions that should help. It seems that Minyas have a natural sensitivity to change of temperature. I am to keep one constantly on the lookout, using it as a way to know what Lasia is doing at all times. Then I am to creep around her, placing diamonds, which the Fat Lady has given me, in five spots around her, forming a pentagon. Once the final diamond is in place, a shield will be formed around her, thus allowing us to pass by unharmed. I truly hope the Fat Lady is correct in this.

Jacob and Akeno walked in silence for a while as Jacob pondered the events of the last two days. He finally gave in to his curiosity. "Akeno, can I ask you a couple of questions?"

"Sure."

"What happens when you touch the trees? I mean, I know it has something to do with Rezend or whatever, but how does it tell you when there's danger around?"

"When a Makalo comes in contact with something that's alive, we're given a sense of what's around us. Basically, we see what they see, but not in a visual way."

What would that be like? Jacob looked back at the poplars behind them—trees that tall had to have a great view. "Why do you read trees? Why not me, or one of the Minyas? We're living things."

"Theoretically, you're similar, but not similar enough." Akeno paused, a slight frown on his face. "There's a lot of history behind it—I'll give you all of it someday, but for now, all you really need to know is that hundreds of years ago, Makalos were completely tied to trees. We lived in them and through them—they fed our Rezend. A good Makalo leader took us from them, but then our magic started to wane with each generation. By doing that, the leader saved us. 'Course, we still maintain a connection with trees."

Akeno sighed. "The Makalos were the most powerful people in this world, and their magic was not outdone by any, including the humans and Shiengols. There were millions upon millions of us." He gazed toward the mountain towering above them. "Their greatest city was located not far from here. The Kaede trees, from what we know, are still standing. I can only imagine how amazing it was to see the city in its prime."

He turned to Jacob. "You've probably noticed that my finger is blue—the Rezend which flows through my body creates a brilliant silver-blue glow, and a Makalo's body shines when at his or her fullest magical ability. The Rezend is like their blood, and—"

"That's really weird," Jacob said.

Akeno frowned and took a minute to answer. "I guess I can see why you would feel that way. I've known about it my whole life, so it's normal to me."

"It wouldn't be weird to you to walk up to someone who was blue all over?"

"It's not a berry blue." He scratched his head. "You would barely notice the shade until you got close to the individual. It was more like a silvery blue glow around them."

Akeno paused and stretched, then put his hand on his stomach. "I'm hungry. We should probably eat now." He knelt at the side of the path and pulled things from his pack—a pot, carrots, potatoes, seasoning, water—and made soup.

Jacob built a fire, then relaxed in the grass while the soup cooked. Neither said anything, and when the soup was finished, they ate in silence for several minutes, Jacob lost in his own thoughts. What would those original Makalos have been like? How would he have reacted when he saw their powers? Or their blue auras?

"And your village is all that remains of the Makalos. Wow."

"Yes, mainly because of the war that occurred several years ago, but also because the Makalos aren't as powerful, magically. In a few more generations, the village will probably be gone."

Jacob and Akeno gathered their things in silence and continued on the path. The Minyas flitted around, playing another silly game.

Jacob looked up at the mountains, now right in front of them. The path appeared to be practically slashed into the mountainside, forming a series of switchbacks.

"Looks like we're going up," Akeno said.

"Good thing I don't mind hiking."

At first the trail wasn't too difficult. The mountainside sloped gently upward, and the path followed naturally. However, after they'd hiked half an hour, the path rose sharply, and the switchbacks started. They were deeply cut, causing a sheer drop on one side of the path. In several sections, parts of the path had crumbled away, leaving only a few inches left on which to stand.

They paused to rest and admire the view. Smoke rose from Aldo's chimney below, and with the forests and gently rolling hills, Jacob found himself wishing he had his camera with him.

After resting about five minutes, they continued upward. The trail became more difficult, and in many places, they had to grab branches and bushes to pull themselves along. Eventually, and much to Jacob's relief, they reached the top where the path crested over the foothills and turned left, veering to the east.

They only followed the trail for a few more minutes before deciding to stop and set up camp in a small canyon harboring a thicket of scrub oak. The sun was setting, and a brisk, cold wind had picked up. Akeno assembled the hut while Jacob started a fire, and the Minyas raced through the branches of the small trees. When the fire was blazing, Akeno cooked dinner. They ate as they watched the sunset.

Jacob leaned back, content now that his stomach was full. "Those were amazing potatoes." He watched the last rays of amber sunlight disappear. After a moment, his thoughts returned to the task on hand. "I wish we'd had more time to discuss the Lorkon. Do you know anything about them?"

"Not a whole lot. Just that they're evil and prefer being in the dark." Akeno stood and started raking dirt over the coals. "I've also heard they're really ugly."

"Yeah, they would be."

Akeno frowned, turning to Jacob. "Why do you say that?"

"Haven't you ever noticed? The bad guys are always ugly."

Akeno laughed as they headed to the makeshift tent where September and Early had already turned in for the night.

Jacob was restless for a while, trying not to dwell on what had happened at the manor. He needed a good night's rest, free from nightmares, and wasn't sure he'd get one. After tossing for several minutes, he finally fell into a deep sleep.

Jacob woke early the next morning. Akeno murmured something in his sleep on the other side of the hut and Jacob got up, trying not to wake him. He wanted to move around a bit to stretch out his sore muscles. He'd slept well, but it would take a while for the aches to leave from the previous day.

He climbed his way through the hole Akeno had left for him in the mess of brambles and leaves. The mountains were to his back, dark and tall. He glanced up at them. They were beautiful in their ruggedness. No trees, no bushes—nothing but huge granite outcroppings. Though he was able to admire them, he was grateful the path didn't go any higher.

Instead, it led across a plateau shaped by the foothills they'd climbed yesterday.

Walking away from the campsite and back to the path, Jacob looked down at the switchbacks, maintaining a safe distance from the edge. The view was dizzying, and he had to steady himself by taking a couple deep breaths.

The wolves were making their way up the switchbacks. He rolled his eyes. What ridiculous creatures.

There was a sound behind him, and Jacob turned. Akeno was just getting out of the shelter.

"What are you looking at?" Akeno asked, picking a bunch of leaves from the branches on the hut.

"Just looking. The wolves are coming up the mountain."

Akeno finished picking the leaves, then joined Jacob at the ledge. He glanced over. "Are they just now catching up to us?"

Jacob nodded. "How long did it take us to get up those switchbacks? A couple of hours?"

"Or a little more."

Jacob frowned. "Let's get out of here before they gain too much on us."

Akeno turned. "I'll put the branches back."

"Why does it matter if they're put back?"

"Because they die quickly when under so much pressure. While I'm around them, I can use my Rezend to prevent them from being damaged, but once we leave, they won't have that protection."

He went to the hut and Jacob followed, grabbing his backpack before Akeno dismantled his creation. The Minyas flew out, brushing themselves off and looking irritated.

"Good morning," Jacob said, but they ignored him and flew away. He turned to Akeno. "Why don't they talk to us very much? I've barely had a handful of conversations with them."

"They're like most Minyas," Akeno said, pulling his tape dispenser from his bag. "They prefer games to conversing, and they're very light-minded. They don't find anyone but other Minyas to be interesting." He sat and taped the leaves to his shoes. "If they didn't have such good memories for relaying messages, no one would keep them around."

Jacob took a drink of water from his canteen, then put it back in his knapsack. "I've noticed they never get tired of going back and forth."

Akeno picked up his bag and they headed to the trail. "And they won't. They never mess up the messages and never get lost. They're better than cell phones."

Jacob smiled. "Ha. Good one."

He looked over his shoulder toward the switchbacks. No sign of the wolves. He took a breath, telling himself to relax. The wolves didn't want to attack—at least, he hoped not.

The trail curved a couple of times around huge rocks, but it was level. There weren't many trees here, and the mountain rose on the right with the drop-off on the left.

Strange-looking wildflowers grew in patches on both sides of the trail, and Jacob picked one to examine while walking. It was a type he'd never seen before, with bright blue petals and soft thistles on the stems and leaves. He noticed something odd and stared at it. "That's weird. Are the petals moving?"

"Yes, they are," Akeno said. "That's how they attract bees. They're my mom's favorite flower. The petals are edible, with a spicy-sweet flavor. It does take a bit to get over the feel of them wiggling in your mouth, though."

Jacob grimaced. "That's really gross."

"It's disconcerting, yes," Akeno said, adjusting the strap on his knapsack. "Of course, if you're out on the road and don't have anything else to eat, you'll take what you can get, right?"

"I guess so," Jacob said. "But I really doubt I'll ever be starving enough to eat something that wiggles in my mouth."

Akeno laughed. "You already have. The potatoes last night were seasoned with them."

"They were? Sick!" Jacob threw the flower away from him in disgust.

He paused, staring at the trail ahead of them. The flowers and trees abruptly ended, and the ground was shiny and bubbly looking. It was a brown-gray color, with no inclines of any sort. As he got closer, it looked as though someone had poured a layer of smooth cake mix over everything. He took a step onto it—the path was barely visible—and his foot crunched through an inch or so of dried mud. It felt like stepping on dead leaves. He bent to scrutinize it.

"What's all over the ground?" Akeno said, peering past Jacob.

"I think it's mud. Have you seen anything like this before?"

Akeno shook his head. "No, never."

Walking carefully, Jacob soon got accustomed to the crunching sounds under his feet. The farther they walked, the bigger the bubbles got, and the path was becoming impossible to distinguish. Then he stepped through a bubble that was at least a foot tall, causing him to stumble forward. Akeno reached out and steadied him, and together they surveyed the area. The path disappeared over the next several feet, and the bubbles were getting much, much broader.

Jacob ran his hand through his hair. "This could be a problem."

"Maybe we should try to go around it."

"Good idea."

They retraced their steps and separated, leaving the path. Jacob went right, trying to skirt the mud on the side closest to the mountain and Akeno walked in the opposite direction, toward the edge of the cliff.

"The mud goes all the way up," Jacob called to Akeno. The mountainside was a sheer granite wall, and Jacob had only been rock climbing a few times. He wasn't about to practice here.

"It spills over the cliff on this side," Akeno said from where he stood. "We won't be able to go that way." They walked toward each other. Akeno shielded his eyes from the glare of the morning sun. "Do you know anything about crossing huge sections of land covered in big, dried mud bubbles?"

Jacob chuckled. "Of course not. I'm new to this place. You're supposed to be the resident genius."

"Right." Akeno wiped some dust off his pant leg. "I've lived in Taga Village my whole life, and we rarely go anywhere else."

"Where could you have gone, anyway? I thought your village was blocked off until the Lorkon broke through the barrier."

"It was blocked off," Akeno said, smiling. "But . . . we go into your world to spy on your people from time to time."

"You guys spy on us?" Jacob said, and then laughed. "Why didn't you, you know, make contact with us?"

"You make it sound like we're an alien race."

"Isn't that the definition of 'alien'? Something strange and foreign and completely different from you and what you've ever seen or met?"

Akeno smiled. "Touché."

Jacob looked ahead. "Let's get started. We'll just have to cross it."

They continued forward, crunching through the smaller bubbles and kicking or pushing through the sides of the bigger ones. The going wasn't very difficult, and they made good progress for a while. Jacob looked back a couple of times, but didn't see the wolves.

After a while, the sides of the bubbles became more and more difficult to break through, and they took turns leading. Jacob's arms and legs soon tired from the exertion, and eventually he and Akeno reached a bubble neither could break. It was about four feet tall and five or six feet wide.

Jacob put his palms on the side, pushing as hard as he could. "You know, they might be able to support our weight now." He tested a couple sections first, then hoisted himself on top. He got to his feet and surveyed the land. There were still hundreds more bubbles to cross, but they were different. They were flat on top and almost square in shape.

Jacob shifted his weight to the other foot. Nothing happened.

"I think if we walk on the edges of the bubbles where they're flush against each other, we'll be able to cross, no problem. They'll probably be strongest on the edges."

"I'll walk in front of you," Akeno said. "I'm lighter."

Jacob pulled Akeno up, then moved aside, waiting until Akeno had a lead of a few feet before he followed. They crossed several bubbles without difficulty and Jacob actually found that he was enjoying himself. But after they'd walked for twenty minutes with barely a change in scenery, he sighed in exasperation.

"This is going to take forever." He stopped. "Where are the Minyas? I thought they'd be back by now."

"Yes, they should have been." Akeno shaded his eyes, looking for the creatures. "We'll probably need to talk to them about not leaving us."

The sun neared the middle of the sky, warming the breeze almost uncomfortably, and Jacob was glad his skin wasn't the kind that burned easily. It looked like the day would be another hot one.

Suddenly Akeno stopped. Jacob stepped to join him, but Akeno held up a hand. "There's a hole—don't move. I'm going to test it out." He inched closer to the hole, peered down, and then stiffened. "Uh . . . Jacob?" He looked back. "The bubble we're standing on is at least thirty feet deep."

Jacob straightened, his heart clenching. "It is?" Even though the sun beat down on them from overhead, Jacob's hands turned to ice and a cold sweat sent shivers down his arms. He tried not to imagine the huge distance below the hardened mud under his feet.

Early zipped past Jacob's face, startling him, and hovered above the hole, looking down.

"Early! Where have you been?" Akeno asked. "And where's September?"

"Right there," she said. "We slept in Jacob's bag. It was his idea." She pointed at September, who was just getting out of Jacob's knapsack.

"You should have told us where you were going," Jacob said. He carefully folded his arms, trying to appear stern while not thinking about the thin crust he was standing on. "What if something had happened?"

"We would have awakened and helped you," Early said.

September flitted around. "We could hear you."

"Yes, but we had no idea where you were," Jacob said. "From now on, if you're not going to be in sight, tell us where you're going and when you'll get back."

"Okay, we will," Early said.

Jacob looked at the hole, resolving to toughen up and keep going. "Let's go around this bubble. I'd rather stay as far away from holes as possible."

They made their way to the next bubble, and Jacob was relieved when he saw there weren't any holes in it. He looked out over the shells in front of them, dismayed at the distance that remained. "It looks like we're barely halfway."

"Yes, and it will probably take an hour or more to cross."

Jacob motioned for Akeno to keep moving. They didn't go very quickly, as Akeno was now being much more selective about the shells on which they walked.

Jacob was making his way over a very large bubble when a cracking sound came from under him. He stopped and watched in dismay as a line shot across the surface, starting at his foot.

Akeno whirled. He was five feet ahead of Jacob, already on the next bubble. "Jacob, don't move."

"I'm not," Jacob said, his voice wavering. He opened his mouth, but couldn't inhale. Just the thought of falling made his head spin.

"What do we do?" Akeno said.

"I don't know," he forced out.

A few seconds passed. It felt like an eternity.

Finally the wind rushed into his lungs, clearing his mind, allowing him to think. "Back up a little. I'm going to see if I can jump."

Akeno frowned. "Jump? Are you sure?"

"If you come over here, we'll both fall through. And we don't have anything for you to toss me—no branches, no rope."

"What about kneeling down and crawling or something?"

Jacob shook his head. "No, that much of a shift in weight would be bad."

"Okay. Just . . . be careful." Akeno backed up.

Several seconds passed, and Jacob still didn't do anything. He went through his options again. Running was out of the question. Turning around to backtrack would be a bad idea, too. Obviously he couldn't just stand there forever. What if he tried inching forward a little at a time? He looked at the shell beneath him, doubtful it would hold his weight while he moved. He took a deep breath. How much strength did the bubble have left? Would it be enough for one jump?

Finally he crouched a little, careful not to shift his weight too much. After waiting to see if the surface was still holding, he took a leap, aiming for the bubble nearest him. He didn't lose his balance when he landed. Squeezing his eyes shut, he sucked in a lungful of air, holding it for several seconds.

Nothing happened.

He released his breath and straightened, relief pouring over him in huge waves as he took a careful step toward Akeno.

A loud crack raked the air. The crust beneath his feet gave way and he gasped, his eyes widening, as he clutched at the air, trying to find something, *anything*, to hold on to. He tipped backward as he fell, and the shell broke as his body hit it. He was aware of Akeno's scream, the bright sun in his eyes, and the scent of mud.

Cold, damp air rushed past him, making a roar in his ears as he gained speed in his descent. Then with a thud, he landed on solid ground, and the wind whooshed out of his lungs. Everything threatened to go black. He forced his eyes open, and a dull ache built in his chest.

"Jacob! Jacob!" someone screamed.

He tried to pull in the air he needed to breathe. It wouldn't come, and panic washed over him. How far had he fallen? Everything was dark except for a small shaft of light that came in through the hole above him.

His chest felt on fire. Finally, with a gasp, he drew in a ragged breath. Sharp pain shot across his back and chest, nearly knocking the wind out of him again. He closed his eyes for a moment, struggling to stay conscious, trying to clear his mind. He became aware of every pain spreading across his body, manifesting in varying degrees. He'd landed on his right side, his arm and leg pinned beneath him.

An eerie blue glow appeared in the hole, and it took a few seconds for Jacob to recognize Akeno's voice.

"Jacob! Are you all right?"

Struggling to remain conscious, he could only groan in response. He looked up, feeling tears smarting in his eyes.

"Jacob, stay awake! Please stay awake!"

Through the pain, he was aware of water under him, seeping up through his clothes. The coldness made him gasp—made him nauseated. A random thought crossed his mind that it was a good thing he hadn't eaten breakfast.

"Don't move, Jacob! And keep your eyes open! Open your eyes!"

He wasn't even aware he'd shut them. He forced them open, the blue light again registering in his mind. He felt tingles all over his skin, and he could barely feel his hands.

He was aware of Akeno's voice, but couldn't tell what he was saying.

A new level of pain washed over him when he was suddenly lifted from the ground.

The sunlight rushed nearer, and once again Jacob was out in the open, the heat of the sun bearing down on him. He shut his eyes against the glare, willing the cool air and darkness to return. Akeno's voice was loud and it surrounded him, hurting his ears, making him moan.

"Oh, Jacob, I really hope this works. You should feel better soon."

The last thing Jacob recognized was a soft, warm surface. Something closed over him, putting him in darkness, and he relaxed, letting go.

Chapter 9
Minyas Up Close

We've caught up with a portion of those who were kidnapped by the Lorkon and apparently were left behind. All of them are women, most of whom work in the castle with Arien. Disappointingly, but not surprisingly, Arien was not among them. However, Kelson was much overjoyed to find his wife, Midian, among the survivors. She is injured and has been mostly unconscious since we found her. She recognizes no one. I'm afraid she won't live much longer.

We are nearing a city where Kenji has several close friends. We will beg for help where our new group members are concerned. We are unable to continue carrying them with us. Kelson is still very much needed in our company, and though I offered to allow him to stay with his wife, I was glad when he chose to continue and trust her to one of Kenji's friends for the time being. We will return for her and the others when this journey is over.

A sweet fragrance entered Jacob's nose as he inhaled. He was on his back in a bed. He felt someone sitting next to him, holding his hand, comforting him.

"Mom?"

There wasn't an answer. He opened his eyes. She was looking at someone on the other side of him. Turning his head, he saw that it was Brojan, the patriarch. They were conversing in hushed voices. He tried to open his mouth to say something, but the scene in front of him faded and blurred, and everything went black again.

Jacob opened his eyes. He couldn't see anything. It took several seconds for him to realize he really was awake. Afraid to move, he concentrated as air rushed in and out of his lungs. No pain! He took a deep breath, and a sweet maple fragrance entered his nose.

After a moment, he decided he needed to test for broken bones. He started with his toes, flexing them, then moved to his fingers and hands, stretching and flexing them as well. He lifted his arms and legs one at a time and bent them, tightening the muscles. Still no pain. He stretched his arms over his head and pushed against the cushions that surrounded him.

Jacob touched his face and traced the outlines of his eyes, then checked his ears. Nothing was out of the ordinary. He stretched his hands, bumping them into the same soft fabric that covered the surface where he lay. Wiggling around, he found four corners and realized he was in a box of sorts.

"Oh my gosh, am I in a coffin?"

Trying not to panic, he pushed with his might against the surface in front of him. Light rushed into the box, momentarily blinding him, and he let the top fall shut again.

At least it wasn't sealed. Jacob waited for a moment before trying to open the box again, this time much more slowly so his eyes could adjust. Finally, after several seconds of short movements, his eyes grew accustomed to the light, and he pushed the lid all the way open.

An *extremely* large Akeno stared down at him with a big grin on his face.

Jacob yelled and backed into a corner as fast as he could.

"Calm down, Jacob," Akeno said. "Oh, wait, sorry. Let me explain what happened."

"What did you do? Did you shrink me?"

"It was the only thing we *could* do."

"'We'? 'We' who?" Jacob looked around frantically, still trying to get away from Akeno's large face, but not wanting to fall out of the box.

"Us, of course!" a voice said.

Jacob flinched when Early appeared out of nowhere to stand right next to him. She was enormous! Well, by comparison to how she looked before, anyway. He realized that she was still smaller than he, but not by a whole lot.

"Oh, wow . . ."

She was exquisite. Every minute detail was perfect. Her skin was the color of a pale pink flower, as delicate and fragile-looking as a petal. There were patterns on the skin of her upper arms that were like green vine tendrils. Her hair, also green, fell to her shoulders and had a soft, pretty wave to it. Her eyes were green too, but very sparkly.

Her beauty caught him off guard, and he had to remind himself to close his mouth and stop staring. She laughed at him, making him feel self-conscious.

September flew up behind Early, and Jacob, looking at him, wondered why he'd paid so little attention to either of them before. September had the same vine tendril designs on his arms, but his were darker than Early's. His hair was dark green—so dark that it looked almost black—and his eyes were the same shade as his hair.

"Wow," Jacob said. "You guys are amazing."

"Thank you!" Early said, curtsying.

"Wait a second. How big am I?"

"About two and a half inches tall," Akeno said. "Only half an inch taller than the Minyas."

"That's so cool!" He stood and faced Akeno. "Didn't you break a whole ton of rules by doing this?"

Akeno nodded. "Here, let's put you back to normal. I want to make sure I didn't do any more damage when I shrank you than what had happened when you fell, and we won't know until you're bigger again."

Jacob thought for a minute, weighing the options of asking Akeno to let him stay small for a while longer so he could explore the world as a two-and-a-half-inch person, or getting back on task. He decided he could have Akeno shrink him again later. Getting the Key as fast as possible was more important.

"Okay," he said. "Tell me what to do."

"Nothing. Just don't panic. I have to pick you up. I'll try to be careful, but it's difficult to tell if I'm squeezing too hard or not." Akeno reached his hand toward Jacob, but stopped. "Oh, wait, I'd better check to make sure everything is clear outside."

Jacob hadn't noticed they weren't under the sky. It had been so bright when he first opened the box that he'd just assumed they were out in the open. He looked up, recognizing tree branches forming a light shelter around them. Akeno put his hand on one of the bigger branches, and a few seconds later they folded away, letting Akeno step out of the shade and into the sun.

The sky was deep blue and the sun was overhead, making Jacob squint. He noticed that at this size, everything was so out of proportion that he couldn't distinguish anything around them, except for the tree right behind him and the mountain in the distance.

Akeno came back and reached to pick Jacob up. Jacob braced himself, closing his eyes. He felt a tight pinch around his waist and ribs, nearly knocking the air out of him, and opened his eyes again. Akeno held him out at arm's length. There was a whoosh of wind and then solid earth under Jacob's feet. He looked around—he stood at least thirty or forty feet away from Akeno. His body felt normal again, and he could tell he was back to his right size.

"That was so cool!" Jacob yelled, jogging back to Akeno. "And I'm surprised it didn't hurt more. But, you know, after having fallen so far being shrunk wouldn't have caused much extra damage."

"Yeah. You should have died from that fall."

Jacob picked up the box where he'd slept. It was solid silver with flower imprints on it, and the inside was lined with soft material.

"That's September's," Akeno said. "It's saturated in Kaede Sap and heals Minyas if they ever get hurt—which almost never happens. I wasn't sure it would work on you, but thank goodness it did."

Akeno grabbed his bag and tossed it to Jacob. "Here, eat. It's been too long since you had food."

They both sat.

"While you were unconscious," Akeno said, "we ran out of food, and Brojan and my father shrank more and sent it to us with the Minyas."

Jacob examined his chunk of beef jerky. It looked the way jerky always looked. "And you made it big again." He popped the piece in his mouth and glanced at Akeno. "You can both shrink and enlarge things. Isn't that rare?"

"A little, yeah. Normally, a Makalo can either shrink or make something big again. I think one of the main reasons they had me come with you is that I'm able to do both."

"After we get the Key, you should shrink me again," Jacob said, then smiled. "I'm going to pull some amazing pranks on Matt!"

Akeno laughed. "That would be fun, but we don't really know what happens to the actual cells of things that have shrunk. That's why we have rules."

"Well, I'm glad it worked."

"I thought you were dead when I looked over the edge, Jacob. You had fallen so far down—I can't believe it didn't kill you. It was September's idea to put you in the box. After I did, I grabbed your bag and ran over the bubbles as fast as I could."

"And no other problems?"

"None—I'm lighter than you. The wolves did catch up after I made camp, though. They sat and watched me. I finally yelled that we wouldn't be going anywhere until you were better. I think they understood because they got up and left."

Jacob ate a handful of carrot sticks. "I really can't believe I'm healed now. I'm sure I broke several bones. Did you get a good look at me?"

"I didn't look at anything. I was trying to put you in the box without killing you in the process."

"Oh, too bad. It would have been cool to know how many broken bones there were."

"That's really weird, Jacob." Akeno began putting things back into his bag.

"Nah, it would have been cool."

"Being healed so quickly is cool enough. You should be happy with that." He sighed. "Do you have any other questions? We should probably get on our way."

"How long was I out of it?"

Akeno paused, then focused on the dirt. "Well, the healing isn't instantaneous."

"Yeah, I figure it was several hours at least, based on how long it took Jaegar."

"And you were a lot more wounded than he was, so naturally it took a few more hours for you." Akeno glanced at Jacob, looking quickly away.

Jacob frowned—why was Akeno avoiding his question? "How many hours?"

Akeno rubbed his nose, then fidgeted with the strap on his bag. "You were unconscious for four days."

It took a second for that to register in Jacob's mind. "Holy cow! Four days? What about getting the Key? What about the Lorkon and the wolves? Is everything ruined now?"

"I'm not sure, actually."

"You should've gone ahead. I would've been fine in the box in your bag."

Akeno shook his head. "Not a good idea."

Jacob scoffed at himself. Obviously Akeno couldn't go on without his help—they worked as a team, and if Akeno had come across another diseased forest, he wouldn't have been able to get through it on his own.

"Brojan and my father want us to get to the nearest city, where we'll be able to hide. Then they want me to shrink you again and have one of the Minyas take you back to Taga so they can talk to you."

"The Minyas can carry me?"

"They've been carrying food for us, and if you've been shrunk, they won't have any problem with your size. It's faster than having you run back to the village."

Jacob thought about this for a moment. "Should I be nervous that they want to talk to me?" He couldn't imagine anything they'd say that would surprise him more than what he'd already learned since coming to Eklaron. He could be wrong, but he hoped not.

"I don't think so . . . but I'm not sure."

"All right, let's do it."

They packed up what was left of camp and started down the trail. It led them through a section of massive granite rocks that had fallen from the mountain above and into a beautiful little valley with rolling, flower-covered hills.

Jacob heard a sigh behind him and figured Akeno was enjoying the scenery. With the mountains looming up to the right of them and the pretty valley on the left, Jacob could understand why.

They continued walking in silence. The Minyas rode on Akeno's shoulder, sitting in one spot for once, and not talking or goofing off.

As they neared a turn in the path, Jacob was startled when a negative feeling passed over him. A few steps later, he felt it again. He looked around, sure it hadn't come from inside him. What was bothering him? Was it the valley? That didn't make sense.

Akeno seemed unaffected, but the feeling intensified until Jacob paused, not sure if it was a warning to leave, or a warning to get off the path. Akeno ran into Jacob, apparently caught off guard by the sudden stop.

"Sorry, I need to figure something out," Jacob said. "Do you feel that?"

"What?"

"The—the negative stuff."

"No . . . I don't."

After standing still for a moment or two longer, the discomfort increased. A gross feeling now came with it, making Jacob want to wash his hands, and all he could think about was getting out of the valley. He walked briskly along the trail and heard Akeno follow.

The path entered a little canyon, and Jacob felt the negativity leave him. Breathing a sigh of relief, he slowed down again.

"That was weird." It reminded him of the way he felt whenever he did something wrong. Guilt, almost, as though he'd just finished swearing up a storm at his mom or Amberly. Not good to experience.

"It affected you this time, and not me," Akeno said.

"Yeah, and I wonder why."

Several feet later, the trail took them right and down into a difficult section. Jacob had to pick his way over the rocks and boulders that jutted up through the earth.

The silence was refreshing, being one of the only times on the trip when they hadn't talked while walking. Jacob recognized, however, that for Akeno it might not have been so easy, since he'd been alone four days in a row. The Minyas really weren't a good form of companionship, and chances that Akeno had an intelligent conversation with them were pretty slim. Jacob felt a pang of regret when he realized he just didn't want to talk.

He looked up from the trail and gasped. "Wow."

The trail sloped downward. It had just exited the short canyon and led them around the mountains, opening up to a huge valley almost completely framed by large mountains, including those by which Jacob and Akeno had been hiking. Near the middle was one of the largest lakes Jacob had ever seen, and the mountains on its left rose sharply with no gradual incline, making the scenery even more dramatic. He remembered seeing pictures of the fjords in Norway, but they didn't compare to this.

There were three cities visible: one on this end of the lake, one to the right, and one—difficult to see—on the far side.

Jacob studied that far city, noticing it had a weird look to it. It was dirty and smudged, as though there was a cloud hanging over it, even though the sky was cloudless. The outline of a large, dark castle was visible. A nervous feeling hit Jacob in the pit of the stomach and he realized he was probably looking at the castle where the Lorkon lived. His palms started sweating when he thought about what could happen. How was he going to find the Key and get out of the castle?

He looked back at the city closest to them. It also had a castle, but it seemed desolate and war-ravaged. So did the whole city, actually. He frowned as he started walking again, wondering what it had been like in its prime.

Akeno interrupted his thoughts. "We should set up camp."

Jacob was surprised that the sun was nearly down. It was later than he'd realized. "Yeah, I think you're right."

"We'll probably head into the city first thing in the morning."

Together they set up camp, then Akeno cooked dinner.

"So how'd you end up as cook for our trip?" Jacob asked.

"You're the guest, so I just felt like I should do it."

"Well, if you show me how to make those potatoes you made yesterday, I'll do it next time."

"Yesterday?" Akeno said, smiling. "You mean five days ago?"

Jacob laughed. "Oh, yeah."

Chapter 10

Macaria

Today a most entertaining thing occurred. As we were traveling, Kelson, Kenji, and I overheard a very heated Minya argument—my first. Kenji informed me that it happens rather frequently, and so we ignored it. However, moments later it became impossible to ignore when a Minya was hurled through the air and hit me smack-dab on the side of the face. It was difficult not to laugh as this little Minya indignantly shook his fist toward the forest from whence he'd come, then latched onto my collar, refusing to leave. He calls himself September.

I was not surprised when he almost immediately decided he preferred everyone else to me, and I've given him to Kenji for safe keeping. Perhaps permanently.

Minyas.

I'm afraid I'll never like them.

Jacob was excited to go into the city, even if it was in shambles. Akeno taped new leaves on his shoes, and they sent Early off to report that Jacob would be coming as soon as they found a place where Akeno could hide. Early quickly returned with the message that Brojan and Akeno's parents were eagerly awaiting Jacob's return.

"But why would it be better to hide in the city?" Jacob asked. "I mean, wouldn't we want to stay away from people, just in case the Lorkon or the wolves come around?"

Early flitted to him. "Brojan said it would be better to hide in a deserted house in the city. He feels it would be safer."

They headed down the mountainside. Jacob didn't notice that the two black wolves were watching them from bushes near the path until September pointed it out.

"Why do they do that?" Jacob said. "It's really creepy."

"Yes, it is." Akeno glared at the wolves.

They made a wide circle around the animals and got back on the trail. Jacob kept one eye on the predators as they walked, but they didn't do anything—just watched the entire time. He decided to ignore them.

After a few minutes, Jacob and Akeno reached the road that led into town and turned to follow it. A faded wooden sign with *Macaria* etched in it showed an arrow pointing ahead. The Minyas floated above them, and Jacob's spirits rose a notch. They were going to see people!

The city was small, and at one point might have been considered quaint. Everything was white. The buildings, the walks—even the dirt had a white appearance to it. It looked as though the whole town had been bleached by the sun, and it made the city beautiful, even with the war-ravaged look. The road was dusty, and each step Akeno and Jacob took caused a little cloud to billow up around their feet. The street was deserted, and the sun was bright as they walked down the center of the road, almost as if they were about to have a face-off with someone at the opposite end of the street. Jacob smiled, feeling like he was in his favorite James Garner western.

He watched for buildings he'd recognize as a store or maybe a hotel. Most of the windows were boarded up. The buildings ranged in size from one story to two and sometimes three stories high, with the remains of the castle being the tallest. The road led toward the castle, which seemed to be situated on the shores of the lake.

"Hey, let's use the castle as our hiding place," Jacob said.

"That would be trespassing."

Jacob chuckled. "Yeah, but what's the difference between that and using an old house? I bet it'd be okay with the people here. Besides, it'd be fun."

"You and your ideas of fun. Broken bones, sneaking into castles—is this normal?"

Jacob laughed. "For a guy my age, yes." He looked around. "I say we first find a town center or a store. See if we can learn something about this city before you shrink me."

Akeno agreed, and they continued following the road, which eventually widened and split, encircling a building that had a few people going in and out of it. It was only a short distance from the castle, and Jacob figured it was most likely the center of the city. Judging by the posters in the windows, it was a store of sorts.

"Are they humans?" he whispered, motioning to the people.

Akeno shaded his eyes from the morning sun. "Looks that way."

"I say we go into the store. Wouldn't hurt."

"As long as we don't tell them why we're here."

"Of course not." Jacob stopped and turned to the Minyas. "Would you be okay in my bag? I don't want anyone to see you, but it would be better if we didn't get separated right now, in case something bad happens." He was surprised when the Minyas agreed, and he pulled his bag open, letting them fly in before shutting it.

Only a couple of people turned at the sound of the door opening. They were all human—at least, Jacob thought so. He saw shock register in their eyes as they looked at him and Akeno, and he wondered if they'd ever seen a Makalo before. A black man wearing an oily leather apron worked behind a counter.

"Your . . . Highness?" he asked.

Jacob turned to him and saw the look of recognition leave the man's face.

"Er, no, I'm Jacob."

"Oh, I'm sorry . . . please . . ." The man fumbled with a jar on the counter full of little brown squares that looked like caramel. "Would you like to try some Canush?"

"Um, no, thanks."

"Are you sure? They are quite excellent." The man popped one into his mouth, closing his eyes and grinning.

Jacob looked at Akeno.

"We have them too," Akeno whispered. "Try one. They're good."

"You eat one, then," Jacob replied.

The man opened his eyes. "Oh, I'm sorry. Excuse me," he said. "I'm sorry. Here, you can have one, too." He held the jar out to Akeno—who took one—then extended his arm to Jacob.

"What . . . exactly is it?"

The man flashed a smile, his teeth white in contrast to his dark skin. "A popular sweet here. It's made from the roots of the Canush tree."

Jacob looked into the jar. Not too scary, but he hated trying new foods. He hesitated a moment longer, then put one in his mouth, biting down on the corner. He was surprised when the entire thing dissolved as soon as he bit. A cool, sweet juice gushed over his tongue. He almost choked on the unexpected liquid, but it didn't disagree with his taste buds, and he felt the corners of his mouth lifting.

"You like it, don't you?" the man said. "Oh, I knew you would. It's quite a popular treat here with the children. I mean, you aren't a child, but I thought you would like it because you are still in your youth. Of course, I don't mean to say that you are a boy, because you aren't, but you are young still, and not quite a grown man—though you are a man already. I'm sorry, I'm—"

"No, you're fine," Jacob said, almost laughing, but remembering his manners just in time. "And yes, I do like it a lot."

He looked around the store, noticing that people glanced away as he did. They must have been watching him try the candy. How awkward. The man put the jar back and waited, leaning on the counter with both hands.

"Sir, may I ask your name?"

"Of course, of course. It's Gallus. This is my shop."

"It's nice to meet you. Like I said, my name is Jacob, and this is Akeno, my friend."

Gallus studied Akeno, a thoughtful expression on his face, then addressed Jacob again. "What brings you to our city?"

Jacob rubbed his neck, his eyes flicking to Akeno's. "We're actually just passing through," he said. Then, wanting to deflect further inquiries, he said, "Um . . . can I ask a question?"

"Certainly."

"Why did you call me 'Your Highness' when we walked in?"

"Oh, well, because the last time a human was seen traveling with a Makalo, it was many years ago." Gallus turned to hand something to a customer before continuing. "He was a prince from a faraway kingdom. Dmitri was his name. He was a really extraordinary man who went through quite a lot during his short lifetime." Gallus looked wistfully at Jacob. "It has been a long time since we experienced true peace here. Dmitri would have been our king if the Lorkon hadn't taken over." He rubbed his forehead, then again scrutinized Akeno. "The Makalos are all but extinct, though there are rumors of a village not far from here."

Akeno looked away, and Jacob worried about the attention Gallus was giving him. "What kind of money do you use here in exchange for products?" he asked.

"We don't. Our money system was completely destroyed when the Lorkon took over the city."

Jacob exchanged a glance with Akeno. If the Lorkon were in control, would Akeno be able to hide safely while Jacob went back to Taga?

"They're in charge?"

Gallus nodded. "Basically, but they got bored with us a year or so ago. They were searching for something and thought we were hiding it here, but when they didn't find it, they gave up and no longer care what we do."

Jacob relaxed at this news. "That's good."

Gallus stooped to pick up a jar of grain from the floor. "Many of our loved ones were taken away during that period and never returned. We've tried several times to find them, but have only been met with a great deal of resistance, and even death." He set the jar on a shelf behind him. "We're still in the process of fixing things around here. Mainly the government, but the city is much safer now." He turned to Jacob, a slight frown on his face. "I'm surprised you don't know this already. Where are you from?"

"East of here," Jacob lied, and immediately felt guilty. He hated being dishonest.

This appeared to satisfy Gallus, however, who excused himself to assist a customer. Jacob turned to look around the store.

There was an array of odd-looking equipment Jacob assumed was for farming. There were also saddles, bridles, and other things for horse riding. Jacob's thoughts drifted, thinking how much nicer the trip would be if they'd had horses. The switchbacks alone would have taken a lot less time. Then he remembered the bubbles and realized they would have had to leave the animals behind anyway.

He found a small stand displaying pretty necklaces and picked one out he thought his mom would like. Akeno made eye contact with him, motioning to the door. Jacob gave a small nod, but wanted to see if he could buy the necklace first.

He walked back to Gallus. "If you don't use money, how do you buy things?"

"We exchange for products. If you have nothing to exchange, you can work for what you need."

"Okay, well, maybe next time." He had nothing to trade, and taking time to work off debt was out of the question. "It was nice to meet you." Jacob put the necklace back on the rack, then gave a small wave as he and Akeno left the store.

Once outside, he looked at Akeno and raised an eyebrow. "Why didn't you talk?"

Akeno fidgeted with his bag. "I don't know . . . I didn't know what to say."

Jacob ducked down a small alley, then pulled open his knapsack to let the Minyas out and grabbed a sack of beef jerky as well, offering some to Akeno. "Are you shy?"

"A little, I guess. It depends."

Jacob took a bite of jerky. "Let's find a place where you can hide after shrinking me." He walked back onto the street again.

"I see where you're headed," Akeno said, a smile coloring his voice.

"It's really not out of the way."

"Fine, we can use the castle."

"Awesome!" Jacob jumped into the air. "I've always wanted to go inside a castle!"

Akeno laughed and fell into step next to Jacob. "But if something goes wrong, we'll know who to blame."

The road they followed turned a few times, leading them away from Gallus's store. It was lined with old, intricately designed flag poles. A few of the flags remained, and they must have been magnificent once. They were royal blue, with gold and silver designs.

"This street has to lead to the castle," Jacob said.

"It does. See?"

Jacob looked ahead to where Akeno pointed. They were just coming around one of the bends in the road, and the remains of an impressive wall were now in sight. Jacob whistled. The wall was awe-inspiring—obviously designed more for show than anything, but still imposing.

They walked over the crumbling bridge and past the wall. The courtyard was filled with flowering trees and was overgrown with ivy and bushes. Daisies pushed through the weeds and vines in clumps.

Most of the castle walls had crumbled, except for the one farthest from them. It was the tallest, with a turret and tower still attached, and was closest to the lake.

Even though the front wall was non-existent, the huge wooden doors stood intact. Jacob walked up to the door, pushing it open. "Looks like the castle is still trying to keep people out."

"Wait. Let me see what's around us." Akeno walked to a tree, putting his left hand on it. He closed his eyes for a moment, a look of concentration on his face. "There's nothing here. We should be safe to go in."

Jacob stepped through the doorway, and they entered what must once have been a grand receiving room. It was very wide and tall, and the remains of second and third-floor balconies were visible on a few of the walls. The ceiling was gone, except near the back.

"Where should we go?" Jacob said.

"I'd feel more comfortable hiding in a room with four walls and a roof."

"I don't blame you." Jacob walked forward. "Let's go to the other side of the castle."

They walked through a set of doors into a dark and dingy hallway with many doors leading off it. The walls went up six feet on either side and extended away from the hallway, forming a large shelf, one on each side, running the length of the corridor. On top of the high shelves stood life-size statues of humans, Makalos, and many creatures Jacob hadn't yet encountered.

"Why haven't we run into any of these?" he said.

"They're probably extinct or in hiding still."

Jacob wandered down the hallway, looking at the crumbling statues. He found two next to each other that were identical, right down to their odd-looking hands. He stopped to inspect them. "Why are there two of these?"

"One is a Dust, and the other is a Wurby. They're very much alike, except Wurbies are good and Dusts are evil. The only way you can tell the difference between them, besides how they treat you, is the color of their eyes. Wurbies have light eyes and Dusts have dark eyes."

"So, dark eyes represent evil?" Jacob snickered. "My dad's eyes are brown."

"Obviously it's not something that carries over into other species. In the case of Dusts and Wurbies, though, yes."

Jacob continued down the hall. "When we get back, I want you to tell me all about the other races and species that lived in this world." He saw the statue of a beautiful woman and walked up to it. It fascinated him. She looked too angular to be human, although she had all the features of a human. Her eyes had crumbled away, but the rest of the statue was in perfect condition.

"That's a Shiengol," Akeno said, noticing Jacob's fascination. "There used to be diamonds in her eyes. Someone must have stolen them."

"Why did they put diamonds there?"

"The eyes of a Shiengol are the most beautiful part of him or her, and the thing least understood by anyone else. Diamonds were used to represent both the color of their eyes and the power that originated there."

"Power? As in magic? Like Rezend?"

"Kind of, but not in the way you're thinking. They had amazing eyesight, and in ways you'd never imagine."

"How so?"

"I can't explain it very well, but I'll tell you what I know. A Shiengol could see more colors than we can, and in three dimensions. They could see all the senses, including sound waves, and they could even see and smell molecules. Other things about them were different, too." Akeno started opening doors in the hallway. "When we get back with the Key, I'll have my father explain it. I want to be there when he does, though, since there's a lot I don't understand."

He pushed open a door across from the Shiengol statue. "This room is perfect." He stepped back and pointed down the hall. "All right, you go that way and I'll walk this way."

Jacob jogged to the end of the corridor and turned to face Akeno. The Makalo reached out, and Jacob felt a strong, tight pressure around his waist and ribs that knocked the wind out of him. The pressure disappeared, and then he was standing on Akeno's extended palm. Nothing in between—no whoosh of air, no sensation of shrinking.

"Did I hurt you?" Akeno whispered.

Jacob tried not to gasp as he caught his breath. "No, I'm fine."

"Okay. I'm having Early take you back."

Jacob felt warmth in his cheeks and turned away for a minute, pretending to check his bag. Early was very pretty. He contemplated asking Akeno to have September take him instead, but didn't want to hurt Early's feelings. He clamped his mouth shut and closed his eyes. Why was he still shy around girls? He was fourteen—he should be over all that stupid stuff by now.

Early accepted the job in the way she normally would any request. He could tell her excitement had nothing to do with him, and he was surprised to realize he was disappointed for some reason. His self-confidence went down a notch, and he tried not to think of Early's reaction as a rejection. Feeling silly for even having the thought, his face flushed more, which embarrassed him further. He shut his eyes tighter, and moments later, saw a bright flash through his eyelids, and then he stood on a firm surface. Opening his eyes, he wasn't surprised to see huge figures surrounding him.

"Jacob, would you rather stay small for the conversation, or be enlarged again?" Kenji said.

"Make me big," he said. He didn't want to feel as though they were talking down to him.

"It increases your risk of being hurt."

"That's okay. It's better than being small."

Kenji sighed. "All right, we'll get you back to normal size."

He extended his hand and Jacob hopped onto it, grateful to have a choice—he was getting tired of people picking him up.

Kenji raised his hand high in the air, and Jacob felt the wind blow past him. The large, bouncing steps Kenji took made him feel sick, so he sat and closed his eyes, concentrating on breathing the fresh air.

"Jacob, I'm going to put you down now."

Jacob felt solid earth beneath his feet and he opened his eyes—he was back to his normal size. Looking up, he saw Brojan, Kenji, and Ebony standing on the canyon wall above him and was momentarily confused as to why he wasn't up there with them. Then it occurred to him there probably hadn't been enough distance for him to be put back to his normal size without a building getting in the way. He smiled at them, feeling a strong sense of relief mingled with homesickness. He was really close to his family! He ran forward and climbed the rope ladder they lowered to him.

"Welcome back, Jacob," Kenji said, shaking Jacob's hand.

It took a few moments to reach Brojan's house. When they did, the scent of spicy meat hung thick in the air, and Jacob's mouth started watering. The group entered the back room, and Jacob felt like jumping for joy when he saw the table. It was covered with steaming, savory things to eat.

"All right! Real food!"

"I thought you'd enjoy something different from what you've been eating," Ebony said, sitting next to Kenji.

"Oh, I'll remember this meal forever!"

Everyone laughed as the rest of them took their places. Jacob ended up sitting nearest Brojan, who was at the head of the table. The conversation started by covering all the expected topics: their health, how Jacob enjoyed sleeping in Akeno's huts, how they were getting along, how well the Minyas were behaving, and the city where Akeno was hiding. Then Brojan leaned forward.

"We wanted to talk to you because we believe the Lorkon are waiting for you," he said. "The wolves dropped their guard on the link as soon as you left, and we think the Lorkon are using the Key as bait."

Jacob almost choked on a piece of meat. "What?"

Kenji shook his head, a concerned expression on his face. "We suspected it before, but weren't sure. Things are finally adding up. For example, the wolves aren't attacking, but seem to be monitoring your progress. Nothing's trying to stop you from getting to the castle, and there have been no real distractions."

"But why are they trying to bait me?"

"They want you in their possession. It appears they haven't gotten past the spells on the Key yet."

"What are they expecting from me?" Jacob frowned. "That I'll be able to teach them how to use it?"

Kenji took another helping of potatoes. "I think they're hoping you'll be the answer to all their problems."

Jacob snorted. "Well, they're stupid, then. They have to know this is the first time I've been in their world—there's no way I'll know how to do anything for them."

Kenji put down the potato spoon and looked Jacob square in the eye. "Have you figured out why things heat up under your hands?"

"No," Jacob said. "I forgot about that, actually."

"It is immensely important you figure it out as soon as you can," Brojan said.

Kenji agreed, then leaned forward. He didn't say anything for a moment. Then, "Jacob, we didn't get the chance to explain about the Lorkon before you and Akeno had to leave. We'd like to talk to you about that now. For starters, Lorkon are almost always male. Very rarely does anyone come across a female, and there are huge differences between the male and female.

"The females are beautiful, and they have talents and abilities that come with that beauty. They are captivating. The males, on the other hand, are disfigured and hideous. While it is said you will never forget the first time you see a female, the memory of the first time you see a male will have the power to haunt your dreams for the rest of your life."

"Was the lady I saw in the forest a Lorkon?"

Kenji nodded. "We believe so."

"We hesitate telling you more about them," Brojan said, and then took a deep breath. He held it, then slowly let it out. "However, Ebony and Kenji have been very persistent in the belief that you should know as much about the Lorkon as possible before you meet them."

Kenji looked at Jacob, then closed his eyes. "Jacob, I really wish things were different. I wish your first experience in our world had been under better circumstances. And more than anything, I wish the Lorkon weren't what they are."

Ebony leaned forward. "We believe the more you know about them, the better prepared you'll be."

"I think so too," Jacob said. "Tell me as much as you can."

"They are horrible and very powerful," Kenji said. "They're taller than humans, nearing nine feet. Sometimes they hunch over inside their cloaks and it's difficult to know how tall they really are. Their teeth are stained black and yellow. They are very swift on foot and are extraordinarily strong, both physically and mentally. So strong, they don't have need for weapons."

He shook his head slowly. "All this aside, however, the most disturbing feature of the Lorkon is their skin. It's blood red in color and is constantly chafing and peeling. They infect whatever they touch, and the blood that oozes from the cracks in their skin burns like acid." Kenji shuddered at this point, rubbing his shoulder.

"That . . . is disgusting," Jacob said. "And I have to get the Key from them? How is that even possible?"

"It will be possible," Kenji said. "But remember, do not attack them. You'll lose if you do. The Lorkon are immortal and invincible. We discovered this during the last war. Sneak into the castle, using the Minyas to look out for danger. Hide until you know the coast is clear. Use the abilities you and Akeno have at your disposal to get the Key and escape."

"So I can be shrunk again?"

"Yes, but only if it's necessary. And while in the Lorkon castle, do everything in your power not to get separated."

Ebony leaned forward. "I'm particularly interested in what the Lorkon woman said to you." She looked at him expectantly.

"I . . ." Jacob thought back to the infected forest. He could picture the woman—could see her mouthing the word, but nothing came to mind. Everything had happened so quickly, and she'd been so pretty. He felt a blush creeping across his face. "I . . . uh. I can't remember." He stared at his hands, feeling sheepish. "Sorry."

"Let us know if and when you remember," she said. "It could be very important."

There was silence for a moment. Jacob finished his food while waiting for one of the Makalos to say something.

"We've decided to allow you to take something back with you," Brojan said. "It is a journal that tells the history of a man very significant to this land. It also explains how the Lorkon got in control, which is necessary for you to know."

Brojan reached back, took a book from a small table behind him, and put it in front of Jacob.

Jacob gave Brojan a questioning look and reached forward to take it. It felt worn and fragile in his hands. The leather binding was rubbing away, and the pages were old and tattered. Flipping through it, he was surprised that the first page was the only one with writing. The rest were blank.

"Only the first page has something on it," he said.

Ebony smiled. "It's intended to be read one page at a time. The rest of the information will be available after you have read what comes before it. The ultimate book—it prevents skipping ahead." She smiled again. "You'll notice that the first couple of pages were torn from another journal and added to the beginning of this, as a sort of introduction."

Jacob inspected the pages, seeing where the first few were attached. If Ebony hadn't said anything, he might not have noticed the difference. He turned to the introduction. The writing was loose and haphazard and somewhat similar to his dad's writing, so it wasn't difficult to read.

My name is Dmitri. I am twenty-three years old, and I live in the kingdom of Troosinal.

"Wait," Jacob said. "This book is about a guy named Dmitri?"

"Yes, it is," Kenji replied. "Does that mean something to you?"

"When we got to the city, we stopped off at a store, and the guy there told me about a prince named Dmitri. Is this the same person?"

"Yes, probably. Who was the man in the store?"

"He said his name was Gallus."

"Wait—Gallus?" Kenji sprang to his feet, startling Jacob.

"Yes . . . uh . . . he was a tall black man with a deep voice."

Ebony squealed, jumping up, and she and Kenji threw their arms around each other, laughing and crying. "Oh, I can't believe it!" she said. "I just can't believe it!"

"I take it you guys know him?"

Ebony wiped tears from her eyes. "Yes, of course we do. Oh, Kenji, I hadn't imagined he'd still be alive!"

"Neither had I! What a wonderful surprise!" They sat back down, and Kenji leaned forward. "Jacob, please tell us everything Gallus said."

"Well, we got to the store, and he called me 'Your Highness,' then made me eat some candy. He said the Lorkon took over their city's government for a while. They were looking for something, but gave up a year ago and moved on. That's pretty much it."

"I'm sure they were searching for the Key." Ebony nodded. "Oh, it's such a relief to hear that Gallus survived!"

"Jacob, when you return, find Gallus again," Kenji said. "Let him know who you are and that we sent you. He is one of the most trustworthy people you'll find. If he makes any suggestions about things you should or should not do, listen to him."

Jacob raised an eyebrow. "That's what you said about the old guy, and he ended up throwing nuts at us. How do you know Gallus isn't crazy too?"

"You talked to him yourself," Kenji said. "Did he seem lucid?"

"Yeah . . . he did."

"Well, there you have it."

"Please let him know we're overjoyed he is still alive and well," Ebony said. "He is in good health, isn't he?"

Jacob shrugged. "He looked like it."

"Such wonderful news!" Ebony said. She and Kenji smiled at each other, acting as though they were the only people in the room. Then she turned to Jacob. "You should get back to Akeno now."

Jacob put the book into his backpack. "So—read the book, talk to Gallus, figure out my ability, get the Key."

"Right," Kenji said.

"At least with the book, you'll be better prepared for what lies ahead of you," Ebony said. "And Gallus should have more information about the current condition of the land there."

"All right. Who's shrinking me?"

Brojan raised his hand.

Jacob slung his bag over his shoulders. "I'm ready."

Chapter 11

Grrr

It is with deep regret and pain that I write the events of the past half hour. Arien's Minya was sent to deliver our latest report to the king and queen, and returned with horrible news. The castle has yet again been attacked, and King Roylance was killed. The queen was injured—she probably won't live much longer—and sent tidings that the crown has passed to me. Though I am still prince until the crowning takes place, I am fully in charge of this kingdom.

I'm beside myself with grief. King Roylance has been a father to me these past few years since my escape from my father, Ramantus. Queen Ara Liese played an immense role, alongside my own mother and Arien, in helping me to change who I was becoming, to prevent me from following in Ramantus's footsteps. What am I to do without their guidance? Oh, how I wish I were with Arien.

Right before we received word that the king had been killed, Aldo contacted me. He informed me that the Key of Kilenya is now in his possession. I'm not sure how he got it, or from where. I'd nearly forgotten *the myths and legends surrounding those artifacts of olden times.*

He instructed me not to attempt to contact him for a while longer. He's in a very dangerous situation and will not be able to communicate. He says he's seen the princess from a distance. She still hasn't given birth to our child and appears to be healthy. Oh, what a relief!

Ebony filled Jacob's knapsack with fresh food before he left. The trip back with Early was just as quick as the trip to Taga, and soon they entered the same hall from which they'd exited. It echoed with shouts and loud crashes.

"Early! Early! Move him fast! *Hurry!*"

Early jerked Jacob upward just as a hand with long fingers swept through the air at him.

He yelled and clung to her arms, then watched in relief as whatever it was that had tried to grab him appeared smaller as he was raised higher. Early set him down on the shelf by the statues. Jacob scrambled toward the edge to see what was going on, but Early yanked him back, stopping him.

"September, what's happening?" she asked.

"Don't know. I was looking for honey and heard loud noises. A bunch of wolves and a Dust were attacking Akeno. You got here right after I did."

"A dust?" Jacob said. "Dirt?"

"No," Early said. "You saw the statue earlier. They're creatures in this world."

"Let go—I want to see."

Jacob pushed Early's arms away and jumped forward, dropping to his stomach and army-crawling to the edge of the shelf. Peering over, he saw Akeno brandishing a sword that was much too large for him, trying to protect himself. The wolves were snapping, growling, and barking at him. He was using the sword to fend them off, only taking a few swipes at the Dust every now and then. Jacob frowned. Why didn't Akeno just use his Rezend?

The Dust was an odd-looking humanoid creature with large hands, small ears, and a big mouth. Brown pants were its only article of clothing. It was fast, but it didn't seem to have rhyme or reason to its advances. It held two long knives that it was attempting to use as weapons against Akeno.

Jacob watched the way the Dust moved and realized that the only thing that made it any sort of a threat was its speed, and the fact that it was almost as big as Akeno. The Dust had no skill with the knives, and kept acting surprised to see them in its hands. Every time it swiped at Akeno, it looked down, saw the knives, yelled out, and jumped back a step or two before looking at Akeno again and resuming the attack.

September crawled up next to Jacob to watch as well.

"Does it have a short-term memory problem?" Jacob whispered. "It keeps getting surprised that it has weapons in its hands."

Suddenly the Dust pivoted in place, yelling, and looked up at Jacob. "Said get human!"

Jacob was astonished to see the knives disappear to be replaced with hooves that the creature quickly used to cover the distance between Akeno and Jacob. The wolves also abandoned their attack and ran to the base of the wall. As soon as the Dust reached the wall and lifted its hooves, long-fingered hands appeared where the hooves had been, grasping the wall and climbing.

Jacob jumped to his feet and started to back up, but watched as the creature slid off the wall, staring at its hands.

"Fingers?" the Dust yelled. "Fingers? No fingers! Knives better!" It turned and screamed at the wolves. "I trying! It complicateder than looks!"

A loud crack sounded in the air, and the wolves and Dust fell to the ground.

"September! Early! Bring him down now! We have to go!"

Jacob was lifted in the air by both Minyas and flown to Akeno.

"Hold on to him. We've got to get out of the castle before they wake up!"

Akeno led the way toward the front of the castle. He raced around a corner and almost ran into a girl who was tearing down the hallway from the opposite direction.

"No, no!" she exclaimed. "You can't come this way! There are tons of wolves coming into the castle through the front. We've got to go somewhere else." She grabbed Akeno's and tried to pull him with her, but he shook off her hand.

"Stop it!" Akeno blurted. "Who are you, and why should we go with you?"

The ferocious sound of enraged wolves echoed down the hallway in front of them. More angry noises came from behind as the wolves and Dust woke up. Jacob's heart nearly choked him when he saw several wolves round the bend at the other end of the long hall, trapping the group.

"Run, run!" He tried to scream, but only squeaked.

"Okay, let's go!" Akeno yelled.

The girl pulled Akeno down a side hallway, taking a couple of turns until they reached a heavy door. She shoved it open with both hands, revealing a descending staircase. Grabbing Akeno's arm, she pulled him down a couple of steps, then turned and shut the door behind them. September and Early, carrying Jacob, barely made it through before they were plunged into darkness. Jacob was at once grateful that he didn't have to worry about tripping over his feet on the way down the stairs. He could feel the Minyas speeding up as they followed the girl.

It was quiet for several moments except for the echoes of feet on stone. After a while, they stopped going down and moved forward into pitch-black darkness. Jacob widened his eyes as much as he could, trying to see anything. He hoped the girl knew where she was going.

The faint sounds of howling, barking, and growling wolves came from above. Jacob heard the voice of the Dust, though the words were unintelligible. They must have made it through the door.

"Give me your hand now!" the girl said.

Heavy footfalls echoed through the tunnel as Akeno and the girl started running. The wind streamed through Jacob's hair and he knew the Minyas were keeping up, though he detected no movement. He opened his eyes—still couldn't see anything. How did the girl not run into the walls?

The tunnel seemed to go on forever. The sound of the wolves was distant behind them, but growing louder.

The girl spoke and the footfalls slowed down. "We're going to enter a very large room now. There's a lot of water in the middle—do *not* touch it or go near it. Stay as close to the wall as you can, and follow me."

The sound of their feet hitting the hard floor quickened, and the Minyas sped up again. Jacob glanced over his shoulder at the faint light glowing from a torch down at the other end of the tunnel. He barely made out the figures of the wolves and Dust running toward them.

"Hurry, hurry!" he urged the Minyas on.

They soon reached a point where the wall turned in and to the right, forming the first corner of the room. This section was longer than the first, and it took more time for them to reach the next corner.

Just as Akeno and the girl arrived at the second tunnel, the wolves and Dust entered the room. One of the Dust's hands formed a lit torch, casting weird shadows in the oblong room and over the puddle, which was black as coal.

The wolves caught sight of them and rushed into the water. "No! No! No water!" the Dust yelled, but the wolves didn't turn back.

The girl grabbed Akeno's hand, pulling him into the tunnel as the room erupted in a frenzy of commotion. Loud roars echoed, and waves splashed everywhere. Hundreds of roiling things moved in the water, joining with the thrashing wolves as they tried to reach the other side of the room. The wolves howled and yipped, the Dust screamed, and the Minyas took off into the tunnel, following the girl and Akeno. They were soon enveloped in darkness. The howling and roaring coming from behind grew so loud, echoing in the tunnel, that Jacob had to cover his ears to block out the sounds.

After a few moments, the roaring stopped, and the shouting faded away.

The girl exhaled loudly. "I doubt the water got on the Dust—I've seen him before, and he knows this castle pretty well—but there's no way he'll be able to walk around the side of the room now. It's too wet, which means nothing is following us anymore. Do you have a torch or something with you? I didn't bring a light source with me."

"No, but I'm a Makalo."

The tunnel filled with the eerie blue light that emanated from Akeno's finger.

"Oh, wow!" the girl said, slowing to a walk. "I've heard of Makalos, but I had no idea there were any here! And you're still magical!"

Akeno laughed. "Yes, we're still magical. Not by much, though."

"But why are you here?"

"Mostly because Jacob came."

"Who's Jacob?"

Jacob waved at the girl. "I am."

"Who's Jacob?" she asked again after a pause.

He waved both hands in the air, and the girl glanced at him. "I'm Jacob!"

"How did you get three Minyas?" she asked, still walking. "My mother was only able to catch one."

Jacob scowled at her and yelled, "I'm not a Minya!"

No response. He cleared his throat. "Hello? I said I'm not a Minya!" Again, no response, and Jacob felt like kicking something. "Are you serious? How is it possible that you can't hear me? Akeno, tell her." He blew out a breath of air in frustration. "And can I go back to my normal size now? I'm tired of not being able to walk."

Akeno shot a look at the girl before answering. "Not yet. The tunnel has too many curves in it. You'd only be about as tall as me if I were to try enlarging you right now."

"This is really annoying," Jacob said. "And my sides are starting to hurt from the way the Minyas are carrying me."

The girl turned to walk backward, watching Akeno. She smiled, as if amused by the attention he was giving his three "Minyas." Jacob scowled again.

Akeno moved the strap of his bag. "I'm sorry. Here, you can sit on my shoulder."

"Yeah, that's not embarrassing or anything," Jacob said, giving in and allowing the Minyas to put him down. "Hey, you!" he yelled at the girl. "I'm not a Minya! I'm a human! And who are you, anyway?"

Either the girl didn't hear him or she pretended not to hear him.

"Sorry, Jacob," Akeno whispered. "Not many people outside the Makalos respect Minyas . . . or even address them directly."

"That's ridiculous," Jacob said. "Anyone who actually looked at me would see that I'm human."

Akeno sighed. "I know, but—"

"And I really don't like being this little. It's stupid." Jacob looked at the Minyas, who were now flitting back and forth near the ceiling. "No offense to them, of course."

He settled in for a long ride. Yesterday he had been excited to be shrunk again, but this wasn't what he'd envisioned. And the tunnel seemed to go on forever.

Finally, after the umpteenth curve, they reached what Jacob hoped was the end. Stairs were cut into the stone, heading up.

The girl looked back at Akeno. "These stairs will lead us to a building not far from Gallus's store."

Jacob started. "Gallus! We need to talk to him!"

"Okay, we'll do that before leaving the city," Akeno said.

After climbing for several minutes, they reached the top of the stairs. The girl pushed a slab of wood away and peered over the top. Then she and Akeno crawled out, Jacob hanging on to Akeno's shirt. The Minyas flitted through the hole behind the group. They entered a small, grimy room full of broken furniture, then went through a doorway into a slightly larger room with a big glassless window which overlooked an empty street.

"I need to set Jacob right again," Akeno said. "Are we in danger of the wolves coming here?"

"No, we'll be fine. It will take the wolves quite some time to find us. If they do at all." The girl looked around the room as she spoke. "And who's Jacob again?"

Jacob yelled out in fury, but Akeno's "Never mind" covered his voice. He looked up and saw that Akeno was smiling, which made him even more irritated.

Akeno walked out the open doorway onto the street, took Jacob off his shoulder, and, using his Rezend, put Jacob down at least fifty feet away, returning him to his normal size. He watched Akeno go back inside.

Jacob brushed himself off and took a deep breath, getting ready to storm back into the building and tell the girl a thing or two.

The distance between himself and the old, run-down building quickly disappeared as Jacob walked up to it, and he sighed in exasperation when he heard the girl's voice again, coming from inside. He leaned against the wall, feeling his determination waver. What would he say to her, anyhow? "Why couldn't you tell I'm human?" That sounded stupid. He stalled for as long as he could until Akeno yelled out the open door. "Hey, Jacob, are you here yet?"

"Yeah, I'm coming." Jacob scowled, mentally preparing himself as he entered the building.

The Minyas flitted around the ceiling, Akeno leaned against a wall, and the girl lounged in a broken chair. Her long hair was dark brown, and she had sparkly brown eyes. There was a dimple in one of her cheeks. She was cute, and his mind went blank, irritation forgotten. Cute girls did that to him, and he hated it.

"Jacob, this is Aloren. She wants to join us on our trip, and I think it might be a good idea."

"Uh . . ." He looked away from Aloren and focused on Akeno. "What?"

Akeno just smiled, and Aloren jumped to her feet, extending a hand. "Akeno said you were with us the whole time we were running through the tunnels."

Jacob dropped her hand, his frustrations coming back. His response was curt—there was no reason to have her on his side. "Yes. I was. Apparently you didn't notice, though." He turned to Akeno, scowling. "Do you really think it's a good idea to have other people come with us?"

"I don't see any harm in it," Akeno said. "She was amazing at helping us get out of the castle alive. Besides, I've had a chance to talk to her. She's looking for her brother who's been missing for a while."

Jacob raked his hand through his hair in annoyance. "What does that have to do with her coming? Honestly, Akeno, I don't like the idea."

"No, listen. It *is* a good idea. I think we can trust her, and she's traveled the road many times we'll be taking."

"I can help you with any obstacles or other things you'll come across," Aloren said.

Jacob turned to her. "You expect we'll have trouble on the road?"

"The chances are very high," she said, nodding.

Jacob dropped his bag and folded his arms. "How often have you traveled the way we're going?" He knew this was a silly thing to ask—if she lived here, she must have gone that way a lot. He pushed his thoughts aside, though.

"Six trips coming and going, and each time, we ran into trouble."

"We who?"

"Me, and the people traveling with me."

Jacob raised an eyebrow. "Did you stop to think that maybe the problems happened because you were there?"

Aloren thumped into her seat, glaring at him. "Of course it wasn't because I was there. Most people die taking the trail to Maivoryl City. Maybe the trips were so successful because of me."

Jacob raised his hand to run it through his hair again, but lowered it instead. "Can I talk to Akeno, please? Alone?"

"Fine." Aloren stood, flipped her hair, and left the room.

As soon as she was out of earshot, Jacob motioned for Akeno to stand near the front door with him.

"Akeno, I trust your judgment, I really do, but I just don't think this is a good idea."

"It'll be fine." Akeno sat and pulled the tape dispenser out of his bag. "You need to talk to her. I don't think she'll cause problems for us."

"And how do you know that? She'd probably slow us down, or make us need to be cautious about what we say, or—you know what? I'd bet anything the Lorkon sent her."

Akeno snorted and started re-taping one of the leaves to his shoe. "After what happened at the castle, you're worried she might be working for the Lorkon?"

Jacob rolled his eyes. "And you said you've read a lot of human books. It's how it always goes. The good guy trusts some seemingly innocent person who only wants to help, but in the end, turns out to be working for the bad guy."

Akeno was silent for a moment before responding. "It's just a feeling I have. Besides, we don't need to decide right now. Didn't you say we're supposed to see Gallus again?"

"Yes, I did." Jacob frowned, thinking. "Let me just talk to her and get a better idea of who she is."

Akeno put the tape dispenser back in his bag and stood. "Okay."

"It's all I'm promising, though."

"That's fine. It's a start."

Jacob started toward the back of the room, then stopped. "Hey, Aloren!"

Her voice came from somewhere up above them. "Coming!"

After a moment, Aloren breezed into the room, giving him a look he couldn't read. She half-smiled, her dimple showing.

Jacob watched her facial expressions, mostly her eyes, trying to sense if there was any dishonesty there. After a brief moment, he gave up. She was a very guarded person. He'd just have to talk to her.

Akeno leaned against the frame of the front door, watching them.

"Where are you from?" Jacob asked, sitting on one of the broken chairs.

"This city." She kept her eyes on Jacob, but played with a section of her hair.

"How long have you lived here?"

"Most of my life."

Jacob stood and paced. So far so good—she seemed to be answering his questions honestly. He couldn't get the edgy feeling to go away, though. A cute girl—this was Matt's arena, not his. Understanding the "mission" objectives had been easy. Get the Key. Read the journal. Figure out his ability. "Invite stranger to come along" wasn't one of them. "Do you have any relatives here?"

"No, none."

"Where are they?" Jacob turned to face her.

She tucked a strand of hair behind her ear. "I don't have any, except my brother and my father—if they're still alive."

"How old are you?"

"Thirteen, almost fourteen."

"And why, exactly, do you want to come with us?"

Aloren looked down and bit her lip, a troubled expression crossing her face. Jacob glanced at Akeno, who shrugged.

"My mother has been dead for a couple of months. She and my father were separated from each other years ago by the war, and my older brother went with my father. I don't remember him or my father."

"I, uh . . . I'm sorry," Jacob said.

"It's fine." She took a deep breath. "Naturally, my mother wanted to be reunited with them. It just never happened. She was always in poor health and unable to travel. For the past few years, I've tried to find them by searching this and other valleys. The only place I've never been to is Maivoryl City. The groups I've gone with always run into trouble before getting there, and each time, we've had to abandon our quest."

"I thought you said you'd been able to take the road six times," Jacob said.

"Six times to Ridgewood, but never to Maivoryl City. No one ever makes it to Maivoryl City."

"Why not?"

"We don't really know. They never come back." She looked at Jacob for a long moment, her eyes pleading. "Please, Jacob. This is really important to me. I know it might cause problems for you to bring me, but I really can help."

"Well, give me time to think about it." Jacob figured he'd first speak with Gallus before making any decisions.

Aloren stood and walked to Jacob's side, giving his arm a quick squeeze. "Thank you."

Jacob's face flushed and he turned away, picking up his bag.

"My parents knew Gallus?" Akeno whispered, his eyes flicking toward Aloren. Jacob didn't blame him—he didn't want the girl overhearing them, either.

"Yes. They knew and trusted him, and said we need to talk to him before leaving the city."

Jacob and Akeno walked several feet behind Aloren, who was peeking around every corner, keeping an eye open for the wolves as she led the way to Gallus's store.

"That's neat to think about, actually," Akeno said. "It's almost like going back in the past, meeting people my parents knew." He smiled. "I only hope he doesn't throw nuts at us."

Jacob laughed. "I doubt he will. He seems normal enough."

They soon arrived at the store. Gallus was helping a large man who had a small child in his arms.

Aloren stopped walking. Looking at Jacob, she said, "I know my way around here pretty well. I can help you find what you need."

"Just keep an eye open for the wolves. Akeno and I will only take a few minutes."

"No, really. What do you need? I can help."

Jacob shifted impatiently. "Something from the store owner. That's it."

"From Gallus? Why?"

He closed his eyes, his jaw clenched, trying not to lose his temper. Why was she being so nosy? He took a deep breath, controlling his voice. "Aloren." He paused, then continued, putting emphasis on each word. "Why do you need to know?"

Aloren stomped her foot. "Okay, fine, never mind then. I'll wait outside." She gave a small wave to Gallus.

Gallus smiled at her, shaking his head, and approached Jacob. "Welcome back."

"Thank you," Jacob said.

"How can I help you?"

"Actually, can we speak with you in private for a moment?"

"Sure, sure," Gallus said. "Let me see . . . I'll need someone to take over for me." He walked to the door and opened it. "Aloren, would you mind watching the store for a few minutes?"

Jacob's mouth popped open. He shut it before Aloren could notice. She had an "I told you so" expression written all over her face. He looked away, ignoring her.

"Thank you, Aloren. Holg here was interested in finding a new set of cups for his wife. Would you help him pick out one Nerra would like?"

"Of course."

Gallus led Akeno and Jacob up a narrow set of stairs and into a room full of boxes and merchandise. "I'm sorry about the mess," he said. "I'm afraid we'll have to stand."

"That's fine," Jacob said.

"How can I help you?"

"Well . . . I'm not sure where to start." Jacob looked at Akeno, but his friend wouldn't meet his eyes—probably being shy again. He sighed. "I'll just start at the beginning. My name is Jacob Clark, and this is Akeno. His parents are Kenji and Ebony. They said you'd—"

"Kenji? Ebony? Are you serious? Oh, what extraordinary news this is!" Gallus swooped forward and picked up Akeno in a huge bear hug, tears running, a big smile on his face. Akeno let out several small, fearful squeaks, his eyes wider than Jacob had ever seen them before. Jacob had to cough several times to control the urge to laugh at the Makalo's expression.

Gallus chuckled, wiping his tears away, and put Akeno down. "Oh, I'm sorry, I'm sorry," he said. "Kenji was just as shy around strangers until he warmed up to me. Ebony never was a cautious one, though, was she?" He smiled at Akeno, waiting for a reaction.

Akeno gave a small shake of his head, terror still in his eyes. Jacob didn't hold back the laugh this time, and Gallus joined him. It felt good to laugh.

"And how did you come to be involved with the Makalos?" Gallus put his hand on Jacob's shoulder.

"I'm still not sure about that," Jacob said. "However, Kenji and Ebony said we could trust you, and to talk to you about what we're doing here."

"Would I be correct to assume that all this has to do with the Key of Kilenya?"

Jacob started. "Yes, it does. How did you know?"

"I had my suspicions when you came to the store earlier. I knew that if a Makalo had come out of their hidden village, the Lorkon must have found the Key's hiding place. The Lorkon spent several years searching the land for that Key, only stopping about a year ago. I'm surprised they were able to get into the Makalo village that quickly. They stole it, didn't they? And that's why you're here?"

"Yes. We've been asked to find it and bring it back."

"That won't be an easy task. Did Kenji and Ebony prepare you well?"

Jacob glanced at Akeno apologetically. "Not really, actually. There's not a lot they could tell me, mainly because they haven't been in this area for several years."

"Hmmm." Gallus looked at Jacob for a moment. "I can help you, I think. First, the road to Ridgewood and Maivoryl City is very dangerous. If you have a couple of days, you could stay in my home with me and my family. That would give me enough time to tell you everything you might come across."

"We . . . don't have that much time," Jacob said, thinking about the wolves. "We need to leave as soon as possible."

"In that case, I recommend you take someone with you who knows the way. I'd love to do it, if you'll have me. It's been several years since I last left Macaria, and it would be nice to get out again. I'll have to shut my shop down, but I'll manage."

Jacob shifted his weight. "Well, actually, Aloren has already requested that she come with us."

"Aloren?" He frowned. "That girl is so stubborn. I should have known she'd be trying to get to Maivoryl City again. Of course she would." He started fidgeting with one of the boxes in the room for a moment before saying anything. He looked up at Jacob, a disappointed expression on his face. "No, she'll be a better guide than I would." He sighed. "Of course you should take her instead."

"Is she trustworthy?"

"Aloren? Trustworthy? Of course she is. She's worked for me since she was eight. She's a hard worker—doing basically everything. Housecleaning, laundry, cooking, stable cleaning—basically whatever people need. She and her mother used to live right here, in this room. That was back before her mother . . ." His voice trailed off, and he didn't continue.

"Died?" Jacob said.

"Yes," Gallus said. "Jacob, listen to me. Aloren has had a difficult life—very difficult. Parents separated before she was born, a mother who was almost always sick, a constant loneliness and desire to find her father and brother. She's got a lot of energy, she has, but she's still hurting from her mother's death. I've tried to talk her into settling down here, but every month or so she uproots herself, searching through a different part of the kingdom. And while her mother was sick, Aloren was incredibly restless. She had the desire to be out searching, but couldn't leave her mother's side for several months." Gallus frowned. "That was hard for her. She felt trapped, and then felt guilty for feeling that way.

"She's been everywhere in this part of the kingdom except past Ridgewood. It would be wise for you to take her with you—to have someone with you who knows the land. And . . . it'll ease her mind if she's searching for her brother."

Jacob moaned to himself. "All right, we'll take her."

"And you won't regret it."

Jacob heard Aloren's laughter from down below and almost rolled his eyes.

Gallus smiled. "Just take care of her, okay?"

"We will."

They walked through the city, Jacob keeping his eyes open for wolves. Aloren had been talking almost non-stop since they left the store. He tried to control his frustration, realizing she was probably just excited to be leaving Macaria. He paid little attention to what she was saying, only offering an "Uh-huh" or "Yeah" when he felt they were necessary. He just wanted to get out of the city.

"You know, you really don't need to worry about the people in this town," Aloren said, putting her hand on Jacob's arm.

Jacob startled, pulling away. He hadn't realized she'd noticed him glancing up and down the alleys. "I'm not worried about the people—I'm worried about the wolves."

"They're not here anymore. I already told you."

"But you couldn't tell me why. I'll feel much better when Akeno can confirm it for us."

"Anyway," Aloren said, "as I was saying, this used to be a glorious city."

"Really?" Jacob quickly looked down another alley, his eyes having caught a movement.

"You should've seen it at night. I barely remember it—there are paintings, though. If we get through this, maybe someday I'll show them to you."

"Yeah, sure."

The dust from the road blew into Jacob's face, irritating him. Come to think of it, everything was a source of irritation at this point, and he was still nervous about having Aloren on the trip.

They walked past the last of the buildings and Jacob let out a breath, relieved to be out of the city. He realized Aloren had stopped talking. Had she asked a question? He wracked his brain, trying to remember the last thing she said, but was unable to come up with anything. He risked a quick glance in her direction, but she didn't seem to be waiting for anyone to say something. She had a smile on her face, though—her dimple was showing.

It was nice not to have to pretend to be listening. He felt bad for that, but his brain could only handle so much conversation before he went crazy.

On the other hand, there were so many things he wanted to talk to Akeno about, and Aloren made that difficult. Gallus might trust her, but Jacob didn't want to just open up and talk about things with her around—at least, not until he knew more about her.

His thoughts turned to the experience they'd had while running through the tunnel. Those things in the water—what were they? Something Aloren had experience with and that scared the Dust.

Something tickled Jacob's head, and he scratched it. He glanced at Aloren again—she was still smiling. What could be that funny? Or maybe her face never relaxed—maybe it was frozen in a smile. He almost stopped walking as this thought occurred to him. Maybe she had a muscular disorder that made her face look like that. Jacob made a mental note to check to see what her face looked like while she was sleeping. He almost laughed out loud when this thought formed in his mind, realizing how awkward it would be if she woke up with him in her sleeping place. He could only imagine what he'd say. "Uh, I'm checking to see if you have a muscle problem in your face that makes you smile all the time." That would make for an interesting conversation.

Scratching his head again, he looked around, not at all surprised that the Minyas were nowhere to be seen.

His head itched again, and this time he felt something crawling in his hair. He jumped, swatting his head several times.

"Hey!" a tiny voice cried out. September flew down from somewhere up above him, joined by Early. "Don't hit us!"

Jacob jerked to a stop, scowling. "Were you in my hair?"

"We're just playing a game," September said.

Early flitted in front of him. "Is that okay?"

"No, it's not okay!" Jacob pointed at Akeno. "Why can't you play in his hair?"

"It isn't as thick as yours," Early said. "Besides, his lies flat on his head. Yours doesn't."

Jacob scoffed. "That is seriously the dumbest thing I've ever heard."

"It's not dumb—it's fun to play in your hair," September said.

"Fine. Play. I'm warning you right now, though—don't blame me if I forget you're there and one of you ends up squished."

"We'll be fine!" Early said, giving Jacob her most winning smile. She and September disappeared from view, and Jacob felt them land on his head. He rolled his eyes again, glancing sidelong at Aloren. She grinned at him. Scowling, he started walking again and let out a breath of pent-up frustration. This was going to be a long trip.

Chapter 12

Storm's a Comin'

An unfamiliar Minya just approached me, bearing greetings from Brojan, leader of the Makalo army. He and his troops are in the valley just east of here, and are awaiting word from us as to when the attack should begin. It can't possibly happen for several days, since we have not yet begun to gather forces. I am appointing Lahs, a member of King Roylance's guard, to round up an army to meet with Brojan's. Lahs is eager to be of assistance. I've instructed him to find any and all who are willing, from every race, to join the cause for freedom.

We are nearing the next element: fire. The land around us is burned, and I have a sick feeling in the pit of my stomach that says danger is ahead. Hopefully the Fat Lady's instructions will prove useful, and Lasia will be held at bay

Jacob, Akeno, and Aloren finally made it to the original trail Akeno and Jacob had been following for so long.

"Aloren?" Akeno asked.

"Hmmm?"

"Can you explain what happened in the basement of the castle? Why we couldn't touch the water?"

Jacob perked up, glad Akeno had asked his question. He wasn't about to start a conversation with Aloren.

"Of course," she said. "The castle is built over Sonda Lake, one of the most dangerous parts of Redland. The water is really deep, but no one knows for sure how far down it goes because of the Eetu fish. They live only where the water is darkest—they can't stand the sun, and so only come to the surface after it's gone down. Eetu fish are really dangerous. Their fins can act like feet, giving them the ability to move quickly regardless of whether they're on land or in water. They get to be huge—sometimes up to ten feet long. They have razor-sharp teeth that triple line their mouths, and are able to make a full-grown man disappear in a matter of seconds."

Jacob raised his eyebrows. These fish sounded like piranhas on steroids.

Aloren looked at Akeno. "This isn't the only reason why they're so dangerous, though. If a drop of the water from their territory hits you, they will hunt you down until they've eaten or destroyed you. They're able to sense where that water went, regardless of whether it has evaporated or not. They know when someone has come in contact with it—even just one drop.

"Your only defense when you get wet is to hope you're able to outrun them. They only last above water for an hour or so, but most people make the mistake of thinking they'll die or retreat after that. This isn't true. An Eetu fish can replenish itself with any water source big enough to cover its gills. Once it's replenished, it continues the hunt. On average, it takes the Eetu fish around twenty-four hours to lose the scent of that bit of water."

Jacob glanced at Aloren—this topic was seriously fascinating to him, and he wanted to ask questions. That would require talking to her, though, and he wasn't sure he was ready yet. He shook his head at himself for being so petty, then swallowed his pride. "What about the water the Eetu uses to replenish itself while on the chase?" he asked. "Does it become the fishes' territory?"

"No. Eetus have to live in the water for at least a full day to claim it as their own. Also, Sonda Lake is the only place where it's deep enough or dark enough for them. They don't survive very long in shallow water."

"So if I go down to the lake and touch the water right now, we'd be in big trouble?"

"Again, no. The only water the Eetus claim as their own is what's immediately around them." Aloren pushed her hair out of her face. "There's a crack somewhere in that room, letting them inside, and hundreds of Eetus live there."

"Yeah, I saw," Jacob said. "When the wolves went in, it looked like the whole thing was moving. But how do they live so closely? Wouldn't they constantly be killing one another for invading their water?"

"Actually, no. Eetu fish live in relative peace with their own species."

"Is it possible to kill one?" Akeno asked.

"Yes, but it's difficult. No average man or woman has been able to defeat them, mostly because Eetus are fast and intelligent. The only safe bet is to outrun them, if that'll even work."

"I bet a gun would take care of an Eetu fish in short order," Jacob said, laughing. "Hey, what happens if someone takes some of the water without touching it? Like if they dipped a container into the water and then sealed it? Would they be able to use it as a weapon? You know, throw it on someone and have the fish chase that person down?"

"It's possible, I guess, but has never happened."

"Why not?"

"Because no one has been down that far into the lake without getting killed in the process," Aloren said. "And no one knows about the water in the tunnel, except for myself and the Dusts who live there, and Dusts aren't intelligent enough to use it to their advantage."

"How do you know the castle so well?" Jacob asked.

"I live there."

"With the Dusts?"

Aloren glanced at Jacob. "Yeah. It's really not that hard to stand up to them. You just have to be smarter and present them with new obstacles. If the challenge is out of the norm, it'll take them months to figure it out. I just have to change my barriers—what I use to keep them out of my tower—every six months or so, and I'm completely fine."

The group fell into silence. Jacob couldn't help but wonder if it was possible for him to get some of the Eetu water as a way to protect his companions and himself against the Lorkon.

Akeno broke the silence by asking Jacob questions about his family. He was curious about how they interacted with each other, and it was easy for Jacob to forget Aloren's presence while talking about home.

After several minutes of discussion, Jacob realized that Aloren was paying close attention to what he was saying. He looked at her, surprised that for once she didn't have a smile on her face. He felt uncomfortable when he noticed there were tears in her eyes. She glanced at him, then away, but not before Jacob saw the tears spill over.

156

Jacob fidgeted with his hands, wracking his brain, trying to figure out what his mom would do if she were here. Probably make Aloren a cup of hot chocolate. That wasn't possible . . . but there was food in his knapsack. He swung it off his shoulder and pulled out some apples. He tossed one to Akeno, kept one for himself, and gave another to Aloren. She accepted and took a big bite, not meeting his eyes.

Jacob shrugged, deciding not to worry about it. He pulled the journal out of his bag, looking around at the countryside, surprised to see how far they had walked since leaving the city. The sun was very hot still, although it was late in the afternoon. Clouds were building in the sky to the south.

"It looks like a storm's coming," Akeno said.

"Storm?" Aloren looked up with a dismayed expression on her face.

"Yeah, see it?"

"Yes," she said. "Storms aren't good here."

"Why not?" Jacob asked.

"They're dangerous." Aloren sped up, walking several paces in front of the boys instead of alongside them.

"It'll be a nice break from the heat, though," Jacob called to her, wiping a drop of sweat off his forehead. He waited, but she didn't answer. He looked around again. "Where are the Minyas?" It'd been a few minutes since he'd last felt them in his hair.

"I don't know," Akeno said. "I didn't see them leave."

"We're going to need to find a way to keep them nearby. I'm tired of them flying off."

"Maybe they could sit in your knapsack for a while."

Jacob cupped his hand around his mouth. "September! Early! Where are you?"

With a flash of light, the Minyas were next to him.

"We're here!" Early said.

"Yeah. We weren't very far," September added.

"All right, you two—you've wandered off way too many times. We want you to ride in my bag for a while." He held his knapsack open. "In you go."

Early giggled and patted Jacob on the hand. "We'll be good now." She turned to September. "Another ride in his bag! Fun!" They disappeared into the knapsack.

Jacob sighed. "We'll see how long that lasts." He left the bag open a couple of inches and carefully swung it back over his shoulders. Then he opened the book, deciding to make use of the light while he could.

My name is Dmitri. I am twenty-three years old, and I live in the kingdom of Troosinal. Following the counsel of my mother, I have started this journal. She said there may come a time when our people will need to understand my history and that of our land.

My father, the king, is named Ramantus. He is evil and always has been, following in the footsteps of the many kings and queens who have gone before him. His subjects fear and hate him. I will not speak of his acts of evil against them—however, let it be known the people hate him for good reason.

Ramantus showed uncharacteristic wisdom in his choice of a wife.

My mother was his exact opposite. Gentle, kind-hearted, loving—she did more for me than anyone else ever has. She died a couple of years ago—a death which could easily have been prevented if my father had cared to do so.

Jacob stopped for a minute when he had to turn a page. He watched the words flow, then stop—the book must have realized he wasn't internalizing the information. He laughed, trying to see if he could figure out a way to trick the book into giving more than he was actually reading. It didn't work. He started to read again.

Though it pains me to say, I followed closely in my father's steps for several years, and he has chosen me as heir to the throne. I'm not even his eldest son. I wonder if he will still want me to take over when he finds out how different I am now.

At my mother's request, I will write of the things that caused the change in me—the first being a marriage she arranged for me—a marriage which still hasn't taken place, and the terms of which were decided long before I realized what was going on, long before I started changing my life. The neighboring king and queen, Roylance and Ara Liese, agreed to allow me to marry their daughter, Arien, but only if I stopped the cruel and evil things I'd been doing. My mother, with her never-ending faith in me, agreed to the terms and took it upon herself to ensure I understood the gravity of my ways.

The second event was a conversation between my mother and me, which I'm sad to say wasn't very successful on either part. She did her best, in her ever-gentle manner, to show me where my father was wrong and where I was becoming like him. I didn't listen, and responded with anger. This conversation, however, started things rolling in my heart and mind. I began recognizing how my father's choices—and more importantly, my response to those choices—were influencing me.

The last event was a culmination of many things. My father had become upset over something trivial, and he was angrier than I'd seen him in months. He entered the hall where the rest of the family played games together, yelling and cursing and throwing things. My dear sister, not paying attention to his mood, teased him. He turned on her, shoving her against the wall, and her head struck the stones. He was drunk and barely recognized he'd hurt her. My sister began to convulse, my brothers rushed to her aid, and my parents started yelling at each other. Ramantus threatened to physically punish my mother, then threw her in the dungeons.

With close medical care, my sister survived—but Ezra feared permanent damage had been done, and he was right. Over the last few years, I've watched her become reticent and even unresponsive. Mother was already very ill and became much worse in the cold, damp air of the dungeon. We tried to release her, but my father kept the only key and didn't listen to our pleas to let her go. She only lasted a week.

Jacob stopped reading when Akeno and Aloren halted, letting the words of the book sink in. He'd never come across such corruption in his life, except through the media and studies of history. What would it be like to have a dad who acted that way, attacking the people he was supposed to love the most? It was hard to fathom—especially when Jacob's parents treated each other with such respect.

Aloren and Akeno were now setting up camp, carrying on an animated conversation. He had no desire to join them, deciding instead to take advantage of the last bit of sunlight.

*I was with her when she died. By then I'd experienced
a complete change of heart—I no longer desired to do evil.
I regretted the years of destruction I'd caused in others'
lives—regrets I still carry.*

*My mother told me it was vital that no one know of
the transitions I'd been experiencing—especially my
father. Not even the servants. She said there would come
a time when the people of Troosinal would be so badly
abused by my father, so poorly treated by the noblemen
that they would turn to wickedness for help and comfort.
They would stop listening to anyone who brought
messages of peace and hope. I'd need to leave the kingdom
when this occurred—she said I would know when that
time arrived.*

"Jacob, what've you been reading?" Akeno asked. Aloren
wasn't around.

"It's a journal written by the prince Gallus mentioned—
Dmitri. Brojan and Kenji gave it to me while I was in Taga.
It's supposed to help me understand more of what's going
on here, but the only thing I've read so far is how wicked
his dad was, and how Dmitri used to be wicked, but is
good now."

Akeno finished making the fire and turned to the scrub
oak and bushes near him. He touched one of the trees, and
the leaves and branches folded into two separate huts. "What
did you talk about with them?"

"Apparently, the lady in the forest is a Lorkon."

"She is? She wasn't at all what I thought they'd look like."

"Your dad said the females are different from the males,
and it's the guys who are really disgusting." Jacob paused.
"Was it a Lorkon that injured your dad in the war?"

"Yes." Akeno tested the strength of the huts by pushing against them in a few places. "He told us he was attacked with acid or something. Pretty horrendous."

"He told me the Lorkon blood burns like acid. They must have dripped it or poured it on him."

"Oh, wow. No wonder he never said exactly what happened. That's disgusting." Akeno sat on the ground near the fire, watching the logs burn. "Oh, I meant to ask you if you wanted to try cooking those potatoes."

Jacob's thoughts flew to their extra company. "Tonight? Can't we do it some other time?" Like, after Aloren was no longer with them . . .

"They're really not that hard to make."

Jacob suppressed a growl. "Fine. Teach me."

They began preparing dinner. Aloren returned, and there was surprise in her eyes when she saw them. She offered to help, but they had nearly finished, so she sat to wait.

"Here, have some potatoes." Jacob held a plate out to Aloren, surprised to see his hand tremble. Why was he nervous for her to try the food? A smile was behind her eyes when she took it, and, embarrassed, he pulled away, grabbed his own plate, and sat where she couldn't see his face. He couldn't help but feel a little irritated again—mainly with himself, though he wasn't sure why. Deciding just to ignore it, he turned back to Akeno.

"I wish we could listen to some music," he said, taking a bite of potatoes. Too bad he hadn't worn his iPod while he'd been shooting hoops—otherwise, he'd have it with him now. He couldn't remember a time when he'd gone so long without music.

"See if you can get the Minyas to sing for you," Akeno said, organizing the food on his plate into neat piles. "It's actually very entertaining."

"Uh, thanks, but no thanks. I think I'm Minyaed out for the rest of my life."

Aloren stretched out her long legs. "Yours haven't seemed so bad to me."

"That's because you haven't had to deal with them for the last week," Jacob said, leaning up against a large rock.

Akeno disagreed. "You've only dealt with them for a couple of days. I've had to deal with them for the last week—four days of which you were unconscious."

"Yeah, but you've been around them your whole life, and so you're used to them." Jacob looked around. "Where are they, anyway?"

"They went up into the trees," Aloren said. "They smelled honey."

"Jacob, you have to remember that Minyas aren't like humans or Makalos," Akeno said. "They have a completely different set of social rules. And they don't have a very developed intellect. They understand language fairly well, but that's about it. They used to be kept as pets by the more wealthy Makalos and humans."

"Really? A pet Minya?" Jacob laughed out loud at this. Minyas were too human-like to be pets.

"Is it so hard to imagine? I mean, they need some social training, but after that, many of them are fairly loyal and like to belong to the same person for long periods of time."

Jacob finished the food on his plate and got seconds. He wanted to ask Aloren about her parents, but didn't want to pry. How would she respond to personal questions? There was only one way to find out. "How did your parents get separated?"

"I don't really know. My mom had some memory problems that she got from an injury. I've always had the feeling it was a very traumatic experience for her."

"What were your parents like?"

"My father wasn't anyone really important, socially. I think he was one of many who worked in the stables at the castle. And I think my mother was a lady-in-waiting for a rich family in Maivoryl City. She spoke frequently about the woman for whom she worked, but was never clear about the details."

"What about your brother?" Jacob asked. "What do you know about him?"

"Only a few things my mother told me. He was a blond-haired, blue-eyed boy with dimples. He was a tease, even though he was only two or three."

Jacob collected the other dishes and plates. Sitting still with Aloren nearby was unsettling, and he had to do something with his hands. "Why do you believe he's in Maivoryl City?"

"Because it's the only place I haven't looked for him yet. No one has left or entered the city for so many years—it would make sense if he were there."

"If no one has been able to leave it, how do you know for sure that people are still there?"

"They were there when my mother left."

Jacob scraped off the dishes. "But how do you know any of them are still alive?"

Akeno shot a warning glance at Jacob, probably wanting him to back off with the questions. The Makalo took over cleaning the dishes.

"I guess I don't know," she said. "I just feel the need to go search the city. Please, Jacob, try to understand. If you were in my place, and your only sibling was lost, wouldn't you do everything in your power to find him or her?"

Jacob felt chastised—he'd been pushing too much, and Akeno was obviously aware of it. He stared at his hands, unsure what to say. "Yeah, I guess." He picked at some dirt stuck to his palm, then sighed. "Sorry. I'm not trying to be a jerk."

"I know I probably seem crazy."

"No, just lonely. I'd hate to be in your shoes."

She didn't respond for a minute, and Jacob wondered if he'd said something wrong.

"I just wish my mother hadn't gotten sick," Aloren finally said. "She remembered a lot when I was little and told me stories about my father and brother, but she forgot most everything. I only vaguely remember the stories now. It's so frustrating."

Jacob felt a sudden need to comfort her, though he wasn't sure why or how. He hoped she wouldn't start to cry and he wished his mom were there. "That really bites," he said. "I mean, it stinks. I mean . . ." He stopped and snorted at himself, giving up. Curse girls. Curse the need he felt to protect Aloren from her own negative emotions.

She smiled at him, her dimple showing. "It's fine, Jacob. I've had a lot of time to deal with things."

Jacob was suddenly aware of how dirty his hair and clothes were. Feeling embarrassed, he looked away. His dad used to say something about society needing good women to keep men civilized—suddenly he understood what that meant.

He stared up at the stars again, noticing the clouds were covering most of them.

It began raining about thirty minutes after dinner was over. Akeno set off to make the tents stronger in preparation for the oncoming storm, and Aloren and Jacob put out the fire. Jacob did his part, then went into his and Akeno's hut after everything was put away, wanting to avoid another awkward conversation.

It took him a while to fall asleep. The rain started lightly at first, but got stronger and stronger, and the water seeped up through the branches and leaves where he lay. He tossed and turned for a while before finding a somewhat comfortable position, then fell into a restless sleep.

Waking up, Jacob could tell it was not going to be a good day. He was exhausted and sore from trying to stay away from the wettest parts of the ground throughout the night.

He rolled over and saw that Akeno had already left the hut. Stretching out on his back, he lay for a few more minutes, reluctant to stand and discover how many kinks he had in his muscles. Finally, he stood. "Come on, Jacob," he said. "Be cheerful." It didn't make him feel any better.

He poked his head out of the makeshift tent. The sunlight was muted because of the thick clouds overhead. A flash of light signaled a thunderstorm.

A smile crept across his face. He'd always loved thunderstorms. If he was going to be wet all day, at least it would be for a good reason. He pulled himself the rest of the way out of the brambles.

Spotting leftovers from breakfast near the fire pit, Jacob grabbed some food and munched, listening to the rumble of distant thunder.

Akeno and Aloren were down the hill, hiding under the trees at the edge of the forest. Jacob made his way to them, curious why they were staring up at the clouds.

"Uh, good morning?"

Aloren gave a brief smile, but didn't look at him. Akeno didn't acknowledge his presence at all.

"Why are the clouds so interesting?"

"We're looking for Lirone," Aloren said.

"Um . . . right," Jacob said. "Lirone. Of course." He turned to watch the clouds. Nothing happened. "Who's Lirone?"

"Did you see that?" Akeno asked, pointing at a spot over the lake.

"Yes, I did," Aloren said.

"Is it really him?"

"It's been like this before when he's shown up, so I wouldn't doubt it."

Jacob grunted in exasperation, then hiked back to camp to eat more breakfast. Akeno and Aloren were still watching the skies when he finished, so he put away the few dishes. He tried to force the branches of the huts to go back to where they'd been before, but they wouldn't budge. Walking down the hill, he stood next to Akeno again. "Hey, I can't put back the bushes without your help."

Still no answer. Jacob growled in exasperation. "Where are the Minyas?"

"We might not be going anywhere," Akeno said.

"We have to leave," Aloren said. "Those huts won't protect us from Lirone. We need to make sure it really is him, and then get to the caves in the Dunsany Mountains as quickly as we can."

"Dunsany Mountains?" Jacob asked.

"Yes. The caves will provide us with protection. They're dangerous themselves—if you're not careful and go too deep into them, you'll never find your way out of the mountain— but they're the only place where we might find safety from him."

"How do your people survive?" Akeno asked.

"He very rarely goes anywhere but north and south. He's been near my city a couple of times, and I've only heard of him going west once. The Lorkon got upset with him for doing that, and it hasn't happened since."

"What on *earth* are we talking about?" Jacob folded his arms.

"How could a Lorkon possibly stand against Lirone?" Akeno said.

"You'd be surprised, actually. The rumor is that the Lorkon brought him to guard their city."

"All right," Akeno said, turning. "I'll go put the bushes back. At least we can be prepared for him if he does come."

Aloren turned as well. "And I'm going to see if I can climb a little higher through the trees. Maybe I'll be able to see better from up there."

"Will someone *please* tell me what's going on?"

They ignored him, both running up the hillside—Akeno to the campsite, and Aloren farther through the trees. Jacob stood where he was, glaring at their receding figures. Finally, he decided to find the Minyas instead. He turned and scanned the forest for them.

Weird pock marks dotted the mountain. It was almost as if a war had occurred there, and Jacob wondered if the holes were from the war with the Lorkon. Hadn't that happened years ago, though? Shouldn't the marks have leveled by now—from rain and the passage of time? Or maybe there was some weird animal that roamed the countryside, digging random holes everywhere.

Aloren emerged from the trees high above him, and he waved at her. She was staring up at the clouds, though, and didn't see his hand. He felt tension in the air, but didn't know where it was coming from, or why.

Jacob caught a slight movement from the corner of his eye, and turned to face south. The waves on the lake were much bigger than they'd been earlier, as if there was a huge windstorm. No wind was blowing past him, though.

The clouds rolled grotesquely—forming weird, twisted shapes—and were a brown, almost gray-green color. Jacob turned and yelled back to camp, wanting to know what was wrong with the clouds, but no sound came out. Surprised, he clamped his jaw shut and then opened it again, trying to talk. He could feel his lips forming words, but he couldn't hear anything.

Someone jerked him around and started to drag him toward the trees. He ripped his hand out of the person's grasp before realizing it was Akeno.

Akeno said something to him, but Jacob shrugged, motioning to his ears. Akeno shook his head, apparently exasperated, and grabbed Jacob's arm. Pulling Jacob with one hand, he motioned to the sky with the other.

Jacob looked up again. His jaw dropped and he stumbled backward. What on *earth*?

Chapter 13

Caves and Bones

What a day! We were successful in defeating, albeit temporarily, the Fire Pulser! I should note it didn't happen exactly as the Fat Lady had said. Once the five diamonds were in place, instead of the shield we were expecting, a bright light shot between them, connecting them and forming a solid sphere around her. This circle, at least ten feet in diameter, glowed brighter and brighter until it became painful to look upon. However, after several minutes the light dimmed, and all that remained was a diamond ball with Lasia contained inside. I can only imagine her fury to see us there, watching her. As we did so, she pulsed fire from every inch of her body, and the diamond surrounding her became hot. We were quite surprised when we saw the dirt around the diamond begin to melt, and the sphere that encircled her start to sink. Eventually all that was visible were the top few feet of the diamond, which we promptly covered in dirt.

So much for the third element!

A large section of clouds had rolled into the shape of a face. As it became clearer, its eyes opened, glanced around for a moment, then focused on Jacob and Akeno.

The cloud was also forming massive hands and arms that appeared to be gathering something, but Jacob couldn't look away from its angry gaze.

"Jacob! Run!" Aloren screamed. He ripped his eyes from the monster in the sky, surprised he was able to hear her. He hesitated for a split second before the adrenaline kicked in, then tore up the hill toward Aloren's voice, Akeno running beside him.

Suddenly his feet flew out from under him and he soared through the air, landing hard on his knees ten feet from where he'd been standing.

Dazed, Jacob scrambled up and spotted Akeno about a yard away. He appeared to have been knocked unconscious. Jacob looked down the hill to see what it was that had thrown them forward and was surprised that a hole now smoldered, three feet in diameter, where he and Akeno had just been.

Aloren stood at the edge of the trees, screaming. No sound carried to Jacob, though he wasn't more than forty feet away. She motioned with her hands for them to run. Jacob picked up Akeno and both bags, and made a beeline for the trees. Another shock wave blew through the air, nearly knocking him over, but this time he didn't turn around.

He reached Aloren, tossed her the bags, and kept running. They ran up the hill, through the trees. Continual shock waves hit them on all sides with explosions and blasts of fire.

Trusting that Aloren knew where they were going, he stayed as close to her as possible, following her far up the side of the mountain and away from the trail. He still couldn't hear anything, and shock waves rammed into his body, making any kind of movement difficult.

After what felt like an hour of solid running, Jacob saw several caves in the rock ahead of them. He followed Aloren into one, and they ran as far as they could until the cave stopped. Aloren mouthed something and darted out of the cave, unable to hear Jacob's shouts to come back. Jacob wasn't surprised—he couldn't hear them, either.

She was gone for a couple of seconds before returning. Racing back in, she grabbed his hand and pulled him out of the cave. Confused, he chased after her into the entrance of another cave. They didn't stop running until they were almost completely enveloped in darkness. Dropping Jacob's hand, Aloren faced the entrance. The only thing visible was a glimpse of the mountains on the other side of the lake. She put the bag down, slumping by one of the walls.

Jacob stood for a moment, letting his eyes adjust, and then Akeno down next to Aloren. He ran his hand through his hair, raking out twigs, and leaned up against the wall near the others.

After a moment, he got tired of standing and sat next to Akeno, whose eyes were now wide open. Jacob still couldn't hear anything, and it occurred to him that his hearing might have been damaged by the shock waves.

It wasn't long, however, before the faint sound of an explosion reached his ears, making him jump. "Hey! I can hear again!" He turned to Akeno. "Are you okay? You blacked out for a minute there."

"Yeah, I'm fine," Akeno said, sitting up. "I think I'm doomed to be thrown over your shoulder like a sack of potatoes every time something bad happens."

"Yeah, sorry about that." Jacob smiled. "What about the Minyas? Are they going to be okay?"

"They're much too fast for Lirone," Aloren said. "Besides, he doesn't care about them. They're too small."

"Anyway, they probably went somewhere else to wait out the storm and will catch up to us when it's safe again," Akeno added.

Jacob turned to Aloren. "All right. *Now* can you tell me what's going on out there?"

"That, Jacob, is Lirone," Aloren said. "He's one of the main reasons why most people don't make this trip."

Jacob frowned. "What is he? And why couldn't I hear anything? I mean, I know that shock waves and loud noises can mess up your hearing, but I wasn't able to hear even before the explosions started."

"It wasn't because of the explosions. Lirone has the ability to control particles and waves in the air. As soon as he spots someone, he takes away all sound before it reaches their ears or leaves their mouths. It's part of his way of trapping people before he blows them away."

Jacob's mind was reeling. What would've happened if Aloren hadn't been with them? They'd be dead, he was sure of it. "How'd you know about him, Akeno?"

"I'd heard stories and myths," Akeno said, pulling the leaves off his shoes. "My father spoke of a creature big enough to cover the entire sky who existed in the form of clouds and used particles in the air to kill things. I didn't know much else about him, though."

Jacob looked to Aloren. "Why could I hear you scream?"

"Because he'd only seen you and Akeno. If he hasn't seen or heard something yet, it doesn't exist to him, and he can't take away its sound."

"And as soon as you yelled at me, he knew you were there?"

Aloren nodded. "We can hear each other now because he's given up trying to find us for the time being."

Jacob thought for a minute. "So, what's the purpose of doing that? Make it so people can't call out for help or something?"

Akeno shrugged. "I'd guess it's more of a cruel joke he likes to play than anything else."

"Calling out for help can't save you from Lirone," Aloren said. "And usually the people who know his tricks won't stand out in the open."

Jacob rolled his eyes. "Gee, thanks for letting me know."

Aloren laughed. "Sorry, I should have said something. I feel really bad. Honestly, it didn't occur to me to mention it until I saw you step out of the trees."

"Even with my pestering you guys to tell me what was going on?"

"Yeah, I was a little preoccupied and freaked out. Next time, though, I'll let you know beforehand if something bad is going to happen."

Jacob snorted. "That'd be great," he said. He shifted to a more comfortable position. "So, next time Lirone comes around, all we'll need to do is remain hidden, and we'll be safe?"

"Not quite. He still throws bombs even if he can't see anyone. If there are living things in the area, throwing the bombs will either kill them or scare them out of their hiding places."

"But why does he do that?"

"He's always been a violent creature," Akeno said. "There are many theories and legends about why he's that way, but no one really knows for sure."

Aloren rummaged through her bag, pulling out a hair tie. "The first cave we went into was too shallow, and he'd know we were there. That's one of the many mistakes people make. They figure if they can't see his face, he can't see them. They don't know the clouds they're looking at are actually him. If they can see clouds, any part of them, then he can see them."

Jacob frowned. "So I wasn't really looking at his face?"

Aloren fastened her hair back with the tie. "Not in a conventional way. He doesn't have the same shape we do."

"Why could I see a face, then?"

She smoothed her hair. "He was probably doing it for your benefit. To scare you. I've seen him do that before, though today was the first time I've seen him form arms."

"Okay, so he's made of clouds," Jacob said, still trying to get a grasp on this creature. He was both fascinated and freaked out by Lirone—what guy wouldn't be?

"Yes," Aloren said, then paused. "Well, no. I mean, he's not *made* of clouds, but he *looks* like clouds. Any time a storm comes through this land, it's almost impossible to tell if he's part of it or not. He moves a lot when he sees someone, which makes it easy to tell if he's there. But when he's just waiting, he rarely moves, except to shift a little or follow the wind. He doesn't look like a normal cloud when he moves, and that's what Akeno and I were searching for."

"I think I saw that while I was standing out in the open like an idiot." Jacob grabbed his knapsack, feeling around inside it for the journal. He couldn't see anything, though. "All right, I'm tired of it being dark. Akeno, why not light up the place? Aloren, do you think that would be okay?"

Aloren nodded. "Yeah, there shouldn't be a problem. Besides, I'm starving, and we'll want to see what we're eating."

A second later, the cave filled with Akeno's bluish light, and Jacob resumed digging inside his bag for the book and food for the others. He handed them bread and jerky. "Where did Lirone come from?"

"No one knows," Akeno said. "He didn't originate here, though."

"He's existed for as long as there's been a history kept by my people," Aloren said.

Jacob leaned back against the cave wall, munching on jerky and fingering the journal. "And how long do you think we'll need to hide out in this cave?" Too bad they didn't have a grill. And some steaks. Fresh, barbecued meat sounded really good.

Aloren inspected her bread. "Until the sun is shining again and there aren't any storm clouds in the sky. He only comes when there's already a storm."

"Dang, that's going to take forever."

"Not necessarily. The weather can change fast, so it might only be an hour. Soon after we see sunlight, we should be fine to leave."

Jacob sighed, then stuffed the last of his jerky into his mouth, leaned his head against the wall, and looked toward the back of the cave. It opened into a medium-sized room a couple of feet from where they sat, then tunneled off to the left, out of sight. He stood, wanting to know how far into the mountain the tunnel led. A pile of junk sat to the side of the room just before the bend. Approaching it, he saw that most of it was covered with a thick, coarse material. Jacob lifted one edge, peeking underneath. He jumped back in surprise, letting out a small exclamation of shock.

"What?" Akeno asked, leaping to his feet.

"Sick," Jacob said. "Human bones." He moved closer and kicked the cover aside, revealing torn and tattered clothing, broken dishes, a fork, and a smashed pocket watch, all of which had been strewn across skeletons.

"Bones?" Aloren asked.

"Yes. Skulls and femurs. And other junk."

Aloren came over and picked up one of the bigger bones, holding it with a corner of the material. Akeno moved his finger closer, and Jacob gasped. Weird-looking marks were all along the bone, and Aloren dropped it. The marks had been made by teeth.

Aloren looked at Jacob, then back at the bone, shaking her head with an expression of horror on her face. "No, no, no," she wailed. "Oh, I forgot."

"Forgot what?" Jacob asked.

"This is bad, isn't it?" Akeno said, taking a step back.

"Shhh!" She waved her hand at Akeno's finger. "Off, off, off!"

Blackness covered them as Akeno's finger stopped glowing.

Aloren's moan was barely audible. "I can't believe—stupid of me!" She grabbed Jacob's arm, making him jump, and whispered, "Back away as quietly as you can, both of you."

Jacob followed Aloren's, stopping when he felt the wall behind him.

Aloren stood close to him, and Jacob could barely see Akeno's outline on the other side of her. "Be quiet and no moving," she said.

Standing as still as he could, Jacob tried not to concentrate on his awkward position up against the cave wall as it curled into the ceiling. He blinked a couple of times, waiting for his eyes to adjust in the near-complete darkness.

After what felt like forever, he heard a slight shuffling sound coming from the back of the cave, around the bend. Images crossed his mind as he tried to imagine whatever it was that might eat humans and prowl in dark caves. Wolves, bears, Big Foot, ogres, and orcs—all from books he'd read and movies he'd watched. He remembered the white monster in the beginning of *Star Wars 5* and wondered if it would have eaten Luke if given the chance.

The sound got louder and Jacob glanced at Aloren, barely able to see her in the dark. He grabbed her hand.

She gave him a quizzical look. "What?" she whispered.

Jacob put a finger to his lips and nodded toward the back of the cave. An expression of understanding crossed her face, quickly replaced by fear. She turned to her other side, and Jacob heard Akeno's small, quick intake of air.

A few moments later, there was another shuffling sound, and a massive body came into view. Jacob pressed back as hard as he could against the stone as he stared at the creature that had entered the room. He was surprised at how much of the monster he was able to see in the dark. It was almost as if a light were shining on it, though there was no source.

It wasn't as big as he'd expected it to be—it was only about five and a half feet tall—but it made up for its height in mass. Long, heavy arms hung from huge shoulders, and its legs were thick and powerful.

It had large eyes and very pale skin that covered only part of its face. The skin on the beast's huge chin was interrupted by spikes that curved out and downward from the roots of its teeth. These spikes came to a sharp point about an inch below its chin and turned slightly outward.

The creature had no lips, and its teeth were visible. The incisors were sharp and pointed, the molars large and blunt. Food was stuck between the teeth, and Jacob's stomach turned as he tried not to think about the human bones he'd found. Short hair stuck out all over the creature's head and neck like needles.

As the three continued to press against the wall, Jacob risked a quick glance at Aloren. She faced the entrance of the cave, and her eyes were out of focus. She appeared lost in thought. Had she not noticed the beast yet? How was that possible?

Relief spread through him when the creature didn't see them right away. It shuffled over to the pile of junk, bent over, and moved the coarse material.

Suddenly it stopped, its back stiffening. It lifted its head as if to sniff the air, then turned until it faced the small group that cowered against the wall of the cave. Jacob's breath caught when the creature's eyes met his.

For what seemed like an eternity, they held each other's gaze, neither moving.

His breath caught again when he realized he was able to sense the creature's feelings. Did the beast have the ability to transfer its emotions to other beings? It was confused at not having noticed right away that there were humans in its cave, angry at finding its things had been touched, surprised the human could see him.

The last feelings Jacob sensed from the beast were determination, stubbornness, and then another wave of anger. These emotions were caused by the gaze Jacob held with the beast. It was not used to small, insignificant humans defying it as Jacob realized he was doing. He tried not to tremble or show fear, refusing to look away. But he'd never had a poker face—there was no chance the beast wouldn't recognize how terrified he was.

The creature opened its jaws, a hiss issued forth, and Aloren stiffened. This small movement caused the brute to lose its eye contact with Jacob and it looked at Aloren instead, surprised. The creature hadn't expected a female. Taking a small step forward, it stared at her.

Aloren's gaze was directed toward the bend in the cave, still unable to see the beast. Jacob bit his lip, trying to remain level headed. This was disturbing. It was an evil creature, and yet here was Jacob, recognizing its emotions. What was wrong with him that he could connect with it?

He suppressed a growl, recognizing that if he didn't maintain his focus, they'd all be toast. Taking a deep breath, he forced himself to put aside any speculation on the matter. He looked back into the creature's huge eyes, again sensing its emotions. A sudden feeling of protectiveness came over him when he saw its plan to get rid of Akeno and Jacob first, leaving Aloren for last—like dessert.

Jacob put his hands on the wall behind him, bracing himself against the cold stone. The wall warmed under his palms and he gritted his teeth, wishing he'd spent time figuring out this ability of his. It might've helped him right now.

His hands sank into the stone, and he straightened in surprise—of *course* the ability could help him! There was no reason why it couldn't! If the wall became squishy at his touch, wouldn't it let him pull out chunks? Chunks which he could then mold into rocks to throw?

An excited smile crossed his face. Keeping his eye on the monster, Jacob dug his fingers into the now-soft rock. It gathered easily into his hand, and he pulled several sections of it from the wall. This was so cool!

He started molding the lumps into a large rock, but stopped himself when another idea hit him—wouldn't a sword be better? He and Matt used to swordplay all the time with sticks—if he got the weight close enough to one of those sticks, theoretically, he'd be just as good with it . . . right?

Squeezing and pulling, he tried to make a sword, but couldn't get the edges sharp enough. Instead, he twisted it into a club. Not as cool, but he could at least defend himself and the others with it. He hoped it would hold its shape long enough for him to distract the beast.

He was surprised that the rock seemed to know what he wanted and went cold, becoming solid once more. Wow— that was awesome.

Jacob focused his concentration back on the beast's feelings. Its anger had been replaced by determination. It hadn't noticed what Jacob had done and Jacob moved forward, realizing he was, in essence, challenging the feral creature. The monster sensed the challenge, and a deep rumble came from its chest. Jacob scowled, recognizing a laugh. He tried not to think too much about the extraordinary strength the beast most likely had, focusing instead on the fact that he now had something with which he could fight.

The creature dropped into a crouched position, getting ready to attack. Jacob felt a burst of adrenaline shoot through his body, along with intense fear. He took a deep breath, doing his best to appear self-assured.

Using his right hand, Jacob grabbed Aloren and pulled her behind him, pushing her toward the entrance of the cave. "I guess it doesn't matter if we talk, since this ugly thing knows we're here," he said.

"It's in the cave with us, isn't it?" Akeno asked just as Jacob grabbed him as well, pushing him next to Aloren.

"Careful not to get too close to the entrance," Jacob said, trying to sound confident. He was glad his voice didn't crack. "There's no sense in being attacked on both sides."

Holding the creature's gaze, Jacob strode—glad he didn't trip—to the center of the cave, keeping the weapon behind his back.

"Hdakr djksla bi skr!" Low, guttural words came from the creature's throat. Jacob took a step back—he didn't know the thing could talk. The words didn't make sense, but Jacob could sense their malicious intent. His body was tense, ready for an attack to come at any second.

The brute took a couple of small steps to the center of the cave as well, then stopped. A long pause—was the creature waiting for Jacob to do something first?

Jacob closed his eyes, trying to figure out what he could do. Concentrate on what the beast was feeling—an obvious thing—but hard to do when he needed to figure out how to defend his companions.

A thought crossed his mind. *Touch its skin.*

Jacob opened his eyes. Touch the creature's skin? Where did that come from? He hesitated, appraising the beast. Nearly every inch was covered in needle-like hair. Only its cheekbones and forehead were clear.

He looked the monster in the eye, trying to gauge where the thought had come from. The monster was concentrating on its hungry stomach about to be appeased and was amused by Jacob's show of bravery. But Jacob was able to see something else—something the beast seemed positive he'd never figure out.

Jacob almost took a step back in surprise. The monster's main source of protection was its ability to remain invisible to its prey, and for some reason Jacob could see the creature, which had shocked it. Touching the skin would somehow minimize the creature's defense, thereby allowing Aloren and Akeno to see it as well.

As soon as this occurred to Jacob, he was ready for action. Defending two helpless individuals from something they couldn't see would be next to impossible. However, if they could see the creature, they wouldn't be helpless. They'd be able to do something.

Jacob was six feet away. He pulled the bat from behind his back and held it in a defensive position in front of him.

The creature sauntered to one side of the cave, and Jacob got the feeling it wanted to play with him first. He had no desire to give the monster any sense of enjoyment, and put all his concentration on what he had to do.

The monster cocked its head to the side. Another laugh came from inside its chest when it seemed to notice the weapon for the first time.

Jacob tossed the bat from hand to hand, ignoring the brute's laughter. He leaped forward, swinging the blunt weapon. It connected with the monster's head with such force that Jacob almost dropped it. His bones jarring from the impact, he moaned when he saw that it didn't even stun the monster.

No longer laughing, the beast grabbed the weapon and tried to rip it from Jacob's grasp. Jacob, holding onto it, was swung into the air.

He kicked his legs, but couldn't get the weapon out of the beast's grip. Deciding instead to use it as leverage, he flung himself around the back of the monster, landing on its shoulders, the weapon falling to the ground. Aware of the sharp sting of thousands of needles piercing the skin on his shins and arms, he reached around and touched the monster's face. Aloren gasped, and he heard an exclamation of surprise from Akeno.

Visions of the beast's memories flashed before Jacob's eyes—dark tunnels, fire, a huge city under a bright sky, a large, poorly lit cavern full of other beasts like this one, humans, animals. Then he saw one thing that would get them out of this situation.

"Lirone!" he shouted. "The beast is afraid of Lirone!"

The creature's loud, responding roar erupted in the cave. It reached back, grabbed Jacob, and threw him across the small enclosure. Hitting the wall hard, Jacob bounced off and knocked into Aloren and Akeno. He jumped to his feet as the beast charged them.

Jacob ducked the creature's massive arm as it swung around to hit him. "Akeno, you're going to have to shrink it!"

The creature swung again, this time at Aloren and Akeno, who tried to scramble out of the way. They were barely fast enough to avoid being hit, and the monster growled.

"Hurry, Akeno!" Jacob yelled, attempting to kick the monster in the stomach, doing his best to buy Akeno some time.

The beast, in a quick movement, grabbed Jacob by the leg and swung him across the cave. Jacob slammed hard against a wall and fell to the ground. Dazed, he couldn't get up for a second.

"Shrink it? Now?"

Jacob shook his head to clear his thoughts. "Just do it!" He got to his feet as the monster came after him. He spotted the club lying where it had fallen and grabbed it, running to meet the creature. Swinging with his might, he brought the weapon across the monster's head.

The creature turned on Jacob and shoved him over, growling. Jacob jumped to his feet as Akeno rushed toward the entrance of the cave, attempting to put space between himself and the beast.

Jacob turned back, hesitating, unsure what his next move should be. Nothing seemed to affect the creature.

The monster reared on Aloren, grabbed her around the neck, and thrust her against a wall, holding her a foot above the ground.

Anger coursed through Jacob, and he screamed, charging. He slammed hard into the creature's side, surprised when the beast dropped Aloren and almost fell over. Without hesitation, Jacob grabbed Aloren's arm, pulling her up and away from the beast.

"Shrink it!" he yelled over his shoulder as he ran with Aloren to the back of the cave. Turning around to face the beast again, he swung Aloren behind him.

The creature roared, making Jacob's ears ring, and charged them. It smashed hard into Jacob, knocking him into Aloren. They both fell to the ground. Jacob threw his arms over her just as the monster reached for them. Suddenly it jerked and disappeared.

"Got it!" Akeno yelled.

Jacob grabbed Aloren's arm, helping her up, wincing at the pain all through his body. "Run to the entrance!" he shouted to Akeno.

Akeno turned and ran. Aloren and Jacob followed, but Jacob's leg gave out, and he collapsed on the cave floor. Pushing the pain aside, with Aloren's help he lurched to his feet and continued on, reaching Akeno.

The Makalo yelled in surprise as Lirone's explosions erupted all around him. He turned back to Jacob and Aloren, a panicked expression on his face.

"Put him out in the storm!" Aloren yelled. "Put him out in the storm!"

Akeno spun around, holding the monster at arm's length, then threw it. The monster landed on its side in a small clearing about forty feet away from the cave, now large and fully visible to Lirone.

Aloren and Jacob grabbed Akeno, pulling him back into the cave entrance just as Lirone sent a ball of flame smashing toward the ground where Akeno had been standing.

Jacob looked over his shoulder as they turned and ran the length of the cave. The monster jumped to its feet and roared, starting to charge.

"Come on, Lirone, come on!" Jacob said.

The monster bellowed again, but the din was cut off. Jacob glanced back in time to see the aftereffects of an explosion. The monster was no longer there.

They stopped and collapsed to the ground, gasping for breath.

"Wow," Jacob said. "That . . . was close."

"Yes . . . it was," Aloren wheezed.

"What was that thing, anyway?"

"It was . . . a Molg," Aloren said.

Jacob frowned. "A what?"

"A Molg. They're a race that . . . lives in the Dunsany Caves and . . . as you figured out, they eat humans." She paused for a minute, taking a couple of breaths. "They never leave their caves, and I've never seen one. I've heard of them, but wasn't even sure they existed—that's why I forgot about them." She gasped. "There are probably more! We can't stay here!" She tried to jump to her feet, but Jacob grabbed her arm.

"No, no, we're fine," he said, holding her down.

Aloren stopped, and Jacob let go of her. "How do you know?" she asked.

"The others aren't even near where we are."

"The other Molgs?"

"I'll explain—"

"And another thing," Aloren said. "Why could you see it, and we couldn't?"

Jacob scratched his head. "I'm not sure. When it first came into view, it didn't even notice us. I could clearly see it and was surprised you two couldn't."

"Of course we couldn't," Aloren said. "There wasn't any light."

"What changed?" Akeno asked, brushing the new dirt off his shoes.

It took Jacob several minutes to explain to Aloren and Akeno what had happened, from sensing the Molg's feelings to touching its skin, causing him to see that the Molg had just come from a meeting with other Molgs.

He tried to keep the worry he felt out of his voice. Being able to connect with something evil was disconcerting to him. He didn't want to let on to feeling that way—not until he figured things out.

"So, let me get this right," Aloren said. "You pulled rock out of the wall? How?"

"Well, I've got this ability to feel heat in things. I don't know why, or where it came from, but I can mold things with my hands."

Akeno scratched his head. "I've never heard of someone being able to do that before—let alone sensing warmth."

"Neither had your dad. He told me to figure out when and how the heat comes."

"Have you?"

Jacob shook his head. "I completely forgotten about it before going back to Taga yesterday, and since then I haven't had the chance." He paused. "Akeno, your parents are just as bad as my teachers at school. They've given me a ton of homework. 'Jacob, figure out your abilities. Jacob, read the journal. Jacob, get the Key. Jacob, save the world.' The pressure my teachers and parents put on me is nothing compared to this!"

Aloren and Akeno laughed.

"Wait," Aloren said. "Get *what* key?"

Jacob mentally kicked himself. That was a stupid slip-up. "Uh . . ." His mind raced as he thought of what he could or should say. "See, there's this key. It's a magical key that was creat—"

"You're not talking about the Key of Kilenya, are you?" Aloren asked.

"Actually, I am." Jacob raised an eyebrow. "You know about it?"

"Of course I do. Everyone does. Most people just think it's a myth. But Gallus has seen it. He told me and my mom that the Lorkon were searching for it when they took over Macaria a couple of years ago."

"Well, that makes explaining much easier," Jacob said. He and Akeno told her how the Key had been stolen and they'd been asked to bring it back.

Jacob sat up, feeling pain in every inch of his body. He tried not to let on that he was hurt. Matt would've been able to handle it. 'Course, Matt was on the football team and was used to getting battered around. If Matt were here . . . but Jacob wouldn't let himself finish the thought.

"You really took a beating," Aloren said. "Akeno, can you light up the room again?"

Akeno did so, and Aloren shuddered when she looked at Jacob. There were little holes all over in his clothes from the Molg's hair.

"Oh, wow," she said. "Jacob, you're stuck everywhere."

"I'm fine," he said. "Just bruised. I might be slow on the trail for a while." He turned to Akeno. "How are your hands? I'll bet you're even worse off than I am."

"Fine," Akeno said. "By the time I had him, the spikes were too small to even break the skin. But it was hard to hold on to him. He really struggled to get away."

They were silent for a few minutes. For the first time in a long while, Jacob wished he had his guitar with him. He almost laughed when he thought of it sitting in the corner of his room, dusty from lack of use. He'd bought it at a pawn shop several months before, hoping to impress a couple of girls with his mad skills. He'd given up on the idea, though, recognizing he'd never outshine Matt. Matt had always been the talented one at basically everything—including winning over girls.

Jacob shook his head, remembering what he'd heard a girl at school say a couple months before—something about how she'd just *die* if Matt ever stopped smiling. "His dimples are so cute!" she'd said, giggling. Jacob had almost snorted his drink when he'd heard that. It was disgusting the way the girls at school talked about his brother.

Jacob knew he wasn't ugly—even if he couldn't keep up with Matt. Girls always made embarrassing comments about his "really nice dark hair" and his eyes, which were the "prettiest, lightest blue" they'd ever seen. But he realized he didn't have the type of personality that drew most girls. He wasn't confident like Matt. He only took the lead when he was forced to, which was only when Matt wasn't around. The thought crossed his mind that if Matt were here, Aloren and Matt would be best friends by now, talking about everything. Aloren would be giggling as Matt told some hilarious joke or story.

Jacob grunted, recognizing how ridiculous he was being. He forced himself to come back to the present. "How much longer until Lirone leaves?"

"I don't know," Aloren said. "I'd rather wait and be absolutely sure he's gone, though."

"Yeah, me too." He lay down again, trying to relax. He smiled and closed his eyes, imagining he was in his own bed, pulling the blankets up under his chin. What he wouldn't give for that to be true.

Chapter 14

The Fat Lady

I received word today from Lahs that his army is assembled. I was surprised at his speed in gathering an army until I learned that King Roylance had already prepared everything before he died. The army was stationed in the land east of us and has located Brojan's army. They are ready to begin the battle as soon as I send word.

Jacob?" Aloren asked.

He rolled to face her. She was lying on her back, not making eye contact. "Yeah?"

"I, uh . . . I'm really glad you're here," she said.

Jacob couldn't help it, but a sheepish grin crossed his face. "Uh, thanks. I'm . . . glad I'm here, too. Kind of."

"We wouldn't have made it if you hadn't been able to see the Molg."

Jacob's smile grew, and he felt uncomfortable—not in a bad way, but more of an embarrassed way. So he changed the subject. "What if you never find your brother?"

Aloren rolled onto her side, facing Jacob and Akeno, and curled up into a ball. "I don't know. I guess I'd have to find somewhere else to put my focus."

"You could live in Taga with the Makalos," Akeno said. "I'm sure we'd have plenty of room for you, and besides, you could probably even get to know the humans from Jacob's world if you did."

"From Jacob's world? I thought he was from Eklaron."

Jacob smiled. "Nope, I'm not."

Aloren looked at him quizzically. "Where are you from, then?"

"Mars. Ha ha, just kidding. You probably don't even know what that is. I come from . . . well, a different land, I guess."

It took a few minutes for Jacob and Akeno to explain to Aloren the specifics of the link near Jacob's home and how he ended up in the Makalo village.

"Wow—a completely different world?" Aloren looked lost in thought for a moment. "If I can't find my brother, I want to visit your land."

Jacob hid a smile and agreed to show her around town if she came.

Aloren turned over, and Jacob assumed she didn't want to talk anymore and needed to rest. No dad around, and a mom who'd constantly been sick, then died. How would it be? Both of Jacob's parents were very involved in his life. Sometimes *too* involved—but at least he didn't often get lonely. Matt was almost always there when there was nothing to do—like now.

Jacob pulled the journal out and opened it, tilting it toward Akeno's light. The other two wanted to sleep, and he wanted information.

It has been two years since I last wrote in this journal. My father has become completely tyrannical. The tortures he places upon his subjects are too much for them to bear, and though my group of followers and I try to ease their suffering, the people can no longer shoulder their burdens. They are to the point of giving in to despair, of being beyond help—most are beginning to reject our assistance.

I am writing now because I've just received an upsetting note from Princess Arien. She has heard horrible things about what my father has been doing here in the castle—things of which I was not aware. Given the state of the people, I feel the time has come for me to go. I will leave behind a few members of my group, but have instructed them to depart in a week or two as well.

Jacob paused, fingering the pages. He'd just finished reading the added portion and was now about to start the journal itself.

Would my father kidnap his own daughter-in-law? The castle has been attacked and ransacked. We are trying to count how many are dead and missing . . .

Jacob read until he was tired. The journal had skipped a lot of details, because Dmitri and Arien were now married—Arien was pregnant and had been kidnapped, and Dmitri was trying to find her. And there was a woman named The Fat Lady—just like in *Harry Potter*. Jacob laughed when he read that part. He thought women hated it when people referred to their weight.

The light falling across the book changed, and Jacob glanced toward the entrance of the cave. "Akeno, turn off your light for a minute," he said.

Akeno jerked awake. "What? Another Molg?"

"No, don't worry," Jacob said. "I think Lirone's gone, though." He got up and took a few steps forward. Sure enough, the light outside was brighter and had a warm appearance.

"Looks like the clouds are gone," Akeno said, jumping up and dashing forward.

"Finally!" Jacob said, following Akeno.

"Wait!" Aloren called out.

They both stopped and looked back at her.

"We need to be cautious. Sometimes he hovers above the southern mountains and watches from there."

"Aargh," Akeno said. "I don't want to be cautious."

They waited for Aloren to take the lead, then walked down the tunnel, being careful to stay as close to the sides as possible. Aloren paused every couple of feet, peering into the sky.

The first step outside the cave was a little unnerving. There were still a few clouds above the mountains to the south. However, after they had watched for a few long moments, nothing happened, and Jacob relaxed. Aloren smiled in relief.

They decided to call the Minyas right away.

"Early? September?" Akeno yelled.

No response.

"Okay, we gotta find seeds, then."

The group found some down by the lake, and Akeno put them close to his mouth and whispered.

"What are you saying?" Jacob asked.

"The names of the Minyas I want." Akeno blew on the seeds, scattering them into the wind. "Hopefully they aren't far away." He sat on the ground and started taping leaves to his shoes.

Jacob looked at the position of the sun. "Will they still be able to find us if we keep going without them?" he asked. "I think we need to leave while it's still light. I'd like to put as much ground behind us as possible."

"We can go." Akeno put the tape dispenser away and stood. "They'll catch up."

After checking their bags to make sure they hadn't left anything in the cave, they made their way back to the trail. Jacob ached in a few spots where he'd hit the wall, but the pains were easily ignored. Being outside was so refreshing, he found it hard to focus on anything negative.

"We're here!" a little voice announced. "You sure were gone a long time!"

Jacob turned and saw September and Early flitting in the air. He smiled. "Where did you go when the storm came?"

"We went to Taga Village," September said, landing on Akeno's shoulder and hanging on to his shirt. "And guess what? The humans came back!"

Akeno stumbled, almost falling. "Really?"

"Yes, they're there," Early said, landing next to September.

"Which humans?" Jacob asked.

"The ones who hollowed out the tree and lived there for a while." Akeno looked anxious to be home. "It's been five years since they last came. I hope we get back in time to see them."

"Hopefully you will," Aloren said. She then pointed ahead. "Ridgewood is around that bend. I should warn you—it's a really weird place, with some of the strangest people you'll ever come across."

Jacob frowned. "Strange? In what way?"

"They're superstitious about Maivoryl City. They do everything in their power to stop people from passing through their city and going on. That's one of the reasons why I've never made it."

"How do they stop people?"

Aloren tucked a strand of hair behind her ear. "By trying to kill them. Last time they actually succeeded in killing a member of my group. They believe we're better off dead than continuing on to Maivoryl City and never returning."

Jacob raised an eyebrow. How did the members of this city possibly justify murder? "That's pretty extreme."

"Not to them," Aloren said, shaking her head. "They have a law that forbids anyone to go to the city, and the punishment for breaking it is death."

"That's ridiculous. How do their laws apply to people who don't live in their city? Or who have no say in how the law is carried out? Or who don't even know about it?"

"I really don't think they thought about democracy when setting up their rules," Akeno said.

Jacob laughed. "Yeah, that's pretty obvious. All right. Let's figure out how to get past them." They reached the bend in the trail and he stared at the city, spread across a large area of land between the lake and the forest. A small river flowed through the city from the mountain. "Do we go through tonight or tomorrow?"

"Whatever we choose, we need to figure it out fast, before they see us," Aloren said. "I suggest we go tonight, before the sun sets. I'd just feel better getting past it. Assuming we make it, of course."

Jacob looked at the landscape surrounding the city. "Maybe we could go around? Through the trees on the hill?"

"No, they keep lookouts up there at all times. And before you ask, going through the water is also a really bad idea."

"Why?"

"There are many different varieties of fish in the lake, besides Eetu, and most will eat you if given the chance. The Eetu fish start coming closer to the surface to feed in the evening, and you already know what will happen if we encounter one of them." Aloren looked at the lake. "We tried it once. A member of the group was attacked and severely injured before we realized what was happening. Three men tried to help her while the rest of us swam to shore as fast as we could. None of those four made it. When we got out of the water, the people of the city were waiting for us."

Jacob frowned, glad he'd not been there. That had to have been gruesome. "What happened next?"

"After interrogating us and keeping us in prison for more than a month, they made us promise never to try going to Maivoryl City again. Now they'll just kill anyone who attempts it."

"So, we can't go through the water on the south, and we can't go through the forest on the north," Jacob said. "And we can't very well go under the city. What else can we do? Walk through and pretend we're not doing what they'll know we're doing?"

Akeno shook his head. "No, that wouldn't work."

"Obviously," Jacob said, then laughed. "You know, we could always grab a bunch of bushes and hide under them—like they do in movies."

Aloren frowned. "Movies?"

"Never mind."

"There's a much simpler way," Akeno said. "One that's guaranteed to work. I could shrink both of you and have the Minyas transport you to the other side of the city."

"What about you?" Jacob said. "How would you get across?"

Akeno pointed up at the forest. "Use the trees, of course."

Aloren gave Akeno an incredulous look. "I just said it isn't possible to go that way."

Akeno gave a mischievous smile. "But when was the last time a *Makalo* attempted it? I'll have the trees hide me, and, if necessary, lift and carry me across their branches. No one will see me, and it won't take any time at all."

Jacob watched Aloren as she thought it through. She bit her lip. "Okay, we'll try it," she said. "But let's get it done as soon as possible. I want to travel by sunlight as long as we can."

"Okay, then," Akeno said. "Ladies first."

"What do I need to do?"

"See that big rock? Just go stand by it."

While Aloren walked over to the rock, Jacob called the Minyas down and asked them to carry the two of them across the city and put them in a safe place out of sight of any people.

Aloren reached the rock, stopped, and turned around. Akeno reached out, squinting one eye. Aloren disappeared, and then stood on Akeno's palm.

Akeno lifted his hand until it was level with his face. "Are you okay?"

"Wow!" Aloren said. "I'm so tiny!"

Jacob turned to the Minyas. "Ready?"

"Of course," Early said, picking up Aloren.

"Fly her over the city," Jacob said. "You don't need to use your magic—just make sure to stay high."

Early flitted off, and Jacob was surprised at how quickly she left his view, even without magic.

Then it was Jacob's turn. He ran down the trail to the rock, turned to face Akeno, and gave him a thumbs-up. One second, he was being pinched around his waist, and the next, he stood in Akeno's hand. September picked him up, and then they were flying through the air. Jacob kept his eyes closed most of the way to keep from getting dizzy. Only a few seconds later, they passed the city and landed on a huge rock next to Early and Aloren.

Jacob checked his bag, making sure it was in one piece, then looked at Aloren. "How was your first trip via Minya?"

She half smiled. "It wasn't very comfortable—I'll have to get used to it."

Jacob turned to Early and told her to make sure Akeno didn't need help, and to send word if anything went wrong. She left, September floated to look at something on the other side of the trail, and Jacob and Aloren sat on the rock to wait.

They were alone for the first time. Jacob cleared his throat, feeling self-conscious, and wracked his brain, trying to think of something smart or funny to say. He fished around, finally grabbing the first thing that came to mind. "You have a dimple in your cheek," he said. "It's deep . . . and . . . shows when you smile. And sometimes when you talk, too." He paused, then blurted out the rest. "Did you know dimples are tissue defects?"

She gave him one of those looks that only a girl can give.

"Um, not that you're defective, or anything. I mean . . ." He scrambled for words, and then gave up. A skeptical expression crossed Aloren's face, and he flushed. Why would he say something like that? He kicked himself mentally, wishing he'd just kept his trap shut. So much for sounding smart.

Jacob stayed quiet, breathing a sigh of relief when Akeno, Early, and September came back.

Akeno returned them to their normal size, and the group followed the trail for a while longer before deciding to set up camp deep in the forest. The brush was thick, and in no time Akeno had separated it into two separate quarters, the entrances barely visible. They ate a small dinner and then turned in for the night.

Jacob woke up the next morning both excited and troubled by the dream he'd had. The lady in the forest nearly captured him, snakes had swarmed all over him, and his skin felt like ants were crawling on it. But what she'd said to him had come back. "Danilo." He had no idea what it meant, but at least he could tell Ebony he'd remembered.

"Kenji said you'd be traveling near the cottage of the Fat Lady," September said as they headed back to the trail. "You need to stop and talk to her. She'll help you prepare to meet the Lorkon."

"I know her," Jacob said. "She's in the journal. Where does she live?"

"Just up ahead." September floated away again.

A few minutes later, September pointed out a small path that led through the tall grass. There was a cabin sitting in a meadow about four hundred yards away from the main trail. A clothesline hung to the right, and they could see a paddock behind the cabin to the left.

"I'm guessing this is it," Jacob said, then called the Minyas down. "September, Early, please get in my bag. I want you close, but out of sight, just in case. Same as always."

The Minyas flew into the knapsack, and Jacob closed it as they neared the cabin.

"Do you think it's a good idea to call her 'fat?'" Aloren said. "I mean, who likes to be called fat?"

Jacob ran his fingers through his hair. "That's what Dmitri called her in his journal. I say we just not use her name unless it's necessary."

They arrived at the cabin, and Jacob knocked.

No answer. He knocked again.

"Go away," a woman's gruff voice shouted.

"Can we talk to you?" Jacob yelled through the door. He heard someone moving around, but no one answered the door. "We were told to stop here!"

"I'm sure you were. Go away!"

"No," Jacob said. "Brojan and Kenji sent us, and we're not leaving until you open this door."

"And why should I believe you?"

Jacob turned to Aloren and Akeno. "She's not going to open it."

"Let me try," Akeno said. "Kenji is my father," he yelled through the crack.

"Right. As if *that's* the truth."

"No!" Jacob yelled. "He's serious! Kenji said we needed to stop by the Fat Lady's cabin, and she would help us know what we need to do to face the Lork—"

Suddenly the door swung wide open.

"Well, why didn't you say so in the first place?"

The group of travelers took a step back, looking up. The woman standing before them was indeed large—at least five hundred pounds, maybe more, and well over six feet tall. Nothing like the Fat Lady in *Harry Potter*. She smiled at them, showing an odd assortment of teeth. The top, which were mostly missing, were blackened and crooked, while the bottom teeth were straight, smooth, and pearly white. She wore massive earrings, and the holes in her lobes were stretched out. Her hair was light brown, piled in a knotty-looking mess on top of her head. Her lids were puffy, making her eyes look tiny.

She reached out with a large hand and pulled the three inside, slamming the door shut and pushing them in front of her into the main room of the cabin. "So, tell me," she said. "What news do you bring from Tagaville?"

They exchanged quick glances.

The Fat Lady let out a booming laugh. "Cat got your tongue, eh?" Plopping into a large, furry-looking chair, she propped her feet up on a table in the middle of the room. "Sit, sit," she said, motioning to a couch that was surrounded by piles of paper and junk.

Jacob was the first to move. He knew Akeno wouldn't sit on the end of the couch closest to the woman, so he did.

"Tell me who you are," the Fat Lady said. "Never seen anyone as big as me, have you?"

Aloren shook her head and glanced at Jacob, who wasn't sure what to say.

"Speak up, speak up!" The Fat Lady pointed her finger at Aloren. "You first. What's your name, where're you from." It came across more as a demand than a question.

"M—my name is Aloren. I'm from Macaria."

"Ah. It's been quite some time since I traveled that far. I usually only get ten feet in front of my cabin before giving up and going back home." She laughed again and pointed at Akeno. "I'm assuming you're the one who claims to be Kenji's son."

"Yes, ma'am," Akeno said, his voice shaking. "I'm his eldest. My name is Akeno."

"It has been several years since I last saw your parents." She picked up a vial from the table, put a drop of the contents on her finger, then rubbed her bottom teeth. She jerked her finger toward Jacob, who almost jumped up until he saw she was merely pointing. He'd thought she was going to smear some of the stuff on him. "And you? Who are you, and who do you belong to?"

"My name is Jacob Clark. My parents are Lee and Janna Clark. I'm not from around here. I come from Earth, and it's, well, I guess it's not—"

The Fat Lady squealed loudly, slamming her hands on the armrests. "Oh, I've been expecting you!" She laughed, wagging her finger at him. "Didn't think you were gonna hear me say something like that, did ya?" She jumped to her feet and strode to a cabinet on the other side of the room, dodging the junk and stacks of papers placed randomly on the floor.

"Oh, and call me Fat Lady," she said. "It's the password to enter my house, and I won't answer to anything else."

Walking back to the couch, she handed a vial to each member of the group. "Akeno and Aloren, drink this now. Jacob, wait to take yours. It won't do to have you seeing things you shouldn't see right now."

What was she talking about? And what would the potion do to him? Jacob looked at the corked vial in his hand. The glass was swirled brown and blue, and full of a dark, runny liquid. Akeno and Aloren's potion was different, more of a rose color.

"I really didn't expect you to bring others with you, so it's a good thing I thought to make those up, just in case," the Fat Lady said. "Can't say I blame ya, though. You know this trip will be extremely dangerous, I'm sure. All your lives are at risk. But who cares these days? As long as the job gets done, right?" She jerked her thumb over her shoulder. "Do you know anything about that city?"

Jacob met eyes with Akeno before looking at the lady again. "Not really, no." He knew hardly anything about Eklaron. Or the Lorkon, for that matter—besides what they looked like.

"Eh, it's probably better that way," she said, picking up a dirty towel that had been crumpled in the seat of her chair. She shook it out, causing a cloud of dust to fly in the air, then tossed it on the table and sat with a thump. "Knowing too much can cause a lot of problems, you know."

Was she crazy? "I disagree," Jacob said, sitting up straighter. "I think it's better to know as much as possible before doing anything that might be dangerous, since—"

"Yes, you would, wouldn't you?" the Fat Lady said, peering down at Jacob. "It is, after all, second nature to you." Her voice changed to a more business-like tone. "Knowing as little as possible in this case is in your best interest, though."

How would she know what was second nature to him, and what was in his "best interest?" He'd never met her before in his life. Jacob scowled and looked at Akeno, who still fingered his vial.

The Fat Lady also glanced at the Makalo. "Boy, you'd better drink that! You'll wish you were dead if you don't!"

Akeno didn't move to drink it, instead looking at Aloren, who shrugged. "Bottoms up," she said, emptying the vial into her mouth and swallowing. "Wow, bitter!" she gasped.

The Fat Lady guffawed, slapping her knee. "What were you expecting? Fruit juice?"

Akeno also swallowed his, with much the same reaction as Aloren.

"Why do I have to wait to take mine?" Jacob asked.

"Because theirs were designed to *prevent* reactions, and yours was designed to *control* reactions. If you drink it too soon, we'd have problems. And if we were to prevent your reactions, we'd all be in trouble, wouldn't we?" She smiled her odd grin.

Jacob just stared at her, not sure what to think or say.

"Oh, come on—tell me you've noticed that some things affect your companions that don't affect you."

Jacob thought about the way Akeno acted when they were in the infected forest. "I've noticed."

"Well, get this. They aren't going to be affected by those things any more, now that they drank the potion." She put her legs on the table again.

"What about me?"

"What about you?"

"What does the potion do to me?"

"Well, you're a special case. If you take that potion now, you'll be really messed up, and the potion would be diluted by your blood, taking away its effectiveness. Then, when the thing happens that is supposed to cause your reaction, it'll most likely kill you. Either that, or turn you evil. So, thanks, but no thanks. I'd rather you take the potion when you need it. Oh, and the time to take it is when you feel you have no control over your body. Have them help you," she said, pointing at the other two.

"What—when I feel like I have no control?" Jacob asked. Was she purposely being vague, or would he really be in danger if he knew more?

"But of course!" she said. "You know, when your body goes haywire, and you don't know what's going on anymore? I have no idea when it will happen. Figure it out yourself."

Her demeanor changed again and she stood, looking intently at Jacob. "When you get the Key, come straight back here. No detours, no stopping for breaks, and no trying to figure out how to use the Key until I tell you."

She turned to Akeno and Aloren. "Don't let the Lorkon touch you. The potion might prevent bad reactions, but it will be worthless against their blood." Walking to the door, she opened it and motioned for them to exit. "I believe you have something to get done, and fast. The longer you take, the worse off you'll be."

Jacob, Akeno, and Aloren hurried through the open door. Jacob turned to ask another question, but the Fat Lady shut the door in his face.

Chapter 15
Stone Barricade

$\mathcal{J}$acob followed the others down the trail. He looked over his shoulder at the Fat Lady's cabin a couple of times, but gave up, realizing she wasn't going to open the door. He released the Minyas, ignoring their shouts of joy and exuberant flips in the air. He'd wanted to ask the Fat Lady about the Key and the Lorkon. Why'd she have to push them out of her house so fast?

After walking deep in thought for a few minutes, Jacob noticed that Aloren and Akeno were laughing and talking to each other, bouncing with each step they took. He rolled his eyes, trying to ignore them as he puzzled through what the Fat Lady had said. The potion. How on earth could she create it, not knowing what it would fix, or what reactions it would cause, and then expect him to take it? And why would he need it to save his life?

Akeno bumped into Jacob, and Jacob frowned at him. "I'll bet she gave you guys some sort of hyper potion," he said. "Will you notice anything bad going on around you? Of course not. You'll be too busy laughing and bouncing all over the place."

Aloren pulled food out of Akeno's bag, handing out carrots and apples. "So we're in a good mood! It's not about her." Stuffing a chunk of bread into her mouth, she ran to catch up with Akeno, who had just sprinted off for no apparent reason.

Jacob didn't quicken his pace to keep up with them. He needed peace and quiet, and with them far ahead, he just might get it. He fingered the corked vial in his pocket, wondering when he would have to drink it.

September appeared in front of him. "Is it okay if we play in your hair again?"

"Yeah, sure, fine." Jacob's thoughts were too far away to care. What was it the Fat Lady had said? Something about not seeing things he shouldn't see. But what sort of things? And wouldn't it be better if he knew what was going on? For a minute, Jacob contemplated taking the potion right then. He didn't want to wait until he was almost dead. Maybe it would act as a precaution for the danger they'd experience.

"Honestly, Jacob, have some fun for once!" Aloren yelled from about thirty yards away. "You're so boring!"

"What are you talking about?"

She ran up to him. "Come on!" she said, grabbing his arm and trying to pull him toward Akeno.

"I don't want to . . ." Jacob grumbled, dragging his feet.

"We're going to have a race."

Jacob raised an eyebrow in disbelief and looked at his friends. "Are you serious?"

Aloren stared at him. "Do you have some meeting to go to, some unfinished business to take care of while we're walking?"

"I'm supposed to be reading the book."

"Well, you *weren't*. And you did plenty of that yesterday—this will be the perfect break for you. Besides, what are Akeno and I supposed to do while you're reading?"

"I don't know. Contemplate the wonders of the universe or something else quiet."

Aloren frowned. "Come on, Jacob. It won't hurt you."

Jacob groaned, shutting his eyes so he wouldn't have to look at her. They'd probably keep bugging him if he didn't join them. "All right, fine." He pulled off his knapsack and put the vial in a small front pocket, then slung the bag over his shoulders.

"Yeah!" Aloren said, her grin showing the dimple on her cheek. "Everyone ready? Okay, go!"

As Jacob ran, he felt himself relax. Too much stress made him grouchy, and he didn't want to offend Akeno and Aloren. He forced himself to let go of his irritations. A moment later he even began to enjoy the competition.

Akeno got to the finish first, Jacob came in second, and Aloren was third.

Jacob couldn't help gloating. "I beat you."

Aloren shrugged. "What if I let you?"

Jacob shook his head. "You didn't."

"But you couldn't beat Akeno, so it doesn't even matter."

"Whatever. He's one of the fastest people I've seen!"

"Yes, he's a quick, and I'm glad he won. But only 'cause he kept you from winning."

"I don't buy that!"

Aloren laughed, then closed her eyes, raising her face to the sun. "Oh, it smells so good here, like the bread Gallus's wife makes!"

Jacob opened his mouth to reply, but Akeno grabbed his arm, interrupting him. "Look at that," he said, pointing.

Jacob had to blink a couple of times. "What's he doing?"

A man stood not far away, staring at the lake, a vacant smile on his face. He was clean-cut and neatly dressed.

Jacob slowed down, unsure what to do. The trail was about to curve to the right around a very large tree, and Jacob stopped behind it to watch the man.

He didn't move. He didn't even blink—at least from what Jacob saw.

"I . . . think I know what this is," Jacob said. "If I'm right, it's the second element Dmitri mentioned in the journal—wind. Aloren, you said it smells good, right?"

"Yeah."

Jacob paused. "I . . . can't smell anything out of the ordinary. Akeno, you?"

"It smells strongly of trees and wildflowers." He breathed deeply. "Aaaah . . ."

"But it's not doing anything to you."

Akeno frowned. "No . . . should it?"

"In the journal, when Dmitri and his people passed through here, they all went weird. Kind of groggy and unable to do anything, though they thought they were doing something."

"And it's not affecting us," Aloren said. "Do you think that's because of the potions?"

"Probably."

"But what about you?"

Jacob slowly shook his head. "Not sure. Though it doesn't really surprise me." Nothing seemed to affect him the way it did the others. Well, Akeno, at least. Why? And while it made him feel almost invincible, it also freaked him out—which he did his best to keep hidden from the other two. Just like in the cave when he'd been able to see the Molg. These things couldn't be normal.

Aloren took a few steps around the tree, then screamed. A woman stood on the other side, a few feet away. One arm was raised, as if beckoning, and she was staring straight at Aloren. She had the same distant smile on her face as the man.

Jacob grabbed Aloren's arm and pulled her behind him, next to Akeno. He walked to the woman and stopped a couple of feet away, then waved at her face. Nothing happened.

"I don't like this," Aloren said, her voice wavering. "My mom . . . was like this sometimes."

"Let's keep going," Jacob said.

They walked past the tree, taking care not to touch the woman. Jacob glanced back at the man one last time, but Aloren's gasp made him jerk around.

"There are hundreds of them!" she said.

She was right. There were people everywhere. Some lay on the grass, staring up into the sky. Some sat cross-legged, elbows on knees, resting their chins in their hands. Many were standing, as the lady and man had been. All wore the same vacant smiles. Their attire varied from very nice to grubby and dirty.

"What are they doing?" Akeno asked.

Jacob frowned. "They're living their lives in their minds. An invisible prison, as Dmitri called it. I'd bet a lot of people have disappeared to this place."

Aloren grabbed Jacob's arm—he could tell she was close to losing control. "Do you think my brother might be here?"

"I don't know—we can check. We'll probably need to leave the trail to see them all, though."

"And walk through them? I can't do that!"

"I don't want to do it either. But it'll be impossible to search for your brother if we don't." Jacob glanced at Aloren, then back at the people. "What does he look like?"

"I . . . I'm not sure. I'd guess like me, except with blue eyes." Aloren stared at the people. "Can we please stick together? Just in case?"

"It'd be faster, and we'd get a lot more done, if we split up."

Aloren looked at Jacob, her eyes pleading. "Jacob, please. I can't do that. I can go with you or Akeno, but I can't do it alone."

Jacob paused and ran his fingers through his hair. "All right, we'll do that. I'll go right, you and Akeno go left." He motioned to the Minyas. "Take Early with you. I'll take September."

"How do we know this isn't just a trap?" Akeno said. "Maybe the Lorkon put these people here as a way to . . . well, maybe attack us?"

"It's not a trap for us, specifically, but for anyone who happens to walk into it. In the journal, Dmitri finds out the Lorkon put a potion here to stop people from going anywhere. I thought it would've lost potency over the years." He frowned, looking at an eighteen- or nineteen-year-old on the right, close to the trail. "I just gotta see something first." He hesitated, then reached out and prodded the guy in the shoulder.

The teen turned his face toward Jacob, still smiling vacantly. "Hmmm?"

Aloren gasped, her hand fluttering to her mouth. "Oh . . . let's keep going, please."

Jacob split off from Akeno and Aloren, walking as fast as he could through the people. He glanced at each face, trying to see someone who resembled Aloren even in the slightest. After five or ten minutes, he met up with his friends on the other side of the large group of people. September and Early happily rejoined each other.

"No luck?" Jacob asked.

Aloren shook her head. "This place is really creepy. And it doesn't feel right for him to be here."

210

"Let's keep going, then. Maybe we'll have better luck in Maivoryl City."

They continued forward, finally passing the last person. The Minyas flew up ahead of them, doing somersaults.

Aloren released a long breath. "That was really weird."

"No kidding," Jacob said.

The trail soon turned left, heading toward the large mountains at the south of the valley. On the hills to the right, the forest thinned, and the path led the group close to the base of a very large hill that obstructed their view of both the castle and Maivoryl City.

"How much farther?" Akeno said. "I'd like to be able to keep the castle in view."

"I'd say at least an hour more, if not longer," Aloren said. "I've never been this far, though, so I'm not exactly sure."

They walked in silence. Jacob had to tell himself to relax and enjoy the scenery. The valley really was beautiful. The Dunsany Mountains behind them rose high above Ridgewood. Sonda Lake was to their left, with Aloren's city on the other side. The mountains to the south were majestic and grand.

Jacob pulled the journal out of his bag and found his place. "I'm going to read out loud so you guys know what's going on now."

"*Today we passed through the fourth and final element. It was boiling, shifting, poisoned earth, incredibly deep. When touched, it burned the skin like acid, and nothing—absolutely nothing—would relieve the pain it caused. But it seems the Lorkon have underestimated the Makalos—as even I did—and having Kenji with us proved beneficial. He informed me that the sap of the Kaede tree both heals and purifies. I'd never heard this. Of course, Ramantus never associated with Makalos and wouldn't even allow them in his kingdom, so I didn't have the opportunity to learn any of their ways.*

"Kenji instructed us to gather the sap, then boil it until it was thick. We had the entire company gathering all afternoon. We covered our clothes and skin with the sap, then slowly started our way through the mud. At first it was quite difficult—the mud was deep, and we were hesitant to get burned—but after a while, the mud shifted away from us, and we were able to get through. The sap on our bodies purified the dirt, hopefully enough that it won't cause problems for anyone who passes this way after us."

Jacob looked up. "Does this sound familiar to you, Akeno?"

"What do you mean? I haven't been reading the book."

"The mud. Dmitri doesn't say how much of it there was, but I'd be willing to bet it was fairly deep and covered quite a bit of ground. That must have been the mud shells we crossed."

"I'll bet it was."

"Keep reading," Aloren said.

"After the ordeal of the fourth element, we were relieved to make our way down the mountain, and we've just caught up with Aldo. He was heading back from the Land of the Shiengols, where Arien is being kept. We have now set up a temporary residence in a cabin near the forest. We have many plans to make, and as we are at least a day's journey from our destination, we must start soon.

"Aldo has been using the Key as a way to scout out the area. He reports that the land has completely changed—the Shiengols are, in fact, being held captive. Imagine that! Who would have thought it possible?

"He also reports that the Lorkon are living in the town center, away from the prisoners. Hopefully this will aid us in our rescue of Arien."

Jacob paused for a minute to skip over a scribbled-out part, glad to see that the words continued flowing.

"Aldo used the Key this morning to check on Arien before we attempted to rescue her, and to our surprise, she is no longer being held with the other captives. She's in the town center where the Lorkon are staying, and it appears she has given birth. Oh, I wish I could have been there to comfort and assist her.

"This new information changes our plan drastically, and much thought has been put into a new one. I will give word for Lahs and Brojan to attack the Lorkon army at the same time that Kelson will lead an attack on the stronghold where the Shiengols are being held. We could use their assistance in this war. Accompanying Kelson will be everyone but me, Kenji, Aldo, and September.

"The attack will hopefully provide enough of a diversion so my team can use the Key of Kilenya to enter the town center. We will find Arien and the babe and take them to safety."

Dmitri's handwriting changed—the words were smaller, perhaps more thoughtfully written.

"This entry is one of both joy and pain.

"The attack on the stronghold did provide a needed diversion, but Kelson's men failed to break through. He and his entire group were killed. My best friend is dead. I can scarcely believe it.

"I am shocked to see how close the war is raging. Lahs and Brojan have been communicating with me through various Minyas. Thousands upon thousands of people are being slaughtered by three Lorkon. Three! I had imagined an entire regiment. But they are not to be underestimated. They are strong. Nothing the army has done harms them, and every person they touch is infected with disease and then painfully dies.

"The joy of which I spoke was that Arien and the baby have been recovered. Kelson's attack on the stronghold was successful to that end, and I will forever remember what he did for me and my little family. Nothing can remove the joy I feel as I hold my little one with my wife beside me."

Jacob put the book away. He was glad Arien and the baby had been safely recovered, but how sad that Kelson and the rest had been killed! He glanced up at the foothill beside them. Doing a double take, he pointed up. "Check that out."

On top of the hill, a wall rose high above them. It was gray and looked like granite. The surface wasn't smooth, but had vertical ripples flowing through it, giving the appearance of gray curtains.

"That's really odd," Akeno said.

"Yes, it is. I wonder if it's the first element." Jacob continued to peer up while walking and noticed that even though the hill was getting smaller, the wall-like thing on top stayed the same height. "This is different, though. Dmitri saw a waterfall."

"I'll bet the Lorkon put it there," Akeno said.

Aloren shielded her eyes. "I've never heard anyone mention it. But it probably was the Lorkon who did it."

As they followed the path, the foothill disappeared, and the trail ran flush with the wall. Jacob stared at it, trying to see the top. The glare of the sun was too bright, and he wasn't able to measure the height. He looked forward, surprised to see the path turn and disappear beneath the wall.

"Is that really the end of the trail?" Akeno asked.

"Uh, I guess it is," Aloren said. "Now what?"

"No, it's not the end," Jacob said. "The wall was put on top of it. I'm sure it continues on the other side." He scratched his head, noticing that the Minyas were no longer flying around them. "Maybe Early and September can see over it. Who knows—our Minyas might be better than Arien's. Where are they?"

"I think they said they were going to sleep in your bag," Aloren said. "They went in while you were reading."

Jacob found the Minyas and told them what he needed them to do. They returned seconds later.

"It was way too high," Early said. "We didn't want to keep going."

"It goes several miles up at least," September added. "Would you like us to try again?"

Jacob shook his head. "No, it's okay. Arien's Minya couldn't do it, either. What I'm wondering now is why we didn't see it earlier. You'd think something this big and solid would've been visible."

Aloren turned and looked toward the lake. "I've got an idea," she said. "Let's have the Minyas go halfway across the lake and see what the wall looks like from there."

The Minyas flew off, returning moments later.

"The wall became transparent the farther away we got," September said.

"Weird." Jacob paused, thinking over the situation. "All right, Dmitri found a way through it. Let's separate and see if we can, too."

Aloren and Akeno followed the wall to the south, and Jacob followed it to the north, climbing up the foothill where it met with the wall. He ran his hand along every edge and crevice he could reach, seeking a hole or something similar. After several minutes of searching, he came to a section where the hill changed into huge rock outcroppings that would be impossible to climb without ropes and harnesses. Turning around, he was surprised to see how far he had gone. Aloren and Akeno were little dots at the far end.

Jacob half-jogged his way back down, meeting up with them where the path disappeared. "Did you find anything?"

"No, nothing," Aloren said. "You?"

"Nothing."

Aloren looked up at the wall. "What do we do?"

"I know there's a way past this," Jacob said. "There has to be. The wolves and Lorkon have been coming and going through it."

"Speaking of the wolves," Akeno said. "We haven't seen them since we left Macaria. Why?"

Jacob tilted his head. "Well, if they were only sent to make sure we came to Maivoryl City, there wouldn't be any need for them to make their presence known. We haven't taken any major detours since leaving."

Akeno slid his bag off his shoulder. "Can we eat something while discussing this? I'm really hungry."

"Yeah," Jacob said. "It'll give us a few minutes to think about how to get through the used-to-be-waterfall."

They sat next to a small mound of dirt near the shore of Sonda Lake, stretching out their legs and pulling food from their bags. The Minyas flitted in the air, playing games.

"So, explain what this thing is," Aloren said.

"Dmitri went through four elemental traps that were placed by the Lorkon to stop him. Well, this was the first, except it was a huge, invisible waterfall when he came across it."

"I wonder what happened to make it visible."

"Do you think we can see it because of the potions the Fat Lady gave us?" Akeno asked.

"I'm not sure, but I don't think so," Jacob said. "She said the potions would make you avoid reactions. Seeing something invisible is not a reaction."

No one said anything for a moment. Jacob bit his lip, thinking. The wolves and Lorkon couldn't climb over the wall, and couldn't have been going around—it was too wide. The only way was to go through the tunnel Dmitri had found. But where was it?

"I'd bet anything we're mirroring Dmitri's steps right now," Jacob said. "He and his group went through the waterfall first, then the smelly air, then the mud." He paused. "But they had the Fire Pulser in between. We didn't pass any fire-pulsing people after we crossed the mud."

"And no land that looked burned," Akeno said.

Jacob got to his feet to pace. He loved puzzles like this in the books he read, but hated having to figure it out himself. He walked back and forth several times between Akeno and Aloren and the mound of dirt, trying to keep everything clear in his mind. As he neared the small hill for a fourth time, something caught his eye and he paused, then circled around to the side that faced the lake.

"Hey, come check this out," Jacob said. The others joined him near a shallow hole in the earth. "This has to be the tunnel."

"It could be, but it looks like it's only a pit," Aloren said. "And if it *is* a tunnel, it's fallen in on itself. Not recently, though. That dirt's been there for a year at least. It's too dry and settled to be fresh."

Jacob frowned. "And the Lorkon and wolves have been out of Maivoryl several times during the past year."

"What is it, then?" Akeno asked. "It's not here naturally."

"An animal hole?" Jacob said. "Do animals this big live around here?"

"No, I don't think so," Aloren said, then paused. "Oh, I'll bet Dusts made it. They do things like this in the castle too—digging through things, making tunnels. We'd better move away just in case."

The group circled back to their lunch spot and sat to finish their food—facing the wall so they could continue to examine it.

After several moments, Jacob glanced up—did he just see a section of the wall shift? It was a spot twenty feet or so to the left of where the trail disappeared—the part Aloren and Akeno had inspected. He stood and walked closer, squinting in the bright light of the sun. He stopped in front of it—something flickered again.

"Wait," he said. "That's weird. The wall has a . . ." He reached out to touch it and jumped back when the stone dissolved around his hand. "Wow! What was that?"

The tunnel was now right in front of him—it was dark, and he couldn't see very far into it.

He turned to his friends. "Holy cow! Come see! I just found the tunnel!"

"I can't see anything," Akeno said.

Aloren shook her head. "Neither can I."

"Wait—what? You can't see the tunnel? It's right here." Jacob motioned to it.

218

"There's nothing there but wall," Aloren said.

Jacob frowned. "You . . . really can't see it?"

Aloren smiled, rolling her eyes, and Akeno gave him a look that said "Didn't I just tell you that?"

Jacob sighed. "Okay, come here then." He grabbed Akeno and pulled him over to stand right in front of the entrance. "Put your hand out. You'll feel the wall sorta dissolve around it."

Akeno put his hand out, but the wall didn't dissolve. "Now what?"

"Oh, my gosh," Jacob said. "I know I'm not going crazy. Aloren, you try it."

"No, I believe *you* can see it. There's probably a reason why we can't. I'd guess it's because we're not supposed to go with you."

"What are you talking about? I sure as heck am not going alone!" Jacob said. "There's no way I can go up against the Lorkon without help!"

"Then lead us. That's the only other alternative."

Jacob scowled at the wall. He couldn't think of anything else they could do. He hated the idea of leading them blind, but he knew he'd never get out alive without their help. "Okay, let's go." He searched the air for September and Early, and spotted them flitting around a small tree by the trail. "Oy! Minyas! Get in my backpack. I can't hold on to you two as well."

With the Minyas put away, Aloren took Akeno's hand with her left and Jacob's with her right.

"Let's go," she said.

Jacob turned to face the wall, trying not to think too much about Aloren's touch. This was the first time he'd held hands with a girl. He cleared his mind, then stepped forward, pulling Aloren and Akeno in with him. They were plunged into complete darkness.

"Oh, wow," Aloren said, gasping. "We're in the wall now, aren't we?"

"Yes, we are."

"I feel it. It's pushing all around me. It feels like I'm standing in stone!" Aloren gasped again. "Don't let go of my hand!"

"I won't. I promise." Jacob looked over his shoulder. "Akeno, how are you holding up?"

"Fine," he said.

Jacob could barely make out the walls on either side of them and the ceiling above. Putting out his right hand, he used the side wall to guide him. It was bumpy and had an odd texture to it, making him stop again. He felt around, trying to figure out why it was so weird, but nothing came to mind.

Taking a few more steps, he relied on the wall to guide him. Then it disappeared from under his hand. Feeling around for a moment, he figured out the tunnel turned right. He started to follow it, looking over his shoulder to check on Aloren and Akeno. The blackness made it impossible to see them, though. He cleared his throat. "Uh, how're you guys doing?"

"My bag . . . take . . . my bag," Aloren said, gasping. "Can't feel . . . it . . . don't want . . . lose . . ."

"Okay, okay." Jacob reached out and found the top of her head, then lowered his hand to the bag slung around her neck. He secured it around his own neck and one arm. "Akeno? Do you want me to take yours as well?"

"No, m'fine," Akeno said, also gasping now. "Hurry."

"Okay." Jacob took another deep breath, tracing the wall as he went. "Something tells me this isn't going to be a short tunnel."

The tunnel turned several more times—Jacob lost count of how many. He closed his eyes, realizing he didn't need them open anyway. "Hey, wait," he said. "Akeno, let's see if your finger will light up the tunnel."

The walls were immediately swathed in the eerie blue light. Jacob yelled at what he saw, jumping backward into Aloren. "Turn it off! Turn it off!" he shrieked, squeezing his eyes shut, willing the images that had filled the view in front of him to leave. He couldn't get his mind to clear, though. Hundreds and hundreds of faces, bodies, embedded in the walls of the tunnel. Fingers reaching forward, eyes unseeing, staring into nothing.

"What happened?" Aloren gasped.

"What's going on?" Akeno said. "I can't see anything!"

"Please, Akeno, turn it off!" Jacob said. Through his closed eyelids, he saw the blue light fade out. He remained motionless, trying to calm his heart. Those couldn't have been real people. They couldn't have. He realized his hand was still on the wall and he jerked it off, wiping it on his pants. Wiping didn't take away the feeling of filth that remained. He wiped harder, groaning in frustration.

"Jacob?" Aloren said, her voice pleading. "Please . . . tell us what you saw."

Jacob furrowed his brow. "No, no, it was nothing," he said. "Nothing." He couldn't seem to take in enough air—even it felt grimy now.

"Keep going, keep going," Akeno said, his voice sounding higher than usual.

Jacob braced himself. "Okay." He used his feet to guide him instead of his hand, touching the wall as little as possible and cringing every time he brushed against it. They didn't make much progress this way, but he'd never touch the wall again if he could help it.

Jacob became aware that Aloren was holding his hand too tightly. "Aloren? I can't feel my fingers."

"Sorry." Aloren loosened her grip, but it wasn't long before she held on just as tight again.

Jacob still hadn't opened his eyes, and the muscles in his face were getting tired of squeezing them shut. He refused to open them, though, preferring darkness and muscle cramps to the alternative.

Aloren pulled in a ragged breath of air. "How . . . much farther?"

"Don't know," Jacob said, concentrating on not letting his emotions flow into his words. "I hope not much." He wouldn't be able to take any more of this if it didn't end soon. He couldn't believe he'd actually been touching faces and hands . . . people. He didn't even want to know if they were dead, or trapped in the wall alive—either way, it was awful.

After what felt like an eternity, a slight gust of wind brushed his face. He peeked through his eyelids, bracing himself for whatever had caused the air to move. A small shaft of light crossed the ground several feet ahead of them. Relief coursed through him as he realized what it meant. "I think we're almost at the end of the tunnel," he whispered. "No one talk until I make sure we're safe."

Aloren squeezed his hand, showing him she understood. After two more turns, the tunnel was lit well enough for Jacob to walk forward without using his feet to guide himself. He tried not to look at the walls, but couldn't help it. They were made completely of stone again. Oh, good.

Right before what he thought was the last turn, he stopped. There was something familiar about the light that flowed into the tunnel. He inched forward, paused, pressed up against the wall, then peered around the corner.

Chapter 16

Deformities and Eerie Lights

"Not again," Jacob groaned.

The light was muted, the trees dark and shriveled.

"What is it?" Aloren whispered.

"The trees look the same here as they did in the infected forest." Jacob surveyed the scene before leading them out of the tunnel. The air was heavy and dark, the sunlight barely visible, making it appear to be almost nighttime. "Are you still holding on to Akeno?"

"Yes, he's here."

"Grab on tight, just in case."

After making sure no one waited for them in the trees, Jacob guided Akeno and Aloren out of the tunnel. The trees were so thick that getting through them would be next to impossible. There wasn't a path, and the forest came right up next to the wall. Rock outcroppings were everywhere.

"Can you guys see yet?"

Aloren took several deep breaths. "Yes," she said. "Why is it so dark?"

"I'm not sure. It wasn't exactly like this in the infected forest." Jacob turned to look at his friends. "Akeno, can you see?"

The Makalo didn't answer for several seconds. "Yeah, I can," he said finally.

"What's the matter?" Jacob did his best to sound casual—hopefully Akeno was just being cautious.

"I'm waiting to see how I'll handle this."

"And?" Jacob mentally crossed his fingers. If Akeno flipped out here, it'd be nearly impossible to keep the group safe. The trees looked worse than the last forest—they were shorter, more gnarled, and because they grew so closely together, they almost appeared to be one huge, squat tree. With boulders everywhere, it would be dangerous enough without the Makalo running off.

Akeno slowly shook his head. "I can feel negative emotions, but they're nowhere near as strong as before. I think I'll be fine. Maybe the potion helped."

"This place gives me the heebie-jeebies, so if you guys can see well enough, let's keep moving," Jacob said. "There isn't a trail here, but I'll bet if we stick close to the wall, we'll come across some kind of path eventually."

"We'll follow you," Aloren said.

Jacob looked down at her hand, still clutching his. "But I might need to use both my hands," he said, almost wishing that wasn't the case.

"Oh, sorry." Aloren pulled away.

Jacob smiled, then noticed how worried both she and Akeno looked. He put his left hand on Aloren's shoulder and his right on Akeno's. "We'll be fine. Things will work out." He looked Aloren in the eyes. "No need to stress, okay?"

She nodded and gave him a weak smile.

Jacob opened his knapsack to talk to September and Early, noticing he still had Aloren's bag around his neck. He decided not to give it back to her yet, though. The going would be hard enough.

"Are you guys okay to stay in there for a while?"

"Yes, we're fine," Early said. "Lots to do."

"Good. It would be really, really bad if we got separated right now. You wouldn't be able to get out of this place."

The ground was rough and just as bad as he'd expected it to be. At least the trees weren't as violent here as the ones in the infected forest. Perhaps this was due to the fact that the group was trying to go around the trees, not between. Jacob was quick to note, however, that anytime he brushed up against a tree, he received a swift reminder to stay away. But it was pretty difficult not to touch them, and after just a few minutes of climbing over rocks and clinging to the wall, he felt thrashed.

After half an hour of climbing, jumping down, crawling through, stepping over, and hiking up, they got to a place where the ground evened out and the dirt road appeared up ahead. "There's the trail!"

"Oh, good," Aloren said.

"I really wish I could use my Rezend to see what's out there," Akeno said.

Jacob nodded. "You could try it if you want to, but I doubt the trees will let you touch them."

"I'll leave Rezend as a last resort for now."

The group followed the trail west and away from the wall. It led deeper into the forest, which was now the only thing that appeared to separate them from the castle. Jacob felt a small tightening sensation in his chest. He did his best not to imagine the possibilities the day might hold for them, opting instead to concentrate on each step he took.

The group neared a large tree with oddly shaped branches growing wild at the bottom, then coming to a point at the top. It stood out from the other trees—being several feet taller, and having lighter-colored bark. There was a spot where the branches parted, leaving what looked somewhat like an open-ended box.

"Is this a Kaith tree?" Jacob asked. "Dmitri mentioned one where he found a note from Aldo."

"Yes, it is," Akeno said. "Long ago, the people of this kingdom would leave things here for passing travelers. They'd put spells on the tree so only those who were meant to take the things would be able to get them. If I remember correctly, there used to be several similar trees throughout our land for this purpose. This is supposed to be the only one left—the rest died or were destroyed."

Shortly after passing the Kaith tree, they came to a fork in the road. There was a sign with the words "Maivoryl City" etched into it, pointing to the right. Jacob assumed the left branch led to the castle. His heartbeat sped up, and he had to consciously change his thought process to keep from freaking out. He looked at Aloren. "Isn't this where your brother should be?"

Aloren peered down the road. "Yes, that's the theory," she said. She made no move to walk that way, though.

Jacob hesitated, trying to decide what to do. "Maybe Akeno and I should go with you into the city . . . at least to help you get started."

Aloren visibly relaxed. "Oh, would you?"

"Yeah, why not? We'll stay with you until we're sure it's safe. If things don't look right, you can come with us to the castle."

"I really appreciate this. After the Molg and the tunnel . . . I don't . . . I can't . . ."

Jacob awkwardly patted her shoulder, hoping she wouldn't start crying. He walked to the right, watching her from the corner of his eye. She looked more freaked out than emotional, though, and he relaxed. Nervousness and fright he could handle—but crying? Not a chance.

The trees grew thickly on either side, and it seemed as though they were reaching toward Jacob. He looked at them, but could see no movement. The thick, greenish air, the trees, the eerie quiet—he almost couldn't take it. It made him feel as though he was about to suffocate. He realized Aloren was walking very close to him and he nearly stopped, recognizing how much she depended on him for protection. What had happened to the stubborn, independent girl he'd met two days ago?

After a few turns in the trail, buildings came into view, and Jacob kept his eyes on them as the group continued. With the light of the sun barely visible, the city felt dark and ominous. Most of the buildings were boarded up, but had muted light coming from inside. It wasn't natural light, but a sickly mustard-green color. The feeling that came from the city wasn't welcoming, and the air was now so heavy, Jacob felt a constant need to clear his throat.

As they passed the first house, Jacob saw a face press up against one of the windows. It disappeared, but then came back, accompanied by another. A moment later, the door opened a crack, and an old, withered hand appeared, reaching toward Jacob and his friends.

He almost stopped walking when he saw the tired-looking woman kneeling at the door. She had gray hair that was pulled into a loose bun. "Please, please help us," she wheezed, her light-colored eyes begging.

Aloren looked at Jacob, a troubled expression on her face.

"I really don't feel good about this place," Jacob whispered. "I don't think we should go near anyone."

As soon as he'd said this, the woman's expression turned to one of such hatred that Aloren gasped and stepped into Jacob, nearly knocking him over. She grabbed his arm, holding on to it tightly.

The woman's eyes turned black and empty, glaring at them. "Yes, that's right, children," she said. "Keep walking away if it makes you feel better. You rats." She moved forward into the muted light. "But I wouldn't go that way if I were you."

Suddenly her eyes changed from black to bright, fire red. She reached out, palm down, and flames shot from her hand, surrounded by black smoke. Her hair started growing, turning dark and pouring down her back.

Whoa—Jacob took a step back. Where had that come from?

The fire didn't reach very far, though, and her hair stopped growing as quickly as it had started. The woman jerked forward in a coughing fit, curling up into a ball, her hair shrinking back to the bun and going white again. She shut her eyes and turned her face away from them.

"Please help us." The whisper carried through the still air, the voice pitiful.

Jacob shook his head to get the sound of her voice out of his ears. He pulled Akeno and Aloren close to him, walking down the center of the winding road. He did his best to ignore the disfigured faces that watched them from almost every window. "Uh, Aloren, where do you want us to take you?" he said, trying to distract himself.

"I'm not sure," Aloren said. "The town center? If there is one."

A few moments later, the road opened into a large area with a building in the middle. Jacob paused to scrutinize it. The windows weren't boarded up, and the light that came from inside was warm and welcoming. It was more likely than any of the other buildings to be a town hall. He still hesitated, though, wanting to be sure it was safe. He took a breath, then began to inch forward, step by step. Aloren and Akeno stayed close to his side and he kept his eyes open, watching for any sign of potential danger.

They were almost to the porch when the front door opened, and a man stepped out carrying a rug. He was large, wearing a white shirt and a blue apron, and had a mustache that covered at least half his face. He shook the rug out, then noticed them and jumped, dropping the rug and putting his hand on his chest. "Oh, you startled me!" he said, laughing.

Jacob noted the twinkle in his eyes.

"Can I help you?" the man asked.

"You might," Aloren said.

The man gave her a friendly smile. "I might?" He laughed. "Well, let's hear what you have to say, and we'll see if I can."

"I'm looking for my brother."

"And who is your brother?"

"His name is Devlin."

"You believe you might find him in Maivoryl City?" The man stroked one side of his mustache. "Hmmm. You do know that no one has come or gone from this city in many years, right?"

"Yes, I know," Aloren said. "But he hasn't been seen for a very long time, and I've searched everywhere for him— except this city."

"Have you considered that he might be dead?"

Aloren faltered, but then a determined expression came into her eyes. "Yes, I have. But I don't think he is."

The man smiled again and picked up the rug. "How can you be sure?"

"I can't explain it. I just know. I want to search the city, but I'm not sure where to start, or how."

A young woman came to the door and stood behind the man, her arms folded. Putting his arm around her shoulders, he brought her forward. "My name is Eachan," he said. "This is my eldest, Duana."

Duana's features relaxed, and she smiled at Aloren, who returned the smile.

Hope was starting to come into her eyes. "My name is Aloren, and these are my friends, Jacob and Akeno."

Eachan studied them, a curious expression on his face. He locked eyes with Jacob for a brief moment, and Jacob could sense an under-the-surface emotion coming from Eachan. But he wasn't able to discern what it was, just that it was somewhat akin to heartache.

"Very pleased to meet you both." Eachan opened the door. "Please come in. We don't get many visitors to the town hall or Maivoryl City."

"Thank you," Aloren said.

He held the door for them. "In fact, you're the first visitors to come in a very long time."

"Can we have a minute alone to talk, please?" Jacob asked, motioning for Aloren and Akeno to come closer.

"Of course." Eachan went into the hall, shutting the door behind him.

Jacob pulled Aloren and Akeno several feet away from the porch. "I don't want to go in there until I know how you feel about this."

Akeno and Aloren looked at each other. Akeno was the first to speak. "I trust him."

"Same with me," Aloren said. "I think he's a good man, doing the best he can with what he has around him."

"I don't trust this city," Jacob said, "nor the situation." He frowned, thinking. "But he might have information on how to look for your brother."

Aloren nodded. "He'd have to know everyone who lives here, even if only by sight. And he'd at least know if there was someone here Devlin's age."

"We could use his help."

"You mean *I*. *I* could use his help."

"No, you don't have to do it alone. We'll come with you."

"Why? Your business is much more urgent than mine. You need to focus on getting that Key, and as soon as possible. Besides, you've taken me as far as you promised you would."

Jacob shook his head. "That doesn't matter. Agreements and promises can change."

"Not in this case, they can't."

"Aloren, honestly." Jacob scowled. "It's a stupid idea for you to be left alone right now."

"You get the Key. Don't worry—I'll be fine."

"After we find Devlin."

"No. You have to go now. There's a chance the Lorkon don't know you're here already, and you need to get to the castle before they find out. Otherwise, everything we've gone through will have been for nothing. They'd never let you take the Key and get out—you have to know that. What happens then? We all die? You fail to help the Makalos?"

Jacob looked into her eyes, trying to sense if she really believed what she was saying. "Then come with us to find the Key, and we can look for Devlin afterward."

"And possibly lose my chance of being reunited with him?" She shook her head. "Jacob, this is as far as I've ever gone. If I don't take this opportunity right now, it'll never come again. You know I can't get through that wall without you."

Jacob closed his eyes. "I can't do this, Aloren."

"No, Jacob, listen to her," Akeno said. "Her points are valid. She knows what she needs to do."

Aloren put her hand on Jacob's arm. "And you can't make my decisions for me. I trust Eachan and his daughter. I'll be fine here."

As much as he hated to admit it, Jacob felt Aloren was right. They hadn't come this far only to fail, and he didn't want to let Kenji and Ebony down. He sighed. This felt like desertion, plain and simple. He put his hand on her shoulder.

"Are you sure about this?" he said. "One hundred percent *positive* this is what you really want to do?"

Aloren nodded. "Yes, I am. Besides, I'll only take a couple of hours to search the city. I'll have Eachan and Duana's help, so that should be enough. We can meet near the tunnel, and you can lead me back to the other side."

"All right. Let's make it two and a half hours, to be safe. By that time, the sun'll be setting, and Akeno and I will have to leave anyway. If we don't find the Key today, we'll probably camp out near the Fat Lady's cabin and try again tomorrow. You'll either be with your brother or not, and can choose to come with us or head back to Macaria."

"Thank you, Jacob."

Jacob gave her shoulder a light squeeze and started toward the town hall.

"Jacob, wait," Aloren said, then threw her arms around him. "I really mean it. Thank you so much for believing me and for helping me come here. You, Akeno, and Gallus are the only ones who don't think I'm crazy."

She pulled back, and Jacob saw tears in her eyes. He cleared his throat. "Uh . . . you're welcome."

She wiped her tears away, gave Akeno a hug, then said, "I'm ready."

Jacob knocked on the door of the town hall, unsure if he should just walk in.

The door swung open and Eachan appeared, carrying what looked like a bowl of mashed potatoes. "Would you like some food?" he asked.

"No, thanks," Jacob said. "But can you help Aloren?"

Eachan turned to face her. "What can I do for you?"

"Help me find my brother," she said.

He nodded. "Of course we'll help—as long as you realize that the odds of his being here aren't good, which I think you do."

Aloren turned and gave Jacob another quick hug, then Akeno. "Thanks," she said. "Get going, you two, and I'll see you soon, okay?"

Jacob shook Eachan's hand. "Thank you for your help, Eachan. It's appreciated."

Aloren stayed on the porch to watch Akeno and Jacob as they left. Jacob met her eyes as he stepped off the porch, already missing her company. He turned and hurried down the street, careful not to look at the buildings on either side.

They were a couple of blocks away from the town hall when they heard a girl scream. Jacob whipped around. The porch swarmed with townspeople who were grabbing at Aloren, trying to drag her away.

"Run, Aloren!" Jacob yelled. He almost raced back, but hesitated when Eachan jumped through the door and wrestled with several people, kicking and shoving them off the porch. Duana and Aloren were fighting as well.

Eachan punched one of the leaders full in the face, then grabbed Aloren and Duana, pulling them inside to safety and slamming the door shut. He then put metal bars over the glass.

"Jacob! Look out!" Akeno yelled.

Jacob lurched out of the way just as a disfigured man with long, ratted hair slashed a large knife at him. He slashed again and Jacob dodged, swinging around with his fist and hitting the guy on the side of the head.

The man fell over near Akeno, who sprung away from the man's grasp.

Jacob felt something touch his back, and he jumped around to see a woman with greasy hands and hair trying to grab his shirt. He shoved her away, knocking her into a deformed man behind her. He glanced around. Hundreds of people with mangled bodies poured out of the buildings on both sides of the street, many carrying knives and sticks.

He fought the hands off him, finding that the people were weak. But their numbers . . . there were too many to fight. He and Akeno shoved their way through the group of people and sprinted as fast as they could toward the fork in the road.

Jacob glanced over his shoulder one more time before they turned a bend. The people didn't pursue beyond the last house. It looked as though some invisible boundary kept them from leaving the city.

He stopped when they reached the main road, bent over and put his hands on his knees. "They're not . . . following us," he panted. "Why?"

"Not sure," Akeno said, also gasping for breath.

Jacob straightened and motioned toward Maivoryl City. "Did you see how they swarmed all over Aloren? We have to go back for her—I knew we shouldn't have left her there!"

"There's nothing we can do. We aren't prepared to fight. We'll end up stuck there, too." Akeno reached up and grabbed Jacob's shoulders, forcing him to look away from the city. "Listen to me. We can't do both. If we try to get her, we'll fail at getting the Key." He paused, then resolution crossed his face. "Only a couple of hours. We'll meet her at the tunnel and . . . and help her then."

Jacob closed his eyes, focusing on the air rushing in and out of his lungs. "Okay." He turned to look down the path that led to the castle and hesitated, trying to get the courage to continue. He released a breath and put his hand on Akeno's shoulder. "All right, let's go."

The road led them deep into the forest, and for a time the castle was out of view. Jacob glanced at Akeno. "She . . . she'll be okay," he whispered.

"Eachan'll make sure of it," Akeno said.

After following the winding trail for several minutes, the forest ended, and the castle loomed up before them, large and magnificent. An intense pang of fear clenched Jacob's heart, and he was almost overcome by a sudden urge to run away as fast as he could. He took a deep breath, trying in vain to calm his heart. He realized he could lose everything that was important to him—his family, his friends, his freedom, his life.

The surface of the dirt road blended into cobblestones and led under the castle's huge archway and into the spacious courtyard. There were no guards visible, and the place had an eerie quietness about it that unsettled Jacob. The air seemed to press down upon him, and the silence was almost deafening.

"There's no sense putting off the inevitable," he said, then started forward. He crept up to the left side of the archway, Akeno following. Leaning against the wall, he glanced around, again making sure no one was watching them.

"How do we get in?"

"I'm not sure," Jacob whispered, then laughed a short, almost hysterical laugh. "Maybe we should knock on the door. They'd probably welcome us in with wide-open arms." Akeno frowned at him, and Jacob stopped smiling. "Okay, just kidding. Let's go around to the side of the castle and see if there's another way in."

"Okay."

They crept along the stone wall, staying close to it. Coming to the corner, Jacob peered around it and saw nothing but a long wall with no windows or doors. For a second he considered turning around and going back to the front, but then something occurred to him, and he looked at Akeno.

"I've got an idea. Come on."

Putting his hand on the wall, he felt around, searching for warmth. After a few seconds, he sprinted along, keeping his hand on the wall the entire way. Akeno jogged behind him, keeping up.

Jacob paused, having felt warmth in the surface. It wasn't substantial, though, so he continued running. "Wow," he panted. "The Lorkon really know how to build strong walls." A thought popped into his head, and he stopped. "Hey, maybe I have the ability to sense weakness in things!"

"Excuse me?"

"That has to be it. I think I've known since we were in the cave. I'm looking for a weakness in the wall right now so I can make an opening for us."

Akeno frowned. "When you feel the heat, you mean?"

"Yeah," Jacob said. "And then when I reshaped the rock from the cave wall, I somehow knew how to make it stronger. That's pretty cool. Imagine what I could do with it! I could build an indestructible car!"

"Okay, great," Akeno said. "Let's concentrate on getting the Key for now. You can play later."

Jacob laughed, focusing again on temperature. After running the entire length of the wall, he turned with it as it formed the back of the castle. Ten or fifteen feet later, he found what he was looking for—a spot warm enough to do what he needed to do. Holding his hands over the stone, he felt it heat up beneath his palms and fingertips and become soft. He made a hole in the stone, about waist high, then bent over to peek through it. He didn't see anyone on the other side, so he continued working with the stone until the hole was big enough to climb through. Akeno followed him, then Jacob turned around to reheat the stone and close up the hole behind them.

"Why did you do that?" Akeno whispered. "Wouldn't we want to leave it open?"

"Uh . . . I didn't think that far ahead. I just didn't want the Lorkon to know which way we'd come in."

They turned to survey what Jacob had thought would be the inner courtyard but might be a room in the castle, as it was walled off, and there was a roof overhead. Light streamed through a few windows near the ceiling, making it possible for Jacob to see a door on the opposite side. Crossing the room, Jacob put his hand on the doorknob, ready to open it. Thinking better of the idea, though, he reached to pull his bag down from off his back. One of the Minyas could make sure there wasn't anything dangerous on the other side of the door before he walked through it.

"Oh, no . . ." he groaned.

Akeno jumped. "What?"

"I still have Aloren's bag! I completely forgot to give it back to her!"

"You can give it back when we reach the tunnel. She probably won't need it before then."

Jacob nodded in agreement, then frowned, looking around the room. "What was I doing? Oh, yeah." He opened his bag and whispered into it. "September, I need you. Keep to the shadows and see if you can go through the keyhole in this door. If you can, inspect the area on the other side, then come tell us if it's safe to open the door."

September flitted to the keyhole, and, after wriggling around, was able to get through. Moments later he returned to tell them there was a courtyard on the other side of the door, and no one was there. "There's also a servants' entrance to the castle. I checked the room where it leads, and there wasn't anyone in it, either."

Jacob opened the door and poked his head through. As September had said, the place was empty. Motioning for Akeno and September to follow, Jacob crossed the courtyard and sneaked through the door.

Shutting the door behind them, Jacob inspected the room they'd just entered. It was a large kitchen and looked as though it hadn't been used for quite some time. He ran across the room to the door on the opposite side, and once again had September go through the keyhole. September returned to inform them that the hallway on the other side was empty as well.

Jacob quietly opened the door, glancing through the crack. There were many doors leading off the hallway, and he turned to Akeno. "Where do we go to find the Key?" he asked.

"I'm not sure. I didn't really think about what we would do once we got inside."

Jacob folded his arms, looking around the room, trying to decide what to do. "We could always just start trying doors to see where they lead." He shook his head. "No, that's a dumb idea and would definitely draw attention to us. Better to get in and out as quickly as possible."

Just as he said this, he was suddenly overcome with vertigo. He sank to the floor, feeling feverish, and blood pounded hard in his head.

"What's wrong?" Akeno asked.

"I . . ." For a second, it felt as though he could see another person's thoughts, similar to what had happened in the cave, except this time without the emotions. Pictures flowed into his mind, and he saw the way to the Key. Realization dawned on him, and his headache began clearing as suddenly as it had come. He became aware of Akeno hovering over him, and he rubbed his temples. The headache was mostly gone now, and the dizziness had passed. He slowly got to his feet and took a deep breath. "Uh . . . I know how to get there."

Akeno startled. "You do? How?"

"I don't know how," Jacob said. "It just entered my mind. And we've really got to hurry. No one's around the Key right now, but I doubt it'll stay that way for very long."

"How can we be sure it's not a trap?"

"I don't think we can be." Jacob closed his eyes and concentrated hard on the images, making sure he had them memorized.

"What other options do we have?" Akeno asked.

"We could send the Minyas to find it."

"That might work."

Jacob thought this through. "Except, if we got split up, they might be stuck here for the rest of their existence. It's probably better if we stay together." He frowned. "We could always just search the whole castle."

"I don't want to dig through every corner of the castle when you already know where to find the Key. That would be pointless."

"And there's no way we'd find it by searching. This place is huge."

"So we follow what you saw, then?"

Jacob nodded. "I guess so. It's our only choice."

He opened the door again, peering both ways down the hall. It was still very quiet. He took a few cautious steps, being as silent as possible, then scurried down the hall and into another room. There was a set of stairs on the opposite side, which he took two at a time. It felt weird to be so sure of the way, as though he'd been there before, but he knew these memories weren't his. They belonged to someone else.

He pushed open a heavy door and, hearing someone coming, hid behind a curtain, motioning to Akeno to follow. A dark figure strode past them, turning a corner. Jacob couldn't tell if it was human or not.

He waited a moment, finger to his lips, then walked past an alcove to a door behind another curtain. He put his hands against the rough wood. "This is where we'll find the Key."

"You're sure?"

"Yes, I'm sure," Jacob said. "Stick close to my side. Let's just run in, grab the Key, then get the heck out of here." He looked up. "September, get in my bag again, just in case. I don't want anything to happen to you guys. If we die, you'll need to get back to Aloren somehow." September flew down and joined Early in Jacob's knapsack. After securing his bag over his shoulders, Jacob opened the door a couple of inches and glanced into the room, verifying it was empty before pushing the door all the way open.

The room looked nothing like he'd anticipated—his vision had shown a magnificent white throne room lined with paintings and statues. The walls in this room were covered in thick drapery—there was no throne or artwork. There was, however, a simple table in the center with a beautiful box on top. Warmth struck Jacob in the chest, and he knew this was where the Key was kept. The box was intricately designed in silver, and he could have sworn there was a slight glow around it. He'd never seen anything like it before. He walked to the table, motioning for Akeno to follow him.

Jacob couldn't be sure, but he thought he heard a quiet strain of music. He looked around, trying to find the source. The heavy draperies made it obvious the sound hadn't come from outside. Focusing his attention back on the box, he could now see for sure that it was glowing, and there was light coming from under the lid.

Jacob drew the box across the table. It wasn't very big, maybe four inches long and only two or three inches tall. The silver was shaped into ivy, roses, and flowers.

Jacob opened the box and got a brief glimpse of the Key before he was nearly blinded by a beautiful radiance that filled the entire room—warm yellows, light pinks, greens and blues all together—the happiest and most peaceful colors he had ever seen.

Accompanying the glow was a beautiful melody. Joy and melancholy hit him simultaneously as he was reminded of all the happy times he'd had with his family—laughing with his little sister while playing dress-up, throwing a football or playing basketball with Matt, camping with his dad, talking to his mom. A pang of homesickness hit Jacob hard in the stomach, and he wished his family were there to feel the joy as well.

"Wow," Akeno whispered.

His eyes adjusted to the sudden light, Jacob lifted the box and reached in. The moment his fingers brushed the Key, warmth filled his entire body and he stood still, overcome by feelings of joy and happiness. Tears sprang to his eyes, and he tried to make the moisture go away while allowing himself to revel in the moment. He hadn't realized how much pressure he'd been under, or how stressed and frustrated he'd been, until now. It felt as though the sun had broken through the clouds of a storm that had stayed for several weeks.

"We've got the Key—let's go now," Akeno said.

Jacob held up his finger. "Just wait." After a moment, the wave of emotions subsided, and he pulled the Key out to inspect it. The melody stopped as soon as the Key was removed from the box, and the glimmer faded away. He put the Key back to see if the music and the glow would return, and they did.

Jacob brought the box closer to his face. The Key was silver, delicate, and several hundred years old, judging by the scratches and wear. It looked as if it would break with the least amount of applied pressure. The handle was intricate, and diamonds lined the shaft. Two of the diamonds were different from the others, giving off a rosier sparkle.

"It is beautiful, isn't it?" a rough, deep voice said from the left side of the room.

Jacob stiffened and dropped the box, causing the Key to fall onto the table. The glow and the melody ceased, and the room was once again bathed in eerie light from the windows. Jacob put the Key into the box and shut the lid, then turned to the voice.

The heavy curtains that had covered that side of the room were now drawn back, showing the throne Jacob had seen in vision and a large, cloaked figure that now sat there.

"Though, I must say, it never gave off that light and music until you arrived."

Swallowing several times, Jacob couldn't respond. Finally, he asked, "Who are you?"

"Do you even need to ask? You know who stole the Key."

"A Lorkon?" Jacob tried to keep his voice from cracking.

"Of course," the Lorkon said, and then laughed. Jacob's stomach churned in response to the sound, and he was aware of how close to him Akeno stood. On either side of the Lorkon, two huge black shapes moved, and then two pairs of green eyes fixed on him. With a start, Jacob realized these were the wolves that had been following them for most of the trip. "You may refer to me as Your Majesty," the Lorkon said. "I am king here. Now activate the Key."

"W—what?"

"Come on, child. It was deactivated, and only you can activate it."

"Me?"

The king laughed. "Did they not tell you? You don't know any of it? What a delightful surprise! We were starting to wonder why you hadn't come yet. It never occurred to me you weren't even aware of our presence!"

Jacob stiffened. "What are you talking about?"

"'Jacob,' they call you, right?" The Lorkon shifted on his throne. "We got tired of waiting for you to come, and so we devised a means to get you here. Het and Isan, of course, were able to chase you to the Makalo village, but stealing the Key of Kilenya seemed the best way to make the Makalos want you to enter Eklaron. Their prize possession couldn't be gone for long before they would want it back."

Akeno trembled at Jacob's side. "You know we kept it to prevent it from falling into your hands," he spat. His voice quivered—whether from panic or anger, Jacob couldn't tell, but he grabbed the Makalo's arm, trying to keep him from doing anything they'd regret.

"Besides," Jacob said, "I already knew you were using the Key as bait. You don't even need it, so why ask me to activate it?"

"Oh, we do need the Key. Very much. We realize how powerful it can be and how much good it would do us." The king leaned forward, stopping just shy of the light streaming in from one of the windows. "Of course it isn't anything without you."

"Get on with it!" a voice said from behind Jacob. "Enough chatter!"

Jacob whirled to see three Lorkon step forward from the curtains behind him. They were just as shrouded in shade as the first.

"You would do well to hold your tongue," said the king, almost standing from the throne. "How dare you speak out in my presence? This is none of your concern. I will deal with it!" The two large wolves arose and lumbered past Jacob to encircle the Lorkon on the opposite side of the room.

"Forgive me." The voice was full of bitterness, and the three Lorkon stepped back again.

The king stood. "As you can see, Jacob, we have grown impatient in our wait for you." He paused, then strolled across the room.

Jacob straightened, his hands forming fists at his sides. The Lorkon king stopped right in front of him, towering over Jacob by three feet, at least. Then he bent until his face was close to Jacob's.

Jacob's stomach curled at the close-up sight of the Lorkon's crimson face. It was just as Kenji had described—black hair, eyes the color of blood with bright green irises. He drew back when he saw the creature's chafed and peeling skin.

"You are disgusted by my appearance, are you not?"

"Yes, I am."

The king straightened to his full height. "And yet, you control your fear well." He reached to Jacob, who took a step back. The hand was just as revolting as the Lorkon's face—scabby and peeling, with blood on the fingers. Jacob's stomach clenched, looking at it.

The hand stopped short of touching Jacob's face, and Jacob wondered why the Lorkon ignored Akeno. The group behind them shuffled their feet.

"What do you want with us?" Jacob asked through clenched teeth.

"Nothing from the Makalo."

"What do you want from *me*?"

"Many things," the king said, then reached his hand out again. This time he didn't stop, and all though Jacob shied away, the Lorkon's finger made contact with his forehead.

Jacob felt as though he'd been punched in the face and chest simultaneously. The wind was knocked out of him, and he fell to the floor. Bright flashes of light burst through the room and he closed his eyes, trying to block them out. His blood was on fire, burning every inch of him as it coursed through his veins. He rolled onto his side, his body convulsing in pain as he gagged, trying to get enough air. His muscles cramped, and tremors ran through his body.

He heard hundreds of sounds all at once and was no longer able to focus on just one. They were so loud, they pulsated in his brain like a migraine. Opening his eyes, he gasped as the bright lights flashed again, alternating with blackness. Thousands of people moved through the room at once. His body was on sensory overload. Even the temperature seemed to be fluctuating.

He tried to stand and right himself, but barely managed to lift his head. The walls around him would not stop spinning. He struggled to stay conscious, almost failing several times. The thought kept entering his mind that he had to remain alert—he couldn't let the Lorkon win.

He heard a loud crack, and his head felt as though it was about to explode again.

Someone pulled him to his feet. He struggled against the person until he recognized Akeno's voice commanding him to walk. He slumped against the Makalo—he couldn't hold his own weight. Akeno nearly fell under the load, but struggled forward.

They staggered through a door, across another room, and into a hall. Jacob was so disoriented he couldn't even tell which way was up. Pain was the only thing he knew. He longed to fall to the floor—to give in to the black, to stop the spinning. He brushed against a doorjamb and nearly fainted from the agony the contact caused. He opened his eyes. Hundreds of people streamed through the huge corridor—Lorkon, humans, Makalos, and other creatures. The lights still flashed, and he had to close his eyes again. He felt himself losing his grasp on consciousness as Akeno yelled unintelligible things at him.

They stumbled down a hall, a door opened, and he was pushed inside a room. He slumped to the ground, trying not to give into the convulsions.

"Jacob . . . vial? . . ." Akeno's words didn't make any sense.

He was aware of his bag being ripped off his arm, and moments later a bitter fluid was poured into his mouth. He gagged, trying to spit it out.

"Stop it! Swallow . . . please, Jacob!"

Jacob felt his nose being plugged, and then his mouth was jammed shut, forcing him to swallow. The liquid burned its way down his throat and he fought the urge to throw up as it hit his stomach. Writhing on the floor for what felt like an eternity, he was aware of Akeno at his side.

Suddenly, the potion entered his bloodstream. The sensation started at his heart, inching outward from there. It soothed the pain away, first in his chest, then his lower body, then his arms and neck, and finally his head.

The liquid was cold—cooling his burning blood. His muscles relaxed, and the sounds disappeared. The lights stopped flashing.

Then his brain relaxed, and he surrendered to the peaceful calm of sleep.

Chapter 17

Breakneck Speeds

Just as soon as the relief of rest came, however, Jacob was awakened.

"Jacob, you can't sleep!"

He moaned, not wanting to move.

"Please, Jacob. Come on."

Jacob moaned again and tried to clear his mind. He didn't open his eyes for fear the bright lights would flash again and make him want to throw up. "The Key . . . did you get it?"

"Yes, it's here."

Jacob took a deep breath. "And the box?"

"Here as well."

"Put . . . put them in my bag. I just need . . . a minute."

"We've really got to go, Jacob—now. The Lorkon, wolves, and Dusts are stunned, but won't be for much longer."

Reality entered Jacob's mind, and his eyes snapped open. He jerked to a sitting position, immediately regretting it. "Whoa," he said, holding his head in his hands. It took a second for everything to stop spinning.

While waiting for the dizziness to pass, Jacob mentally examined himself. His body was sore all over, and his eyes ached a great deal.

The ringing in his ears was gone, though. He glanced around the small, dark space. "Where are we?"

"I had September find us a place to hide. We're only a couple of rooms away from where we found the Key." Akeno got to his feet. "There are Dusts everywhere. As soon as you fell to the floor, several of them came in. I think they all knew we'd entered the castle and were hiding from us."

"I saw hundreds of people going back and forth," Jacob said. "Were they chasing us?"

Akeno looked confused. "People? What people?"

"Makalos, Lorkon, humans—tons of them. Even Shiengols and Dusts. Or Wurbies. I couldn't tell which ones they were. And others . . . different creatures."

"I only saw Dusts and the four Lorkon. No one else."

Jacob scratched his head. "Are . . . are you sure?"

"Of course."

"Then why did I see them?"

Akeno gave him a worried look. "I don't know."

Jacob groaned in frustration, switching gears in his head. "Okay, let's just focus on finding a way out. I don't think going through the door would be the best choice right now." He stood. "September, you keep a lookout. Let us know if anyone comes toward the door."

September flew to the keyhole and positioned himself inside it while Jacob felt the walls, searching for warmth. He found several shelves on one side with rags, buckets, brooms, and mops, but no warmth.

"This ability I have is great and all, but it sure isn't the fastest," he said.

After checking the walls, he got to his hands and knees, feeling his way around the floor. "Here!" he said, finding a warm spot in a corner of the room. He held his hands over the stone, heating it up. Soon there was a hole about two feet across. The rest of the stone wouldn't give way. "Hope that's big enough," he whispered, then peered over the edge. "I can't see anything. Akeno, can you?"

Akeno crawled to the hole, looking down. "Can I use my Rezend? It's too dark."

Jacob went to the door, shoving rags underneath it. "Don't use too much light. Oh, and we should have Early check, instead of us."

A blue glow emanated from Akeno's finger, not bright enough to make Jacob squint, but giving enough light for him to see Early as she flew down. She came back a moment later, reporting that the room below was empty.

Jacob ducked his head into the hole to survey the room. "Okay, there's a bed kinda underneath us. If we swing a little, we'll be able to land on it." He turned to Akeno. "Ready?"

"Yes, ready. September, you come, too."

Jacob lowered himself until his arms were straight, then swung his body and let go. He barely made it to the bed, surprised at how far beneath him it turned out to be. Reaching up, he caught the bags Akeno dropped to him, slinging them over his shoulders.

Akeno then dropped down. Being smaller and more nimble than Jacob, he landed on the bed without difficulty. Jacob handed Akeno his bag, then looked around for Early. He sent her through the keyhole to inspect the place outside of the room.

She returned. "It's busy in the hall."

Jacob nodded. "Let's wait a few minutes. Who was out there? Lorkon?"

"Yes, and Dusts."

Jacob sat on the bed. "Were they standing around guarding the doors, or were they going somewhere?"

"They were in a hurry, going somewhere."

"Which way were they going?"

"Down the corridor to the left."

"All right," Jacob said. "Let's wait for a few minutes and go to the right. Hopefully we won't run into anyone." He turned to Akeno. "Where's the Key?"

"I put it in your bag."

Jacob stood and paced for a while, then motioned to Early. "Okay, check again. Actually, just keep watch and let us know when the Lorkon and Dusts go away."

Early took a position halfway out the keyhole. After what felt like an eternity of waiting, she pulled back into the room. "It's clear."

"It probably won't stay that way for long," Jacob said. "Let's go."

He motioned at the Minyas to keep a lookout, one of them staying several feet ahead, the other several feet behind. He took a step down the hallway, but stopped, realizing he had no idea how to get out of the castle, or even where they were. Concentrating, he tried to orient himself to which way was east—where the castle entrance was located—and started running again.

Early's warning made him stop, and he whirled. A Dust charged down the corridor at them, its hands formed into hooves.

"Let's go!" Jacob yelled, and he and Akeno raced the other direction.

The Dust had no trouble keeping up, though, and quickly overtook them, grabbing Jacob and pulling him to the ground—Jacob was surprised at how quickly the beast's hands had changed.

So was the Dust, however, and it yelled at itself. "Stop! No! Where hooves?"

Jacob scrambled to his feet, but the Dust was too fast for him—it quickly recovered from its shock and pushed him down again.

Another warning from Early, and more Dusts poured into the hall. One wouldn't be too difficult, but all these at once? Jacob scuffled with the first, knocked it aside, and got to his feet.

The creatures only paused briefly before they had him surrounded, ignoring Akeno and the Minyas who had rushed to Jacob's assistance.

For several seconds the group struggled—Jacob wasn't able to see Akeno through the punches and kicks he was both receiving and blocking.

"What do I do?" Akeno asked. "Knock them out?"

Jacob shoved the nearest Dust into a couple of others, forcing them to the ground. "No loud noises." The crack would alert the Lorkon to their presence—he was sure they'd recognize Akeno's ability and come running. He whipped around, grabbing a Dust by the throat and throwing it against the wall. The hallway filled with even more Dusts, and Jacob found himself overwhelmed.

One of the beast's hands formed into a long rope, another's hands became knives, and Jacob was knocked to the ground again, his head cracking against the stone. That would leave a bruise.

A Dust's hands formed a blindfold, and it extended its arms around Jacob's neck from behind. Although he struggled, Jacob couldn't prevent the other creatures from tying the cloth over his eyes. He felt a sharp knifepoint at his neck, and he became motionless while the Dusts tied his hands and feet.

He heard a muffled yell of pain—Akeno's—and realized they were both trapped. Jacob wracked his brain. He wouldn't give in—especially not now that they had the Key!

Then he remembered what Aloren had said about Dusts. He had to do something they wouldn't expect—something to surprise them. A new obstacle—but what?

He felt his body being lifted from the ground, and he'd been rushed several feet before an idea came to him. He moved his hand a fraction, the rope slipping to the edge of his palm, and begged it to heat up. It did.

The Dust whose hands had tied him yelped, and Jacob's arms were free again. He put his hands over the blindfold, warming it up as well. He blinked at the light when the cloth was whipped off his face. The Dust who'd tied his feet quickly backed away, and Jacob jumped out of the arms of the others.

"It burnded me! It hotted its hands and burnded me!"

The creatures swarmed around the Dust to see the evidence for themselves—Jacob momentarily forgotten, even though there were close to twenty Dusts in the corridor. He raced to Akeno's side and freed him from the little beasts there as well, who raced to the other group.

Jacob placed one hand against the wall, the other pulling off his bag and tossing it to Akeno. He knew the distraction of their hands being burned wouldn't last long.

"Our food, Akeno—throw it at them when I give the go-ahead." He molded several rocks from the now-hot stone, filling his pockets with them.

"Ready?" he asked as the Dusts turned, angry glares on their faces. "Now!"

Apples, carrots, jerky, and rocks flew through the air, pelting the Dusts. Several of the creatures formed shields to block the missiles, crying in frustration at the change in their hands, but others caught the food and acted surprised when their hands stuffed it into their mouths. Jacob chuckled—what else were you supposed to do with food?

The Minyas finally joined in the fun, zooming at the monsters, disappearing and reappearing in random places along the hall. It wasn't long before the entire group of Dusts swarmed to get away, frightened by the change of events.

Jacob and Akeno laughed in relief, but realized they were still in danger. They turned and ran in the opposite direction, Jacob re-orienting himself to the entrance and which door would take them there. He thought hard, biting his lips and squinting in concentration, willing visions to enter his mind like earlier.

A bright, happy glow coming from a small corridor caught his attention and he paused, backtracking to check it out. Looking into the hallway, he saw warm sunlight pouring in, a stark contrast to the darkness of the rest of the castle. A well-dressed man walked down the corridor, his back to the group. He wore light-colored clothes and a weird hat. There was something familiar about the man's walk, but Jacob couldn't put his finger on it. As he watched, the stranger pushed against the left wall with both hands and the wall shifted away from him, sliding to the side and revealing a set of stairs leading down. The man didn't hesitate before descending out of view.

Glancing back at Akeno, Jacob was startled to see that the hall behind him was dark. The Minyas flitted in the air above them, and Akeno watched Jacob with an impatient expression on his face. Jacob looked back to the spot where the man had disappeared. The wall was shut, the corridor was just as dark as the rest of the castle, and there was no longer even a window to let in light. It had completely disappeared.

"What?" Akeno whispered.

"This way." Jacob hurried down the corridor, Akeno and the Minyas following.

Suddenly, a Lorkon leaped from the shadows of the hall, knocking Akeno down as he lunged for Jacob. Jacob jumped out of the way just in time, and the Lorkon fell to the ground where Jacob had been standing.

Looking around for a weapon, Jacob spotted a large metal candle holder on a table farther down the corridor. He ran and grabbed it, turning in time to see the Lorkon lurch forward again. He swung the candle holder and hit the Lorkon in the side with it, knocking the creature to the ground.

"Hurry, Akeno! Over here!"

As Akeno ran past the Lorkon, it reached out and grabbed him by the ankle, bringing him down with a crash. Akeno screamed, struggling to get out of the Lorkon's grasp.

"Use your Rezend!" Jacob yelled. Akeno complied, and Jacob didn't have enough time to plug his ears before the crack echoed through the corridor. The Lorkon went limp, allowing Akeno to jerk his leg free.

His ears ringing, Jacob helped Akeno to his feet and sprinted down the corridor to the spot where the opening in the wall had been. "Here! We have to go here!" he yelled.

"It's just a wall, Jacob! We gotta go back to the hall!"

"No, there are stairs behind it. I think it leads to the tunnel Dmitri talked about in his journal." Jacob pushed against the wall. It didn't budge. "Help me open it!"

Akeno made a frustrated sound, but jumped to Jacob's side to help. After a moment of exertion, the wall shuddered beneath Jacob's hands. Pushing a little harder, he felt it start to give. He heard a few clicks, and then the wall fell back and slid to the side.

"Go down!" Jacob said, motioning to the Minyas, who flitted into the dark hole, Akeno following close behind.

Jacob looked to see if the Lorkon was still unconscious, then went down a couple of steps, turning back to shut the door. It closed much easier than it had opened. He passed his hands over the edges of the door where it met the wall, searching for any warmth, sealing what he could. Satisfied that the door would now keep anyone from coming through for a while, Jacob turned in the pitch black. "Akeno, can you light up the stairs?"

"Yeah . . . I can," the Makalo said after a moment. The familiar blue light filled the stone stairway, revealing Akeno down several steps from Jacob, rubbing his leg and grimacing.

"What's wrong?" Jacob asked.

Akeno moaned. "My leg . . ."

"Where the Lorkon grabbed you?"

"Yes."

"Do you need to rest?"

"No," Akeno said, then straightened. "We gotta go before they catch up."

"Let me know if the pain gets worse, okay?"

Akeno didn't respond.

Jacob pulled his knapsack off his back. "Minyas, in my bag," he said. September and Early flew inside, then Jacob and Akeno started down the stairs.

After at least three flights, the stairs ended, and a long passageway opened in front of them. Several sections of the ground and walls were wet, but the tunnel appeared to be in good condition.

"Is this the Fat Lady's tunnel?" Jacob asked. "What if it leads us somewhere else?"

Akeno didn't answer. He appeared to be in pain, but was keeping up.

"Are you sure you're going to be okay? We can take a break."

"No," Akeno said, his voice shaking. "Keep going, keep going."

Jacob glanced over his shoulder every now and then while running. Akeno moved slower every minute, his limp becoming more definite with each step. Jacob tried to figure out how to help his friend.

He stopped running when Akeno stumbled. "Okay, this isn't going to work." He frowned, then took Akeno's bag and slung it over his shoulder. "I have a better idea." He picked Akeno up and started jogging again.

Akeno gave a weak laugh. "Sack of potatoes," he said.

Jacob laughed as well. "But this time you're not being thrown over my shoulder," he said. "Your job is to keep the tunnel well lit so I don't fall and drop you."

A few minutes later, Akeno began to shiver and mumble. He opened his eyes, staring straight above him, and gasped.

Jacob looked up, ready to see something falling from the ceiling, but nothing was there. He watched Akeno's facial expressions for a second, then turned his full attention back to the tunnel and getting in as much distance as possible while Akeno was still conscious.

He paused a few times to catch his breath. The weight of Akeno's body was starting to make his already-tired arms ache, and his head began pounding again. How was he ever going to make it to the end of the tunnel? He did his best to push the pain away, but was only successful when he heard Akeno start moaning. He paused to raise his friend's pant leg. There were no breaks in the skin, but the spot was yellow, with angry pink edges.

Akeno's muscles clenched up and his pupils dilated, making his eyes look almost black with only a sliver of blue. He looked as though he was about to slip into unconsciousness.

"No, no, Akeno, stay with me!" Jacob yelled, running as fast as his legs would take him—the end *had* to be near! The blue light only reached forty feet into the distance, and it was getting dimmer—Akeno probably wouldn't be able to keep it lit much longer.

Finally, Jacob saw what looked like the end. Praying it wasn't blocked, he sighed in relief at the sight of stairs leading up. Akeno's breathing was shallow. His left hand was limp, barely elevated above his chest, and his light had dimmed to the point where Jacob could only see four or five feet ahead of him.

"Hang on, Akeno, we're almost there," Jacob said, trying not to panic. His legs were burning from the exertion, and he was forced to slow to a walk. He took the stairs as quickly as he could. It was difficult to carry Akeno *and* the bags, and the stairs seemed endless. He reached the top just as the blue light went out. Akeno must have fallen unconscious.

"Oh, no, Akeno, I'm hurrying as fast as I can!" Jacob put the Makalo down and started pushing frantically against the ceiling and the walls, trying to find the exit.

A stream of sunlight hit him in the face, nearly blinding him as he pushed against one section of the wall. He released the stone, letting it fall shut, enveloping them in darkness again. He pulled his bag off his shoulders and opened it. "September?" he whispered.

"Yes, Jacob?"

"When I push the stone open, I need you to sneak around and tell me what's out there."

"Don't want to."

"Arggh. Early, will you?"

"Of course!"

Jacob pushed the door just far enough to let Early out. He held it open with his shoulders, waiting for the Minya to return. It took longer than usual for her to come back, but after what felt like forever, she zoomed in past him.

"The tunnel opens in the middle of a forest very close to the mountains," she said. "I wasn't able to see much. I did find some honey, though."

Jacob moaned in frustration. Was that what had taken her so long? "Were there any Lorkon?"

"Lorkon? Oh, yes, there were." Early spun around a couple of times, doing some sort of dance.

"How many of them?"

She held up three little fingers.

"And? Where were they?"

She pointed. "Farther south."

"What were they doing?"

She tapped the side of her head. "They looked like they were searching for something."

Jacob rolled his eyes. "Of course they were searching for something." He knew sarcasm would be lost on Early. "Were there Dusts or anything else?"

"I couldn't see anything, no."

"Which side of the wall are we on?"

"I didn't check."

Jacob grimaced—stupid Minya—and decided he'd have to see for himself. He pushed the door open slowly, letting his eyes adjust, then poked his head out. Roots grew over the side of the hill above the exit, and in front of him were several trees. It looked as though the tunnel opened in the side of a small canyon, facing the mountain, since there was a slope going up on the other side of the trees. To the right was the forest, thicker here than anywhere else he'd seen so far. Judging by the light, he figured the tunnel had led them under the wall and to the other side, though it was hard to tell. Something about this bothered him, and he wracked his brain, trying to figure out what.

Then it occurred to him. Aloren. He backed up and let the door fall shut. She had no way to leave Maivoryl City without him.

Jacob mentally kicked himself. He'd promised he'd help her get out of the city—that she would only have to be there for a couple of hours. Who knew what had happened to her after he and Akeno had run away? Who knew if Eachan had been successful in protecting her? Who knew if she was even still alive? He felt sick to his stomach when he thought he might never see her again. She'd trusted him! And he'd thought she could—that she'd be safe doing so.

He took a deep breath, struggling to control his emotions. There was no way he'd be able to save both Aloren and Akeno. This he knew, and he hated it.

He forced himself to put her smile and sparkly brown eyes out of his mind, knowing there was nothing he could do but pray she'd be okay. He had to focus on getting Akeno to someone who could help, and as soon as possible.

Jacob made sure both September and Early were out of his knapsack and swung it over his shoulders, alongside Aloren's and Akeno's bags. Then he picked up Akeno and pushed open the heavy door.

He let his eyes adjust to the sunlight and stepped outside, feeling very exposed, even with the thick forest closing in on him. He lowered the door, then squeezed past a couple of large trees into a small, enclosed area to the left that would keep him hidden for a few minutes while he checked on Akeno.

The Makalo's fuzzy skin was cold to the touch. He had huge, dark rings circling his eyes that made them look sunken, and he was breathing rapidly.

Lifting Akeno's pant leg again, Jacob drew back in horror at what he saw. The skin on his lower leg had broken and was blistered, oozing blood and pus.

"Oh, gosh, that's disgusting," Jacob whispered, pulling the fabric down to hide the sore.

He tried to pour a little water into Akeno's mouth, as he'd seen in the movies. But he couldn't get Akeno to part his lips, so drank the rest of it himself. Akeno was unresponsive to everything.

Deciding it would be a good idea to find out where they were before moving Akeno again, Jacob got up and squeezed through the small opening between the trees. He moved past the tunnel entrance, looking through the roots that hung over the door. At first he didn't see anything, but then he was able to pick out a shape he hadn't noticed before. While he watched, the shape shifted, coming into better focus. It was a very tall figure, wearing a large black cloak. A Lorkon. Jacob watched as it bent over, digging through the brush. It was only thirty or so feet away from where they were. Why was it doing the dirty work, and where were the Dusts?

Jacob crouched down and pushed through the underbrush to check the other side of the small canyon. He stayed still, trying to catch any movement through the thick trees, but didn't see anything. He crept back to the little hiding place, deciding Akeno wouldn't last long enough for the Lorkon to leave.

September and Early had taken positions on Akeno's chest and were having a heated discussion.

"Shhh!" Jacob hissed, crouching down next to them. "I need both of you to do something that could be very dangerous. You both care about Akeno, right?"

"Yes, of course," September said.

"I know you have no tie to me to keep you here right now, but Akeno needs you. Are you willing to help me get him back to Taga, where they'll take care of him?"

"We are!" Early said.

Jacob looked at the other Minya. "September?"

"Okay, fine."

"Good. First, Early, go find Kenji and ask if there's anything I can do for Akeno."

With a flash, Early disappeared. Upon returning, she reported that the only thing Jacob could do was get Akeno to the village as quickly as possible.

"Okay," Jacob said. "I'll need one of you to keep an eye on the Lorkon. There's one about thirty feet from here. Who wants to do that?"

"I'll do it," September said.

"Awesome. Early, would you act as a messenger between me and September? I'll need to know everything those Lorkon are doing."

The Minyas disappeared, and a second later Early returned. "The Lorkon have split up. The one that was closest to us is now moving toward Sonda Lake. Another Lorkon is moving farther south, closer to the Dust mound. The last is heading up the mountain."

Jacob frowned. "Where is the lake compared to where we are now?"

"That way," Early said, pointing through the forest straight ahead of them. "The trail is there, too."

"Okay. We'll go more to the left, then, away from the Lorkon."

Jacob grabbed the bags, swinging them over his shoulders, then picked up Akeno. He stood and squeezed between the trees, trying to make as little noise as possible. Looking around and seeing no one, he stepped to the left, keeping his eyes open for anything dangerous.

Every few minutes, Early would fly to him, relaying a message from September. The Lorkon to the south kept moving in that direction, rummaging through the underbrush, probably looking for the tunnel entrance or maybe for them. The one that had moved up the mountain was now searching somewhere above them. Only the thick leaves and branches of the trees kept Jacob out of sight. The Lorkon moving toward the lake had raised his hands to the sky and yelled words into the wind. Jacob could think of only one reason for doing that.

Lirone.

Jacob stayed as close to the trees as possible, noticing with panic when they began to thin, taking away his cover.

"Oh no," he muttered, looking up constantly, checking if the Lorkon above could see him yet. A few yards later, the forest ended. Dang it—what now? Jacob struggled to stay in control and not give in to the fear.

Jacob paused before stepping from behind the last tree, trying to figure out what to do and where to go. He wished Akeno or Aloren were able to help him decide.

The sky darkened with clouds, and the Lorkon near the lake was now closing in, as was the one on the mountain. Only the Lorkon to the south had maintained a large enough distance not to worry Jacob.

He glanced around the tree, hoping to figure out where they were. What he saw caused relief to spread over him. There was the paddock, the clothesline, and—Jacob moved to the left—the cabin!

"Oh good, oh good, oh good," Jacob breathed. Only one problem remained: the cabin was a good two hundred yards from where he stood, and between here and there was nothing but meadow, with no cover—except for a few small apple and pear trees.

He looked at Akeno—the Makalo appeared nearly lifeless. Only a slight movement of his chest showed he was still breathing. And he looked so sick! A pasty-yellow color accentuated the rings around his eyes, and his hair was matted to his head.

Early's next report was that the Lorkon to the south had turned around to head back their way. Jacob stopped her before she left. "Go get September. I need both of you here with me now."

She flew off, and a split second later, both she and September returned.

"The Fat Lady's cabin is right over there," Jacob said, pointing. "I'm going to make a run for it. But first, September, I need you to fly ahead and let her know we're on our way. Early, help send him off, please."

Light flashed, and September was gone. He returned only moments later. "She said you need to have the Key out, ready to use, and she'll tell you what to do."

Jacob shifted Akeno to one arm and pulled his bag off his shoulder, grabbing the beautiful box that contained the Key. He opened it, jumping when its sweet melody poured out. He removed the Key, then peeked around the tree to see if the music had caught the attention of the Lorkon. It hadn't.

The clouds rolled, warning of Lirone's appearance. A dark spot moved by the shore, and without having to ask Early, Jacob knew it was a Lorkon.

"Okay, let's go," he said, putting the box and his bag away. He took a deep breath. "September, you keep a lookout on the left, Early to the right. Fly back and forth between me and those Lorkon as fast as you can, keeping me aware of their every move. I need to know exactly where they are the entire time. Be careful they don't see you."

Taking another deep breath, Jacob stepped around the tree, holding Akeno securely. Then, putting all his energy into his already tired legs, he took off as fast as he could toward the Fat Lady's cabin.

Only a few seconds passed before Lirone spotted him, making his presence known by taking away all sound. A sudden explosion to the right nearly knocked Jacob over, and he stumbled along, trying to stay on his feet. An explosion behind him was followed by one in front. Jacob lurched to the side, avoiding the huge hole that was created, nearly dropping Akeno in the process. The remaining distance grew shorter. Early flitted to his side, yelling in his ear. Jacob was surprised she could still speak, then realized she was too small for Lirone to see.

"The Lorkon by the lake just spotted you. He's on his way."

September appeared on Jacob's other side, yelling that the Lorkon from the mountain was also in pursuit.

The ground all around Jacob was pelted by several smaller explosions, many of which missed him by a few feet.

"Hurry, Jacob!" Early yelled. "Hurry!"

Jacob watched as a large blast of fire bounced off the Fat Lady's cabin and fell into the brush out of sight. Her house wasn't harmed in any way. Another huge blast went off in front of him, and he veered to avoid the hole. The explosions were much bigger now and coming more rapidly, but something was odd. If Lirone wanted, he could easily hit Jacob, so why didn't he? There were no trees providing cover this time, just the wide-open meadow through which Jacob ran. What was going on?

"You must run faster!" Early yelled. She paused. "I have an idea. Can I use it?"

Jacob nodded, nearly dropping Akeno when an explosion went off right behind him.

Early disappeared, and seconds later Jacob felt warmth spread through his body, originating from a spot on his back. He felt as though his calves had been given an

264

immense supply of energy. He put on a burst of speed, feeling he was about to lift off the ground. There were fewer than a hundred yards to go when Lirone's bombardment suddenly stopped.

The Fat Lady stood on the step of her cabin, waving her arms and yelling. He could only pick out one word—*diamonds*. He looked at the Key still clenched in one of his fists, then back up at her, confused.

"Diamonds!" she screamed.

"She said to slide the two diamonds!" September said.

Jacob shook his head, not understanding.

"The diamonds move!" September yelled.

Jacob slung Akeno over his left shoulder, using both hands to hold the Key up to his face as he ran. He located the two different diamonds and fiddled around with his thumbs. The diamonds slid until they were aligned with each other.

Jacob looked up at the Fat Lady, ready for her next instructions, running free without the shock waves ramming his body.

The Fat Lady yelled again. "Put the Key in my door and turn it to the left! Go to Taga Village!"

Jacob still had about forty yards to go. The ground in front of him was level and hard, and he risked a quick glance over his shoulder. He wished almost immediately he hadn't done so.

The nearest Lorkon was only a foot outside of grabbing distance. Nearly stumbling in fright, Jacob yelled, noticing he could hear his voice again. He willed his body to move even faster.

"September . . . do something . . . Lorkon." he gasped, readjusting Akeno so he was easier to carry. The muscles in Jacob's arms and shoulders were burning.

"Okay." September disappeared.

"Arrgh!"

Jacob looked back just in time to see the Lorkon face-plant into the dirt. He saw a second Lorkon only ten or so feet behind the first, with the third nearly having caught up as well. Akeno started to convulse in Jacob's arms, nearly causing Jacob to drop him.

"Are you ready?" the Fat Lady yelled.

"Yes!" Jacob gasped. His lungs were burning so badly, he was afraid he'd pass out from lack of air. They were down to fifteen yards.

"Do you know what to do?"

"To the left, Taga Village."

"Close the door behind you or they'll follow you." The Fat Lady went into her cottage and shut the door.

The third Lorkon caught up to him. "September, Early! Stop the Lorkon!" Jacob shouted just as he took the last few leaps toward the door.

Reaching out, he put the Key in the hole.

"Taga Village!" he yelled, turning the Key to the left. He swung the door open. Running through, he spun around and tried to shut the door in the face of the Lorkon, but the door bounced open again. Jacob took an instinctive step back. The Lorkon had stopped the door from shutting with his foot. An evil, disgusting smile lifted the corners of his mouth.

"Now you are ours," the Lorkon said.

Something small flitted through the air, and the Lorkon flew across the open space, blasted away from the cabin.

Before the other Lorkon got the chance to rush through the door, Jacob slammed it shut, making sure it clicked this time.

Chapter 18

Bacon and Pancakes

Jacob took in a deep breath, a familiar musty-wood smell entering his nose, then turned around. He was in the big tree in Taga Village, and none of the Lorkon had followed him. Letting out the air, he stood still, allowing his mind to relax from the stress it had just experienced. He shifted Akeno's position, put the Key in its box, then made himself go outside.

The sun had almost set, casting long shadows all over the canyon. He was grateful it was almost night. His eyes ached from a headache that had built up behind them, and he looked forward to having as little light around him as possible.

Forcing his legs to continue to hold him up, he limped toward the side of the village. "Help! Is anyone there?"

"Jacob?" a voice called from the ledge. It was Ebony. "Oh, Jacob, you're back, you're back!" She began crying, calling out for Brojan and Kenji who rushed to her side, then saw Jacob.

"Help him," Brojan said to a few Makalo men who had gathered.

Jacob raised Akeno as high as his arms would let him, and one of the men climbed down and lifted him the rest of the way.

Climbing as carefully as he could, Jacob pulled himself over the top. One of the men supported him as he rushed with Kenji, Ebony, and Brojan to Akeno's house.

Kenji laid Akeno on the table and he and Ebony went to work, acting as a team to cleanse Akeno's leg. Ebony soaked strips of cloth, then handed them to Kenji, who wiped the ooze from Akeno's leg. Pretty soon the leg was as clean as they could get it. Kenji poured the rest of the liquid into the main part of the wound, which had expanded to cover Akeno's entire lower leg.

Kenji glanced at Ebony with a worried expression on his face. "If the fever doesn't break—"

"Wait!" Ebony gasped. "I think we might have—" She ran out of the room, still talking, her voice muffled by the wall. "Potion . . . you . . . last time . . ." She came back, carrying a very familiar vial. "I saved this."

Kenji relaxed. "Oh, thank goodness . . . here, let me." Using an extra cloth, he wiped up the liquid he'd poured in Akeno's sore, then put a couple of drops from the vial into the wound. He then forced Akeno's jaw open and poured the rest of the liquid in his mouth.

Ebony wrapped the sore with strips of cloth, then hurried out of the room, returning with her arms full of sheets. Kenji took a couple and handed them to Jacob. "Wrap him as tightly as you can from head to foot."

Jacob started at Akeno's head, leaving a space around his nose to breath. Ebony started at his midsection, and Kenji at his feet. Brojan held the sheets in place until they were secured.

"The sheets hold in his body heat—heat the potion needs in order to be activated." Kenji turned to Ebony. "How long did it take for me to heal?"

"Two minutes, maybe more. His situation is fairly similar to yours." She put her arm around her husband. "He'll be fine." She smiled at Jacob. "Last time, I was the one stressing over whether Kenji would live, but I didn't need to stress. The Fat Lady really knows her stuff."

After a few moments, Kenji pulled the sheet off Akeno's head. His face was pink again, the dark circles gone. "It's working!"

Ebony gave Kenji another hug. "Wonderful." She glanced at Jacob. "Oh, Jacob, I'll love you forever for what you've done for my son." Her eyes welled up with tears, and Jacob stared at his feet. He was grateful Akeno would be all right, but felt his cheeks flush with embarrassment at the praise.

"You look exhausted." She sniffed, and her nose wrinkled. "And you definitely need to bathe."

A weary smile crossed Jacob's face. "Sorry." He pulled out the box with the Key of Kilenya inside and handed it to Ebony. "Here, take the Key."

Ebony held the container in her hands, her expression one of gratitude. "We knew you'd be able to do it."

"There was no doubt," Kenji said. He took the box and opened it. The familiar tune filled the room, and peaceful colors danced across the walls.

"Wow," Kenji said. The Makalos all looked at Jacob.

"What?" Jacob asked.

"You know it's only doing this because you're near it, right?" Kenji asked.

Jacob shrugged. "That's what the Lorkon king said."

Kenji raised an eyebrow. He didn't speak for a moment. "He would know."

Ebony took the box from Kenji and handed it to Brojan, then picked up the baby from a small bed in the corner. She looked over Jacob. "Oh, poor Jacob, you're exhausted. Do you want some dinner before sleeping?"

Jacob rubbed his eyes. "No, I'm too tired for food."

"Okay. Well, you can sleep in the tree. It's very safe, and we haven't had any problems with the wolves since you and Akeno left. We've fastened a temporary covering over the entrance that should last for a couple of days. It'll keep out any unwanted visitors, including the Lorkon and their dogs. Or, if you'd rather not take chances, I can make up a bed here on the floor. We'll talk tomorrow morning before you head home."

Jacob considered the options—safety versus comfort. "I think I'll give the tree a shot."

"I'll take him now." Brojan stood.

"Now? But—"

"There will be plenty of time for conversation tomorrow," Brojan said.

Kenji looked up from checking on Akeno. "We really need to talk about everything that happened, but you're in no shape at this time. Don't worry—we'll have a good conversation as soon as you're awake."

"Will the Fat Lady be okay?"

"She'll be completely fine. The spells on her cabin are strong and won't let anyone in who shouldn't be there."

Ebony hugged Jacob, thanking him over and over again for returning her son. Kenji also gave Jacob a big hug, telling him goodnight.

Brojan led the way out of the house. He looked at Jacob for a minute, then nodded. "It is you, Jacob. Yes, you are exactly what we need."

Brojan was silent the rest of the way, and Jacob was fine with that. His mind wasn't clear enough to form coherent thoughts, and he wasn't sure what he would say, anyway.

He felt like he was sleepwalking, and they reached the tree quickly. Brojan left after making sure Jacob didn't need anything. Deciding he was too tired to bother with a shower,

Jacob climbed to the third floor, sank into one of the beds, and fell into a deep sleep.

When Jacob finally woke, his mind was clear. He stretched as far as his legs and arms would let him, then sat up, rubbing his eyes. The sun was bright in the sky, and he guessed it was close to noon. He heard voices downstairs, recognizing one of them as Jaegar's. He grabbed the bags and went down the stairs, crouching at the bottom where the two Makalos wouldn't see him. Jaegar was opening the windows, a little blonde Makalo followed him around.

"No, Kaiya," Jaegar said.

She stomped her foot. "Why not? I won't wake him. I just want to peek."

"Mother and Father said not to go upstairs, so the answer is still no."

"But Jaegar—"

Jacob sprung into the open. "Boo!" he yelled, then laughed when Kaiya screamed and dropped the book she'd been holding.

She jumped behind Jaegar, covering her face.

"Hey!" Jacob said. "You look a lot better."

Jaegar smiled. "Yeah. Thank you—for everything."

"How's Akeno?" Jacob asked.

"Still sleeping," Jaegar said, taking his sister's hand. "Come—Mother and Father wanted to see you as soon as you woke up."

Jacob sat at the table in Akeno's house with Kenji, Ebony, and Brojan. They were eating a wonderful breakfast of bacon, eggs, and a type of pancake Jacob had never seen before. He felt refreshed and clean for the first time in several days—he'd taken a shower as soon as he'd gotten to Akeno's house.

He felt torn between wanting to go home, going after Aloren, and talking to the Makalos, who were now giving an update on Akeno.

"The redness on his leg has almost disappeared, and the skin is healed over," Kenji said.

"That's awesome," Jacob said. "Where are Early and September?"

Kenji chuckled. "They came back after you went to the tree last night," he said. "We haven't seen them since. They're probably pretty tired of being ordered around."

Jacob laughed, rolling his eyes. "No kidding. I owe them my life, and Akeno's as well." He rested his chin on his hands. "The Minyas told us the humans came back. When do I get to meet them?"

Kenji glanced at Ebony who was patting the baby's back. "Soon enough—they want to properly introduce themselves to you, and promised to come back in the near future." He pushed his plate aside. "We have more important things to discuss."

"But where are they now?"

"They're probably searching for the other Key—remember that two were created. Don't worry, we'll focus on them at a later time." Kenji leaned forward. "Right now, you need to tell us what happened so we'll know what's coming."

Jacob nodded. "Where do you want me to start?"

"Where you last left off. When you went back to see Gallus."

It took at least half an hour for Jacob to share what had happened over the last few days. He hesitated for a couple of seconds after completing his narration. "Do you . . . think it's too late to get Aloren?"

Kenji sighed. "It would depend on so many things, and since we haven't been to Maivoryl City since the Lorkon took over, we don't know. From what you were saying about the people who live there, Aloren might be diseased and deformed beyond recognition by now."

Jacob ran his fingers through his hair. "I hate the feeling that she's stuck somewhere in that disgusting city," he said. "I . . . I feel like I let her down by not turning around to get her."

Ebony's eyes started to fill with tears. She seemed to be doing a lot of crying lately, though he didn't blame her. "Jacob, that decision saved Akeno's life. We know it was hard, but we appreciate it a great deal." An awkward silence filled the room while Ebony regained her composure, turning her attention to the baby. After a minute she spoke to Jacob again. "We'll help you remove her from that situation as soon as we can."

Jacob cleared his throat. "I'd actually like to go right now. We can use the Key—my family doesn't have to know that I'm back yet."

He hadn't even finished talking before the adults in the room were shaking their heads.

"Why not?" he demanded. "We can't just leave her there—every hour will make it harder to get her away."

"Jacob," Brojan said, "it's too great a risk now. We don't have enough information on Maivoryl City to send any sort of rescue team."

"I was just there—I can tell you what to expect."

"But not everything. Please do not make the same mistake the Lorkon made in underestimating the ingenuity of others."

"But you can't ask me to wait around while she goes through . . . who knows what!"

"And as soon as the Lorkon realize who she is and how she's linked to you, they're not likely to let her out of their sight."

"This is stupid!" Jacob said, throwing up his hands. "You think I'm going to sit on my thumbs and wait?"

"You have to trust that we'll help you as soon as we know more of what's wrong in that city."

Jacob growled in exasperation, but didn't make any reply. He didn't agree with them. He'd be able to get her out safely—he knew he could. And just thinking about the people there—his skin crawled as he pictured the greasy hands reaching for him and the disgusting, leering faces. And knowing Aloren was left there—he couldn't tolerate it. What if she ended up like them? What if she was forced to live out the rest of her existence in that dirty, disgusting, filthy place?

He scowled at no one in particular, not ready to accept what they'd told him, but realizing he didn't have a choice. They had the Key now, and he wasn't about to steal it from them.

He forced himself back to the conversation when Ebony asked him a question.

"How many Lorkon did you see?"

"There were four in the castle. Then there were only three chasing us to the Fat Lady's house."

Ebony looked at Kenji. "That sounds right, wouldn't you say?"

"But one extra. There used to be only three. And I really doubt Keitus would stoop to chasing a human boy, even one with such great significance. He'd view it as beneath him."

"Is Keitus the head guy?" Jacob said. "He's the one who wanted me to activate the Key. He freaked out when one of the other Lorkon tried to hurry him."

"Yes, we've dealt with him before," Kenji said. He took a bite of eggs before continuing. "He's arrogant, especially toward those he feels are lower than he is."

"So, only four Lorkon?" Jacob asked. "What about the one in the infected forest?"

"Five, then," Kenji said, "which brings up another point. Remember when we told you female Lorkon are rare? Well, that was a slight exaggeration. We'd never even heard of one existing before—just that it was a possibility. The Lorkon you saw in the woods came as quite a surprise to us."

Jacob snorted in derision. "Yeah, it didn't do me a whole lot of good, either." He paused, a thought coming alive in the back of his mind. "Oh, I remembered what she said."

Ebony's face showed her excitement. "What was it?"

"'Danilo.'"

"'Danilo?'" Brojan said, leaning forward. "You're sure of this?"

"Yes." Jacob nodded. "What does it mean?"

"It's a name of someone connected to Dmitri, and I'm very surprised she even knew it. No one on our side would ever have mentioned it."

"Why did she say it to me?"

Brojan glanced at the other adults. "Kenji and Ebony don't agree with me, but this pretty much solidifies it. If she is who I think she is, Danilo is someone who would have been very important to her—someone she'd never met, but knew existed and longed to know. I'd guess she's been searching for a long time—suspecting anyone who entered her forest to be him."

Kenji bit his lip. "It . . . does make sense, I guess. But I'd rather be sure." He turned to Jacob. "We'll be researching her history and where she came from over the next few months."

"Speaking of Dmitri, I have another question." Jacob leaned forward. "He was supposed to be the next king of the land. Both the journal and Gallus said so. But it didn't happen. I'm guessing that's because the Lorkon took over. What happened to him, anyway?"

"Dmitri disappeared from among the inhabitants of Eklaron, going through a link to a different world long ago. There are rumors he'll return eventually."

"And he'd never even heard of a Lorkon before," Jacob said. "How's that possible?"

"Lorkon haven't always existed," Kenji said. "They're immortal, it's true, but before they were Lorkon, they were mortal beings."

"Like what? Human?"

"Human, yes, or any other race, really. I've never seen it, but I've heard that the 'recipe' for becoming Lorkon is incredibly complex and dangerous. It almost never works, and instead usually kills or physically destroys the one attempting it."

"Which explains why there are only a few of them," Jacob said.

"Exactly."

"Why would someone want to be a Lorkon?"

Kenji waved his hand at Jacob. "Think about it. What do you know about them so far?"

"They're immortal, physically strong, and can kill basically anything they touch," Jacob said. "But, they're so disgusting. I'm going to have nightmares for months after yesterday's experience."

"To some, the advantages far outweigh the disadvantages," Ebony said. "Not everyone wants to be attractive." She motioned to the journal on the table next to Jacob. "How much have you read?"

"A lot. I'm at the part where Dmitri just rescued Arien. Kelson and those guys are all dead." Jacob almost stood out of his chair, suddenly remembering. "Kenji! You were with Dmitri the whole time, and you didn't tell me."

"Yes, I was. Dmitri . . . he and I were almost inseparable at that time."

"Okay, now I want you to explain the journal to me. What I've read so far, anyway. Why were the two journals put together? A lot of information was skipped."

"That was Dmitri's decision," Ebony said. "He wanted to make sure that those who read his story knew he hadn't always lived in this kingdom, and that he wasn't always a good person. He didn't feel the rest of the other journal was important, since all it did was explain his travels to this kingdom, marrying Arien, and the first few years of their marriage."

"Okay, so this is what I've figured out so far," Jacob said. He proceeded to explain his theory that he and Dmitri had taken the same path, only coming from opposite directions. He couldn't remember passing anything like the Fire Pulser, though.

"No charred or burned land, or anything similar?" Kenji asked.

Jacob shook his head. "No, nothing. How close to the mud was the Fire Pulser?"

"Very close, actually. It wasn't long after we left her that we reached the poisoned mud."

"And you guys didn't kill her?" Jacob confirmed.

"No, we just put her in the diamond ball."

"But where . . ." Jacob paused. "Wait! The valley! It was beautiful, but I felt all sorts of negative emotions there. I'll bet anything that's where she is—still alive."

Kenji frowned. "How can you be certain?"

"Because of how I felt—for some reason I'm able to sense things others can't. Like, I could see the Molg in the cave, and I saw the man in the castle where the passage was hidden. It makes sense to me. There isn't any other explanation for how I felt there."

Kenji leaned back. "I agree, and I'm sure we'll find out soon enough." He smiled at Ebony. The adults were silent for a moment, then Kenji spoke again. "Even with all the bad that has happened out there, it's refreshing to hear news of the outside world. Jacob, you have no idea how exciting this is for all of us. We haven't been able to leave Taga for so long."

"I can imagine. I'd die if I were stuck in one spot for as long as you've been here." Jacob realized he'd lived in the same small town his whole life, but at least he'd been able to visit the bigger cities around them. His eyes traced the silver lines in the ceiling, then a question popped into his head. "So why did the Lorkon attack the castle in the first place? They didn't even know about the Key yet. Was it for money?"

"I think it was more for power than anything," Kenji said. "They came here wanting to rule more and more land. They were jealous of Dmitri and his future kingdom. Well, Keitus was, anyway, and the rest of the Lorkon do as he does. But they were successful in getting rid of King Roylance, Queen Ara Liese, Dmitri, Arien, and anyone else who opposed them."

"*Anyone* who opposed them? Wouldn't Gallus have opposed them? And the Fat Lady? And you guys?"

"Yes, but sometimes the best way to stand up to someone is to bide your time and wait, rather than to act rashly in a moment of emotion. We, as you know, were asked to come here and protect the Key and the link to your world. The Fat Lady hunkered down for a long winter, preparing herself for the storm which is still to come. And Gallus fought bitterly against the humans who sided with the Lorkon, just to stay where he is. He lost everything, including his wife and children. We now know that he's remarried and has started a new family—we've sent Minyas back and forth several times since learning from you that he was alive—but to stay behind was a very difficult decision for him to make. He had to do it to keep an eye on his people." Kenji rubbed his shoulder and stared at the wall for a moment. "Tell us again what happened when the Lorkon touched you."

"There was a lot of pain. My muscles went out of control, and every time I opened my eyes, I saw bright flashes of light. Hundreds and hundreds of people were running around us, but Akeno didn't see them. Do you think the people I saw were dead?"

Kenji frowned. "I'm not sure." He looked at Brojan. "What do you think?"

The patriarch didn't respond for a moment. "We'll want to consult with the Fat Lady and Aldo, if he recovers from whatever is consuming his mind."

Kenji turned back to Jacob. "We knew *something* would happen if Keitus touched you, but we weren't sure what. I'm sorry to say it, especially since it was a painful experience for you, but we were very interested in whatever the outcome would be."

"Nothing changed inside me, and the only thing that happened was the pain," Jacob said.

"No, that's not correct," Kenji said. "Don't forget the potion you took. It was designed to control your abilities, or your reactions to those abilities, once the Lorkon released them."

"How did they release my abilities, and how many do I have?"

"We're positive there are a lot, lurking in your system—"

Jacob couldn't help but grin at this.

"—and the Lorkon released most of them by touching you. The magic in their blood caused a reaction with the magic in yours, jump-starting everything for you. Your talents would have developed naturally if they hadn't accelerated them, but what we've guessed so far is that the Lorkon, in their desperation to gain control, didn't want to wait, but wanted to unlock those abilities at once. They probably figured their chances of controlling you would be greater if you were in their presence when your gifts manifested themselves. They would have been correct in that assumption. The most foolish thing they did, however, was to overlook the fact that you wouldn't have come alone. From their experiences in the last war, they know Makalos are physically weak and wouldn't be good 'bodyguards.' But they didn't realize that many Makalos are still magical."

And a good thing, too. Jacob didn't want to think what would have happened if the Lorkon had been aware of that fact. They weren't likely to make the same mistake again. "What are the Lorkon going to do now? They weren't exactly happy about my leaving."

"They'll be coming for the Key pretty soon," Kenji said. "And for you, as well. As you've already discovered, you possess some pretty amazing qualities. They'll want those gifts under their control."

"But how did they know about me?"

Kenji took a drink. "They've apparently known for a long time, and knew you'd have special abilities, even before we did."

Ebony sighed. "Who knows how or when they figured everything out."

"Will they go after my family, too? Or just me?"

"I'm sure they'll do both," Kenji said. "They'll first prepare themselves, though, and they have to get through Taga before reaching your city. As we said, the entrance was sealed again. Remember, however, that it's temporary. We'll be able to keep them out for a week, maybe, but it will be very difficult to keep them away for long."

Ebony patted Jacob's arm. "Things will be okay."

Kenji rubbed his hands together, a grin spreading across his face. "It's going to be fun to figure out all of your abilities!"

"Yeah, a thriller," Jacob said, snorting. "Okay, it'll be fun, but only if I can walk through walls or fly or something."

"No, none of that stuff. It'll probably be more mental," Kenji said, tapping his head.

"Mental like *I'm* going mental, or mental like I'm making *other people* go mental?"

Ebony and Kenji laughed, and Brojan smiled.

"We don't know exactly what talents you'll have when all this is over," Kenji said, "and we probably won't know until we've been able to talk with the Fat Lady and Aldo. One thing for you to note—when Keitus touched you, he probably unlocked many of your gifts, but not all. The rest will come naturally as you age. Taking the Fat Lady's potion not only saved your life, but put most of those abilities under control until you learn to unlock them yourself."

"So, what happens if I'm never able to control my mad skills?"

Kenji's eyes twinkled. "Nothing much. The Lorkon will continue terrorizing the people of Eklaron, eventually your family will be in danger—as will other people in your world—and the races here that are good will be destroyed, including the Makalos. Oh, and the Lorkon will figure out how to use your talents for you."

"That's it?" Jacob said. "Somehow I expected so much more." Everyone laughed, and Jacob smiled inwardly, glad he'd been able to make a joke of sorts.

Brojan leaned forward in his chair. "You believe your ability to mold things deals with sensing the weaknesses in them?"

"Yes, I think so," Jacob said, nodding. "And I have a theory. I think I'm able to make things stronger when I remold them." He motioned in the general direction of his town. "But why wasn't I able to feel heat from things back at my own place? Does it only work here, in your world?"

"I don't think so," Kenji said. "Your arrival in Eklaron possibly forced this ability to come into the open, but it would have occurred naturally anyway."

"So, I should be able to mold things when I get back home?" Kenji nodded. "We think so."

The room was silent as Jacob thought through what had been said. "How did I get these powers, and does anyone else on Earth have them?"

The adults exchanged glances. "We were afraid you'd ask these questions," Kenji said. "And we're not prepared to answer them right now."

Jacob sat back. "Why not?"

Brojan studied Jacob's face. "There are too many people involved, and it is not our place to answer until a decision to do so has been reached by all."

"That's probably not the answer you wanted, but you'll get one eventually, I promise," Kenji said.

Jacob stared at the Makalo. "I'm sorry for saying so, but this is kind of ridiculous. Something that affects my life so drastically should be my business."

"And, as I said, you will know—someday."

"I was wondering about Aldo. What happened to him?"

"We have no idea," Kenji said, a dark expression crossing his face. "And such a great man. I really don't believe he's gone crazy, though. Something else is going on." He stared at his cup for a moment before continuing. "When we first moved to the canyon, he helped us close off the entrance between our village and the other lands by figuring out how we could use our Rezend to make the trees grow with steel in them, making a much stronger wood. He really showed us just how much he cares about us by doing that."

Brojan cleared his throat. "It would be a good idea if Kenji and I took some time to look into matters with Aldo while Jacob finishes reading the book."

"And we're sure the Fat Lady's safe, right?" Jacob asked. "I know I've already asked, but—man!—she really helped us out."

Ebony nodded. "There's never a need to worry about her," she said. "She and Aldo worked with Brojan to put extra fortifications on her cabin. The passage of time does not lessen their strength, nor do attacks make them weaker."

"And that would explain why she never leaves it," Jacob said.

"Yes, exactly," Kenji said.

"Any other questions?" Ebony said.

Jacob shook his head. "Aside from figuring out what's wrong with me, I don't think so."

Ebony scowled at him. "Jacob, nothing is wrong with you. You're different. That doesn't mean you're broken."

"We look forward to having you return once you've finished reading the book," Brojan said. "You'll find the information very valuable for a complete understanding of what has happened—and is happening—in this world. And once you've read the book, we'll be able to answer any questions you might still have."

"You're now as much a part of this world as we are," Kenji said.

Jacob finished off his juice and put his cup down. "All right, then. I guess it's time for me to go home. I hoped Akeno would wake up while we were talking, but I don't think that's going to happen."

Ebony smiled and patted Jacob's hand. "He's healed. He'll wake up as soon as he's ready."

"Can I at least see him before I leave? Even if he's asleep?"

"Of course," she said.

Jacob followed Ebony through one of the back doors and down a narrow hall to a room with a few beds in it. Akeno lay peacefully in one, breathing steadily. Jacob smiled, looking at him. It was great to see him healthy again. If only Aloren were in such a good position. Jacob leaned against the door frame, suddenly feeling exhausted and helpless— he really, really hoped she was okay. He had to get back to Maivoryl City as soon as possible. He couldn't stand thinking about her alone there, in that awful place. Plans to rescue her solidified in his mind. He'd do it, and he'd get Matt to help.

"Let me know right when Akeno wakes up. I'll come visit him." Jacob returned to the main room, grabbing Aloren's bag. "Oh, wait, one last question. How much can I tell my family?"

"As much as you want," Kenji said. "It was a Minya, as you know, who was sent to deliver the message letting them know where you were, and after that, I don't think what you'll have to say will come as much of a shock to them." He smiled at Jacob. "It also wouldn't hurt to have their complete support."

"All right, off with you then," Ebony said, opening the door.

Jacob left Akeno's house in high spirits. He was excited to see Matt and Amberly again, and his parents when they returned. Whistling, he climbed down the wall and crossed the meadow. He paused on the way to the forest to look up at the tree, wishing he could somehow take it home with him.

At first he was jumpy about being in the forest again, but after a few minutes, when nothing out of the ordinary happened, he stopped worrying.

Jacob sighed as he walked. The trip back to his house seemed to take forever, and he had to control himself to keep from breaking into a run—wait—why couldn't he run? He laughed at himself and took off down the path, excitement building up when he thought of his siblings eagerly awaiting his return.

He stepped out of the trees and onto the grass in his backyard, spotting Amberly playing on the swing set.

"*Jake!*" Amberly squealed. "You're back!" She jumped off the swing and ran at him, almost tripping over her own feet.

Jacob laughed and dropped to his knees, picking her up as soon as she reached him. He held on to her tightly, burying his face in her curls.

"I've gotta show you what we made in the sandbox!" Amberly said, squirming in his arms. "And Sarah fell and got a cut on her knee!"

"She did?" Jacob said, thinking about the neighbor's daughter. "You'll have to show me when I see her next." He put her down. "Where's Matt?"

"Inside!" Turning around, she ran toward the house. "Jake's back! Mommy! Daddy! Jake's back!"

"Wait, Mom and Dad are home? Cool!"

Jacob had barely made it to the back porch when his mom flew through the door and hugged him, nearly knocking him over. His dad was right behind her and wrapped his arms around both of them. When his parents finally released him, Matt tackled him, knocking him to the lawn.

Jacob laughed. "Ouch! Uncle! Uncle!"

It took a minute of good-natured shoving and pushing to get up again, but soon they were walking back to the house, Matt on one side of him and his mom on the other.

"Man, I've got a lot to tell you guys," Jacob said.

His mom looked at him, an intense expression crossing her face. "We were so, so worried about you, young man. You are not to leave this house for a week. And don't you dare think about doing something like that again."

Jacob looked at her, shocked. Getting grounded right now would be really bad. What about Aloren? "But I have—" Then he saw the smile creeping across her face, and relief washed over him. "Oh, good. I'm glad you're teasing."

His parents looked at him. "We were very worried," his dad said. "And we want to hear all about it as soon as possible."

His mom nodded. "It sounds like you became quite the hero while we were gone."

"I'll tell you everything. It might take a while, but I'll definitely tell you everything." He looked at his family. "It's so good to be home."

Jacob paused before entering the house, running his hand over the wood of the back door. A large grin crossed his face when he felt a familiar warmth.

Matt jabbed him in the side with his elbow. "Dude, what are you doing?"

Jacob shook his head. "Oh, nothing," he said, satisfied.

Note from the author:

Thank you so much for reading *The Key of Kilenya!* I hope you enjoyed it. If you did, please consider helping me spread the word about it by posting an honest review on Amazon, Facebook, Goodreads, or wherever else you think is appropriate.

Thank you! :-)

Oh, and also, as an FYI, the actual Key of Kilenya is available for purchase. A lot of my readers use it as a necklace or on a keychain. You can check it out on my blog, under Kilenya Merchandise:

http://andreapearsonbooks.blogspot.com

About the Author

Andrea Pearson is an avid reader and outdoor-er, who loves traveling. She and her husband (AKA Mr. Darcy) have settled near a river that someday will probably overflow and flood their house.

It took Andrea nearly a lifetime to do so (nine years), but she graduated with a bachelor of science degree in Communications Disorders from Brigham Young University. She plans to open a flying bicycle shop eventually, but for the time being, she is happy teaching orchestra to elementary students.

Connect with Andrea online (Facebook, Twitter, etc.): http://www.kilenyaseries.com

Acknowledgments

First and foremost, I want to thank my family for their friendship and for putting up with me while I've made this dream become a reality. I love you all! Thanks especially to my husband, and to Dad, Mom, Lisa, Daniel, and Josh for reading, believing in me, and for your comments and suggestions. I couldn't ask for a better critique group than my own family.

Second, I have to thank my amazing friends, Tristi Pinkston and Jenni James. For supporting me, being there for me when I've needed it, and gently encouraging me onward. I love you two so very much! Trist, you are the super-coolest world's best editor. :-)

Thank you to BJ Rowley for his assistance on this project. I'll forever be grateful to you for what I learned from you and for what you have done for me.

A huge and heartfelt thanks to James Curwen for his hours put into the cover for The Key of Kilenya, and for making my monsters come to life with his illustrations.

Thank you also to my friends over the past few years who have been monumental in my decision to become a writer, or who have assisted me with the writing in some way: Schaara Bradley, Sheena Burns, Brianna Bills, Becky Bush, Jared Dickson, Ron and Charles, the CHQ NOC engineers (Jesse, Craig, Daniel and Ron), my supervisors (Dave, Stew and Elaine), and Broalt and LeShandra Spraguelor.

Next, I'd like to thank my beta readers, because without their comments and suggestions, The Key of Kilenya wouldn't have ever been published. Lon Pearson, Jenni Goodman, Megan Taylor, Kevin Bush, Millie and Jensen, Debbie West, Lani Nelson, my friends/readers from

Authonomy: Jenni James, Jeff, Dave, and Stella. Appreciation to Margo Hammeren, Chris Olsen, their kids, and everyone else on my parents' lists who've helped and supported me—I hate not being able to mention you all by name (that would take up at least twelve pages) but know that I love and appreciate what you've done for me.

My advanced orchestra students from my first year of teaching also need to be mentioned: Allison, Megan, Braeden, Levi, Noah, Lizzy, Savannah, Olivia, Katie, Kim, and Haylie. Thanks, guys, for your ideas for artwork, my series, and your enthusiasm for this book! (Don't forget to practice!)

Gratitude also goes to my brother Mike, to Becky Kendall and Kendall Teichert for the sweat and blood they put into helping me get through that last awful, Leaves-a-Bad-Taste-in-Your-Mouth math class—Becky, especially, for dealing with my day-dreaming about getting published when I should've been doing homework.

And a big "I love you" to Steve and Mardi Nielsen—my adopted grandparents—for their loving support and friendship, and for giving me the time I needed to write and edit this book while staying with them.

Thanks to Gavin Cox and Glenn Pearson for being the world's most stupendous, fabulous, fantastic and talented photographers, Marc and Becky Bule for the hours upon hours of late-night conversations, suggestions, and support, the Drycreek S.S. group for their continual friendship, love, and encouragement (next time I see you I'll make sure to be toting a really big purse and will leave it where you can find it), the Saturday Second Shift-ers for praying for me, believing in me, and being there for me.

And to all my friends and family—thank you so much for your support, excitement, and help. I love you all!

And last, I express my gratitude to the people who invented music, string cheese, dried pears, the English muffin (toasted, of course), and butter—without which this book might never have been published. (Or written!)

Book Club Questions

1. With which character do you best relate, and why?

2. What would you do if you had a pet Minya, or could be shrunken at will?

3. If Jacob hadn't allowed Aloren to accompany them, how would the story have been different? What would you have chosen if you'd been in Jacob's position?

4. What advice would you give to Jacob where getting Aloren back is concerned? Do you agree with the Makalos or with Jacob, and why?

5. Did you predict the ending, and were you satisfied with it? Why or why not? How would you have changed things?

6. How did Jacob's character change from the beginning of the book to the end? How would you have handled the trials he went through?

7. Did you like the use of foreshadowing? Where was it present, and what sort of things are you expecting from future books in this series?

8. Are there recurring symbols in the book? If so, what are they, and why are they used?

Feel free to send your answers to Andrea:

ap@andreapearsonbooks.com

18801977R00167

Printed in Great Britain
by Amazon